"Is it me or is it all men?

"Do you find a reason not to trust anybody who's not a resident of Bardville, Wyoming?"

Boone's question brought Cambria to a halt.

"I've seen your type before, Boone. Maybe you don't mean any harm, but I intend to make sure you don't do any."

Was that the real reason she was sticking to him like glue?

His eyes must have given him away. "That's not an issue," she said. "I told you I have a rule. I don't—"

"Get involved with guests. I know. Rules get broken." He leaned forward swiftly. "And people who play with fire get burned."

He hadn't even touched her. But minutes later, the heat remained.

Dear Reader,

Welcome to Silhouette **Special Edition**...welcome to romance. This month of May promises to be one of our best yet!

We begin with this month's THAT SPECIAL WOMAN! title, *A Man for Mom,* by Gina Ferris Wilkins. We're delighted that Gina will be writing under her real name, Gina Wilkins, from now on. And what a way to celebrate—with the first book in her new series, THE FAMILY WAY! Don't miss this emotional, poignant story of family connections and discovery of true love. Also coming your way in May is Andrea Edwards's third book of her series, **This Time Forever.** In *A Secret and a Bridal Pledge* two people afraid of taking chances risk it all for everlasting love.

An orphaned young woman discovers herself, and the love of a lifetime, in Tracy Sinclair's latest, *Does Anybody Know Who Allison Is?* For heart-pounding tension, look no further than Phyllis Halldorson's newest story about a husband and wife whose feelings show them they're still *Truly Married.* In *A Stranger in the Family* by Patricia McLinn, unexpected romance awaits a man who discovers that he's a single father. And rounding out the month is the debut title from new author Caroline Peak, *A Perfect Surprise.*

I hope you enjoy all these wonderful stories from Silhouette **Special Edition**, and have a wonderful month!

Sincerely,

Tara Gavin
Senior Editor

PATRICIA McLINN

A STRANGER IN THE FAMILY

Published by Silhouette Books
America's Publisher of Contemporary Romance

ISBN 0-373-09959-2

A STRANGER IN THE FAMILY

This edition published by arrangement with Harlequin Enterprises B.V.

Printed in U.S.A.

Books by Patricia McLinn

Silhouette Special Edition

Hoops #587
A New World #641
**Prelude To A Wedding* #712
**Wedding Party* #718
**Grady's Wedding* #813
Not a Family Man #864
Rodeo Nights #904
A Stranger in the Family #959

*Wedding Series

PATRICIA McLINN

says she has been spinning stories in her head since childhood, when her mother insisted she stop reading at the dinner table. As the time came for her to earn a living, Patricia shifted her stories from fiction to fact—she became a sportswriter and editor for newspapers in Illinois, North Carolina and the District of Columbia. Now living outside Washington, D.C., she enjoys traveling, history and sports but is happiest indulging her passion for storytelling.

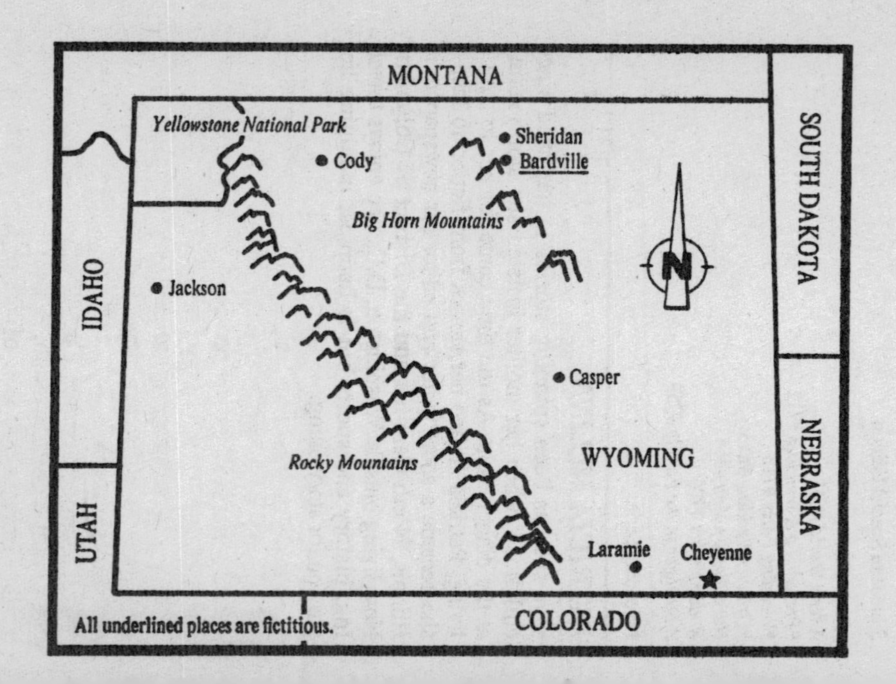
MONTANA
Yellowstone National Park
Cody
Sheridan
Bardville
Big Horn Mountains
N
SOUTH DAKOTA
IDAHO
Jackson
Casper
NEBRASKA
WYOMING
Rocky Mountains
UTAH
Laramie
Cheyenne
All underlined places are fictitious.
COLORADO

Prologue

"Bodie, there's somebody wai—"

Bodie Smith didn't break stride crossing to his office door, the voice of his assistant not quite fast enough to keep up. A thousand details aligned in his head—things he'd see to, people he'd call, decisions he'd make—to keep Bodie Smith Enterprises where he'd put it. On top.

Two steps into his office, all those thoughts vanished.

They were wiped away by the sight of two large, well-broken-in running shoes propped on his desk. Bodie Smith's eyes traced the rangy figure in a tipped-back chair until they met the assessing gaze of the man who'd been his friend since they'd raced bicycles on pitted North Carolina mountain roads.

"You found something, Cully?"

"You didn't give me much, Boone."

Cully Grainger was one of the few people alive who called him Boone. And the only one who recalled the day his younger sister's childish attempt at his first and middle names—Boone Dorsey—had come out "Bodie." He was so used to the nickname that his real name sounded a little odd. And solemn.

"I didn't give you anything," Bodie amended.

Cully shrugged. "Wouldn't go that far. You gave me what Hank let slip—that after his cousin Marlene left North Carolina, supposedly to help out a sick aunt in Nebraska, she had a baby. Your conversation with her confirmed that."

Bodie winced. *Conversation* was a damn polite word for the tense confrontation he'd had with the high school girlfriend he'd tracked down after not seeing her for nearly seventeen years.

"So I focused on the clue of Marlene's aunt in Nebraska," Cully continued. "After a couple of false starts with maiden names and all, I followed that up."

"You found something." Boone braced himself.

"Yes."

"What?" The demand came out harsh from the burning dryness in his throat. How would he live with himself if something awful had happened, something he could have prevented if he'd been around, if he'd known....

"I found your son."

Chapter One

"We've got a guest coming this afternoon."

Cambria Weston turned from the counter, where she'd poured herself a cup of coffee, to face Irene Weston, who ate breakfast with the rest of the family at the round wooden table. To trim the temptation of her stepmother's cooking, Cambria always ate her breakfast—a piece of toast—at her cabin before she took the three-minute walk to the main house to begin her workday as manager of the Weston Ranch Guest Quarters. It was tough to beat that commute, especially with early May bringing in spring's warmth and birds and flowers.

Having made her announcement, Irene appeared content to return Cambria's frown with a mild smile. This called for direct measures.

"A guest? We're not open yet. Not until Memorial Day weekend." Cambria had a schedule of what she had to accomplish each day until then, but in case Irene hadn't checked the calendar lately, she added, "That's another three and a half weeks before we open."

"Officially," agreed Irene placidly.

"Well, then why didn't you tell them—"

"Him," Irene corrected. "One guest. A man."

"Why didn't you tell *him* we aren't open yet? The cabins reek of paint and the floors haven't been done, not to mention the rest of the scrubbing. And the bunkhouse hasn't even been opened. We can't have anybody here yet."

"He sounded so tired," Irene said, then gave a pleased look around the table loaded with apple nut bread, homemade pancakes, scrambled eggs, bacon and all the fixings of butter, jellies and syrups. "And thin."

Cambria sat down, meeting the amused smiles that her father and brother flashed at her from across the round table. It took something to get the men in her family to take that much time out from enjoying Irene's bountiful spread.

The men in her family, she thought again with a catch in her heart. Ted Weston's hair had gone totally silver in the past few years and had grown a little thin on top; whenever he forgot to wear a hat while he worked in the sun and wind that had long ago corrugated his face and neck, the tender scalp pinkened like a baby's. And in the same few years Pete had nearly reached manhood, gangly adolescence filling in with confidence and character practically before her eyes.

She couldn't resist a smile back at them. They all knew Irene Weston's heart was even bigger than her larder. But Cambria took a shot anyhow at adding the salt of practicality, trying to keep her voice stern.

"How can anyone possibly sound thin over the telephone, Mama?"

Mama—that was a tactical error. Cambria had been slipping back and forth between "Irene" and "Mama" since she'd been five years old, a quarter century ago, when Ted Weston had met then married the warm-hearted, ginger-haired young widow. Cambria never used "Mama" when she really meant business.

The older woman's smile softened as their eyes met. "He sounded thin," Irene repeated.

"Weak?" Cambria asked.

"Oh, no, not weak. Not at all. Maybe...stressed. Isn't that what you and Jessa said when you moved back from Washington and she came along to open the shop?"

Yeah, that's what she and her long-time friend, Jessa Tarrant, had decided to tell her family and everyone else by way of explanation. Their separate reasons were more complicated and less easily revealed.

Cambria sighed in capitulation, drawing another pair of grins from the men in her family.

"All right, I'll give the west cabin a once-over this morning. It's in better shape than the others. It should do for...how long did this guy say he wants to stay?"

"He didn't say. A couple days, I'd suppose."

Cambria frowned, but said nothing. Her stepmother's inattention to such practical details as finding out how long guests would stay or making sure they paid before they left was the reason Cambria handled the business aspects of the bed and breakfast.

"Well, don't be surprised if he ends up walking away saying it's not worth paying for."

"We'll get the cabin ready together," Irene said. "And everything will be just fine, you'll see. You worry too much."

"Or worse," Cambria said, pursuing her own line of thought. "He'll stay a couple nights, then, when it's time to pay, he'll say the facilities weren't up to par and he'll try to get out of paying."

"I wish you weren't so cynical, Cambria." Cambria felt a twinge of discomfort at the concern in her stepmother's blue eyes. But that didn't make her buy the reassurance of the words that followed. "Everything will be just fine."

Shortly before four o'clock, Cambria heard car tires on the road that wound from the highway to the ranch buildings. They had the cabin about as well pulled together as they could, considering the limited time.

Open windows helped dispel the fresh-paint smell, but at the cost of a definite chill. The wooden floor was scrubbed and waxed, though to her critical eye it could have used another coat. The wooden table and chair were also polished, the fireplace cleaned and a new fire laid. The tiny bathroom had been disinfected within an inch of its life, the stuffed chair aired and vacuumed, the shelves dusted. They'd washed the sheets, but without enough time to adequately air the other bed linens, she'd used two quilts from the main house.

Irene had gone to the house for a welcoming plate of oatmeal-raisin cookies, while Cambria made the bed. That's when she heard the car reach the gravel on this end of the drive. Something else that needed doing, she thought—she'd have to get a load of gravel to smooth over the ravages of a Wyoming winter before the guests came... the regular season guests, anyway.

She let the top sheet drift down and looked out the window. A glossy, midnight blue sedan with Wyoming plates pulled to a stop. A rental, definitely not economy class, she judged from her experience running the guest quarters the previous two summers. Her left eyebrow rose as she looked more closely at the vehicle—*definitely* not economy class.

Mostly their visitors were family groups, with a few young couples, some retired folks. This car didn't seem to fit any of those types.

She should have pressed Irene about their guest. Not that it would have done any good. Irene might ask his favorite meal so she could cook it for him, but the chances she'd ask the sort of questions Cambria wanted answered were a thousand to one.

The car door opened and one long, jeans-clad leg appeared. Cambria supposed she should go greet the newcomer. She'd never cared for the necessity of being sociable on demand when she'd worked in Washington, and returning to the ranch hadn't changed her feelings about that. Being warm and welcoming came easily to some people, but not to her.

Then she heard a voice—Irene returning from the house—and gratefully continued with the bed. With Irene on hand, Cambria had no need to play gracious hostess.

She was aware of footsteps on the cabin's wooden porch, the opening of the main door and a murmur of voices, but she paid no attention, concentrating on her task. Spreading and tucking, spreading and tucking. She slid the second pillow into a case, tossed it in place, considered the effect, then stretched to plump its brethren on the far side of the bed.

She began to straighten, the action accelerated by an arrogant, low drawl from behind her—where its owner would have had an excellent view of her derriere as she'd bent over the bed.

"Do you come with the room?"

She spun around, momentum advancing her a step so she almost crashed into the solid, male figure. He automatically reached to steady her and she just as automatically withdrew. But her gaze did crash into his—leaving her feeling as if she'd been run over by a pair of gray eyes. Gray eyes that seemed both depthless and flat under a pair of startlingly black eyebrows. She stared into those eyes with the sort of haunting familiarity of déjà vu.

In that instant, chagrin spread across the man's face. Whether it was at his own rudeness or simply because he was smart enough to see he'd riled her, Cambria didn't know. And didn't care.

"Sorry. I didn't expect to find anybody in here," he said, the drawl not as pronounced. "But that was out of—"

"We try to meet our guests' expectations." Recovering rapidly, she cut across his apology with a smile so icy she thought it might crack her lips. "So I'll leave right now, Mr.—"

It would have been a good exit line if she hadn't realized too late that Irene had never mentioned the guest's name, and she'd never asked.

"Name's Boone Dorsey," he said slowly, as if weighing whether to tell her.

"Mr. Dorsey," she repeated, then walked past him and out of the room, out of the cabin and out of his sight.

"You can call me Boone."

Cambria jerked her head up at the casual words, spoken as if an hour hadn't passed since their previous exchange. As if he hadn't tracked her down to the barn where she was grooming Jezebel and Snakebit. As if he didn't have to address her across Snakebit's broad back. And as if she didn't hold a very sharp hoof pick in her right hand.

He'd entered through the open double doors on the east end of the barn. The evening sun, streaming low through the matching doors at the opposite end, so washed him in light that he barely seemed real. She waited, not certain of his motives or his sincerity.

"Or," he went on in a drawl she realized owed more to the South than the West, "you can call me jackass."

He took another step forward, out of the dazzle but not so far that the shadows swallowed him. Now she could see that one side of his mouth lifted in a half grin of self-derision, grooves echoing up his left cheek. She could see threads of gray that softened the hair that sprang back from his forehead and reached his collar to a lighter shade than the harsh black of his strong eyebrows. She could also see the tiredness around and behind his black-lashed gray eyes. And, yes—Irene had been right, of course—she could see a thinness in his face that went beyond the natural angularity of his bone structure.

Buying time, she brushed Snakebit's back with her fingertips, then stroked the coarse, smooth hide.

She let out a quick breath. Why did she have the feeling that staying angry at this man would be safer, even as her anger slid away?

"Jackass has a nice ring to it."

The other side of his mouth caught up, lifting into a full grin. Another skitter of...*something*—was it familiarity, or instinct warning her to beware?—scratched at her nerve endings, then disappeared.

"Look, we got off on the wrong foot, and that was my fault. I really am sorry," he said. "You caught me off guard. Irene didn't tell me anybody was in the room. And I had a situation where there was a good-looking woman in my room I didn't expect.... Not that there's any good cause for me to have talked to you that way. Can I make it up to you?"

It was no surprise that he already called her stepmother Irene. Most people did in the first minute. But there were several items of interest in his speech. There was a flash of belated recognition that his leer might have been, at least partly, a defense against being caught off guard. And naturally, there was the question of what sort of situation he'd been in before that a woman had unexpectedly shown up in his room? But foremost, there was his offer.

It might be interesting to see where the talk took them if he led it. That could reveal more about him than having him give answers to direct questions. She'd often marveled at the willingness of guests to volunteer information, from mundane chatter about family and jobs to the most intimate details of sex lives and phobias.

"You know horses?" Cambria asked.

A glint lit his eyes. "I know some people I'd describe as their rear ends. In addition to me, naturally. That what you mean?"

She fought an answering smile. "Not quite. I meant, caring for the four-legged kind."

He gave a deep sigh that drew her attention to the broad shoulders in his dazzling white shirt, whose perfect fit and very plainness announced that it, like the car he'd rented, did not belong to the economy class. "I was afraid the apology wouldn't be enough. You're going to make me clean out stalls, too, huh?"

She laughed, and meant it despite herself. "I won't go that hard on you. How about combing Jezebel—" she nodded to the mare behind her "—while I finish with Snakebit's hooves."

"Sounds fair to me."

He took the brush she held out over Snakebit's back, placing his hand on the gelding's hindquarters as he came around behind. At least he knew enough to give a horse that warning. Still, she watched for a moment in silence as he worked on Jezebel before she was satisfied he knew what he was doing. He raised an eyebrow but didn't object to her scrutiny. Finally she turned back to Snakebit, lifting his front near hoof and bending over to remove any packed-in dirt or grit.

"So, Irene tells me you don't usually open for another month or so," he offered after several minutes of silent work.

"That's right. We still have a lot of preparation to do before we're really ready to have guests." She wasn't about to come out and make excuses, but...

"The cabin looks great to me."

"And smells of paint." Now why did she say that when she'd just decided not to make excuses?

"Small price to pay for privacy." Was privacy so precious to him? She didn't have a chance to wonder as he went on. "Irene also tells me you're Cambria Weston. Cambria—that's a pretty name. Unusual."

"Did Irene also tell you," she replied sardonically, "that the name comes from a deserted coal-mining community?"

"Yeah, Irene told me that. Doesn't change that it's pretty."

Ignoring the second part of his comment, she asked dryly, "Anything else Irene told you?"

"Yes. She said you're the brains of the outfit. I'm wondering if you're the brawn, too."

"What do you mean?"

"All this preparation for the guests, you do it alone?"

"No, of course not. The whole family works."

"Family," he repeated in a murmur.

She glanced over her shoulder, but he was bent, stroking down Jezebel's hindquarter. That posture probably explained the odd note in his voice.

"Irene, me, Pete—that's my brother—and Dad, when he can spare time from the cattle operation. It's a smaller operation than it used to be, but it's a lot for one man."

"Does, uh, your brother help with that, too? I mean, if he's old enough."

She chuckled. "He'd probably tell you he's old enough to do anything and everything. He does help a lot, and he'd do more if Dad and Irene let him, but they're determined that he have a chance to do things at school, too. He was in a play over the winter and now he's playing baseball."

"Baseball?"

"Yeah. Why does that surprise you?"

"I don't know," he said slowly, as if searching his own reaction. Then he shrugged and she had a feeling the rest of his answer wasn't going to be as honest. "Maybe I figured a kid around here would be involved in rodeo."

"Oh, he does that, too. But he really loves baseball."

"He's on a team?"

From her discussion of Pete's American Legion baseball team, his questions led her to other aspects of life on the Weston ranch. At one point they swapped places so she could work on Jezebel's hooves and he could brush Snakebit. And all the while that she gave answers about the family, local school system, network of neighbors and friends, ranch routine, social activities available in the nearby town of Bardville, and the kinds of people who came through as summer guests, she wondered what on earth a stranger would possibly find interesting in all this.

At the same time she felt an undercurrent of uneasiness coming from the man. A restlessness in his movements, a slight jerkiness in some of his questions. It reminded her of the way a young horse might react to a jump—eager to get to the other side, but dreading the actual jump.

She'd thought letting him lead the conversation might answer some of her questions about him. It raised more. He hadn't volunteered one piece of information about himself, and that was most unusual.

Finished, she led the horses one at a time into their stalls while he gathered the various combs, brushes and picks. After she'd forced closed the stubbornly sticking stall door, he followed her into the tack room, handing the equipment to her one by one as she put it away.

"Thanks for helping." She wished it had come out a little more naturally. There was no reason to be ill at ease with this man. Cautious, yes, as she was cautious around most strangers. But this discomfort came from something much more elemental. And that was odd. He was attractive, certainly, but she hadn't gone tongue-tied around good-looking men since high school. Besides, this man was more interesting-looking, with his dark brows, graying hair and angled face, than classically good-looking. Definitely interesting.

"You're welcome." He sounded distracted. "Do your guests usually get involved with the routine around here?"

"Sometimes." She wasn't going to tell him he wasn't a usual guest. Based on two hours' acquaintance, it would be presumptuous—and maybe too revealing. "It's a matter of what the guests want from staying here—some want to be left alone and some want to join right in. Plus it depends on how much inexperienced help we can take at any one time."

"That sounds fair."

She caught a glimpse of that lopsided grin again as she took the curry comb from him. It left her a little off-balance, and that made her next words more challenging than she'd intended.

"You ask a lot of questions."

"Sorry."

"I have some of my own."

"Oh?" It was not an encouraging syllable.

She didn't let that, or his slight stiffening, stop her. "Where are you from?"

"North Carolina, born and raised."

"That explains the drawl."

"What drawl?" he said in exaggerated perplexity, which she ignored.

"Another question." She also ignored his renewed tension, though it intrigued her. "Would you have cleaned out the stalls if I'd asked you?"

"Sure," he said a little smugly, holding out a brush. "I didn't bring it up until I'd seen they already had fresh straw."

Again he drew a laugh from her when she hadn't expected it. Taking the brush from him, she felt the touch of his hand on hers like a gush of warm water, almost hot against the chilling air of evening. She stepped away, backing into the tack room wall.

He reached out to her, but she'd easily steadied herself so his hands settled lightly on her shoulders, his thumbs not quite meeting where they brushed at the pulse in her throat, a pulse that abruptly pounded like a racehorse coming out of the gate.

She looked up, but his eyes were focused on his hands and her throat, his lowered lids masking what went on behind the taut face.

A brassy clang, strident for all its distance, made them both jerk. The movement brought her closer to him for an instant and tightened his hands fractionally on her before they simultaneously stepped apart, severing the connection.

"That's the call to supper," she explained, hurriedly stowing the rest of the equipment. Buoyed by her success in keeping her voice steady, she told herself that in another second she would meet his eyes without a qualm. She was not one to react to a man she'd just met, so thinking something had happened here must have been her imagination.

"Good, because I'm definitely hungry."

The rough, low tone of his slow voice changed her mind. She wouldn't look at him until they were in the house surrounded by her family.

Just in case it wasn't her imagination.

Boone Dorsey Smith considered the image in the mirror of the small bathroom off the main house's back hall, where Cambria had directed him to wash his hands before supper.

In a few minutes he'd sit down at the table and meet his son for the first time. A life he'd helped create, though he hadn't known it until sixteen years later.

God, what if he said the wrong thing? What if he said something that would let everybody know before the time was right?

You're not going to just march in there and announce you're the boy's father, are you, Boone?

No, I am not. For God's sake, Cully, what kind of fool do you take me for?

The kind of fool who takes action. Sometimes that's needed, sometimes not. You don't always know the difference.

Thanks for the vote of confidence, Cully.

You swear you'll settle back, see what the situation is before you say anything?

I swear.

Swearing not to wade right in had been easy. Now he had to *do* it. And he wanted to do this right. No mistakes. That's why he'd sought out Cambria Weston. To find out more about his son's life before this meeting, so he'd be less likely to make a hash of it.

His groin pulsed with a faint reminder that maybe information hadn't been his sole reason for seeking out Cambria.

What the hell did he think he was doing?

In the cabin he'd had an excuse. Maybe. He'd been tense from marathon sessions at Bodie Smith Enterprises the past month, trying to wrap up as much as he could. Then flying to Wyoming, picking up the car, driving out here. Meeting Irene Weston, the woman who'd been his son's mother. But he'd gotten through that. When Irene had given him a final smile and left the cabin, he'd started to ease up on his rigid control, thinking he was finally alone.

Instead he'd walked in to find a woman bent over his bed, the sunlight from the window adding gold and red to what, after all, was probably perfectly ordinary light brown hair. Her position showing long legs in snug jeans, suggesting at the swell of breasts under a loose-fitting shirt. And the smooth, firm curves filling out the seat of her worn jeans, close enough to reach out and stroke....

But what excuse did he have in the barn?

Another couple of seconds and that gong wouldn't have been any more than a whisper against the roar of hormones rushing through him.

He'd gone in there deliberately, to mend fences and find out what he could about the boy they called Pete.

He'd done that, and more. He'd watched Cambria Weston bend and straighten over the horses' hooves. Listened to her soothing murmurs to the animals. Felt the brush of her fingers against his hand.... And then they'd stood close enough that another step would have brought her softness fully against him. He'd been fighting a losing battle against the urge to take that step when the gong had sounded.

He wiped his hands on a small green towel hanging beside the sink and scowled at himself in the mirror.

All right, so it had been awhile since he'd had a woman. Between the demands of business and his disinclination for women who made it all too clear they'd be happy to oblige the owner of an up-and-coming company, he'd qualified as a trainee for the monastery—in deed, if not in thought—for a good many months.

That didn't mean he had to leap into action with the first attractive, interesting, challenging woman to come along. Especially not with *this* woman. He couldn't risk his chance with his son for a woman he didn't even know.

Lord, his son's adopted stepsister. What did that make her to him?

Besides desirable.

And—if he had any sense—completely off-limits.

Dinner started a little awkwardly.

Irene was her usual cheerful self, and Pete remained absorbed in packing away as much of Irene's cooking as he possibly could. But maybe Ted wondered some of the same things about their guest as Cambria did because she noted that he was even quieter than usual.

As for Boone Dorsey, she wondered if his calm exterior really did hide a strong tension and if he really did keep directing the conversation away from himself, or if her imagination was working overtime.

"Thanks for inviting me to supper, Irene. This is delicious. I'm sure I won't be fed half as well when I start searching out the places the lady at the airport recommended."

"This early in the season not many of those restaurants will be open," Irene said. "We'd be happy to have you take your meals with us as long as you're here."

"Irene, I don't—"

"Thank you, Irene, I'd love to do that."

Cambria's protest and Boone's acceptance came simultaneously. Boone won. His deep voice kept going with barely a pause. "Of course, I'll pay extra for the meals. I know that's not in the room rate."

"It's not any bother to add a plate, but you'll have to settle that with Cambria." Irene dismissed that practicality with a wave toward her stepdaughter. From the corner of her eye, Cambria was aware of the look Boone shot her, but she didn't return it as Irene continued. "Now, if there's anything you need in your cabin, you just let us know, Boone."

"I appreciate that. The cabin looks great. All the comforts, thanks." He chewed a bite of mashed potato, then added, "There is one thing—I didn't see a phone when I was stowing my gear. I didn't look real carefully, but..."

Irene was shaking her head, even as she passed him more green bean casserole. "The guest quarters don't have phones."

"No phone?"

Cambria had to hide a smile. If the man sounded that bereft without a phone, no wonder he looked stressed. Though how he expected to get much rest she couldn't imagine, since she'd spotted a laptop computer, portable printer and other accoutrements of a traveling workaholic when she'd swept out of his cabin.

"No, but you're welcome to use the phone in the den. That's where you can watch TV if you want, too. We don't pick up many channels, but Cambria donated her VCR and her tape collection when she moved back from Washington, D.C., so we do have that." Irene turned to Pete. "So, you remember to leave the phone for Boone's use, you understand?"

"Aw, Mom..."

"No, no, that's okay, Irene." Boone Dorsey's quick reply made obvious his discomfort at the idea of using the phone in the main house. "I, uh, if I need a phone, I can go into town."

"There's no need for that."

"No, really, it's okay. I'd probably need to hook in my portable fax, too. And that would tie up your phone forever. So, if there's someplace in town that I can pay a fee..."

"Truth to tell, I don't believe there is," said Irene with a smile. "So that's all settled, Boone."

Cambria had to bite back a grin as he mumbled his thanks. Clearly, Boone Dorsey was trying to figure out how Irene Weston had managed to both outmaneuver him and leave him obligated to say thank you. He wasn't the first to get in that position.

"Where'd you get the name Boone, anyhow?" Pete asked, making his first real contribution to the conversation now that he'd finished a second full plate of pot roast, mashed potatoes, green bean casserole and stewed tomatoes.

"Pete..."

"It's okay," Boone said hurriedly over Ted Weston's soft reproof. "It's what you might call a, uh, a family name."

Pete cocked his head at him. "You're related to Daniel Boone?"

"Hard to say. Now, I don't want to malign the dear departed's reputation, but my grandma used to refer to him as Darling Danny. And," he added slyly, "my grandfather was away an awful lot to have had eight children."

"Yeah? But— Wait a minute, how old was your grandmother?" Pete demanded.

Amid the general laughter, Boone grumbled about having folks ruin his tales with math and history. But he grinned across the table, and Pete grinned back.

Cambria barely heard Irene say that before Pete's hair got so long *he'd* be taken for Daniel Boone, she wanted him to get to the barbershop.

A shiver of uneasiness crossed her skin. She couldn't explain it, but there was something about this man.... She had avoided focusing on their guest since coming in from the barn, but now she did.

He was attractive. Charming. He drew out Irene and Ted and Pete one by one with questions, just the way he had drawn her out in the barn earlier.

He didn't fit the mold of their guests, that much was certain.

The conversation she'd paid little attention to hit a lull and Cambria impulsively demanded, "How long are you planning to stay?"

Boone raised a brow at her abrupt question, but answered readily enough. "I was thinking a month."

Everybody stared at him in surprise. Most guests stayed a couple of nights on their way cross-country, looking for a resting place between Mount Rushmore and Yellowstone Park. Occasionally they'd stay as long as a week, or even two. But a month? That had never happened before.

"Most jobs you can't take that much time off," said Ted Weston mildly.

"I'm pretty much my own boss."

Cambria found her voice. "A month? Why on earth would you stay here a month?"

"Cambria," Irene murmured in reproach. "Boone, we'd be happy to have you with us a month, or longer if that suits you."

"Thank you, Irene. I've been needing some rest a long time. This seems a quiet place."

"Oh, yes," said Irene. "An excellent place to get away from stress. As Cambria can tell you. When she came back to us from Washington, she needed rest, too. She's much better now, though—"

Cambria was caught off guard by the turn of the conversational spotlight onto her. But now she braced for the worst.

"I do wish she wasn't still so cynical."

Boone looked at Cambria, dark eyebrows raised slightly as if asking for the rest of the story. She turned from him to glare at Irene, who returned the look blandly as she patted Cambria's hand.

And that, Cambria thought sourly, neatly capped that topic without a satisfactory answer—or any answer at all—to why a man from North Carolina with a budget that stretched to luxurious rental cars and top quality clothes, who had a reluctance to talk about himself and entirely too much appeal for her peace of mind, would plan to stay here a month.

Chapter Two

A number of the people who stopped at the Weston Ranch Guest Quarters found themselves at loose ends at first. Some hadn't wound down from everyday warp speed to vacation speed, and some never would because they scheduled their vacations as closely as air traffic controllers bringing in flights at O'Hare Airport.

Boone Dorsey's ends weren't just loose, however—they were frayed.

Serves him right, Cambria thought as, shortly before eleven the next morning, she drove the ranch truck in from the back section and spotted their lone guest sitting on the corral fence. No one else was in sight, the corral was empty, and Boone Dorsey fidgeted as if that top rail had an electric current running through it.

The smile that image stirred never reached full-blown because just then the truck's wheels hit the rut where the back road met the open area encircled by the main house and various outbuildings on one side and a crescent of log cabins on the other. The jolt bounced her high enough to brush her hair against the cab ceiling. No springs, no springs at all. She hoped the engine held out another couple of years.

"Hey, Cambria." Boone's greeting came practically before she'd brought the truck to a stop. "Missed you at breakfast." She'd decided to get an early start unloading irrigation pipe lengths for Ted to put together. "Where is everybody?"

"School, working, volunteering at the hospital."

"I could help."

She arched a brow at him. "You have experience as a hospital aide?"

"I meant around here. I could help you do, well, whatever you're going to do now."

"I'm going to my cabin and taking a shower." She saw her mistake too late to stop the words.

Flame glowed in his eyes in a heartbeat. "I could—"

She was sure he could, which was why she talked right over his response. "And I can manage both on my own, thank you."

She marched off, irked at herself for giving him the opening. She wasn't interested in a little light flirting. She was even less interested in anything serious. Her reaction to him in the barn notwithstanding, she wasn't interested. Period.

If this man truly intended to stay a month, she'd have to set him straight from the start. And the sooner the better.

Where the path branched down toward her cabin, she turned to him.

"I'm going into town after I change. You want to come with?" She didn't bother to infuse any welcome into the invitation.

"Yeah, I do." He remained where she'd left him. "I'll buy lunch."

"We'll split."

She gave him no chance to answer, but went on to her cabin, closing off all errant images of what her shower might have been like under the circumstances she'd seen burning in his eyes.

"I'll drive," Boone offered as Cambria came out in clean jeans, shirt, and her flannel-lined canvas jacket. The clouds had piled up over the sun and the prelude to summer they'd enjoyed recently looked about ready to end.

She should take him up on that, just to save the gas in the four-wheel drive, but she'd seen the wary look he'd divided between the aging truck and the grit-coated, four-wheel drive, and it irked her.

"No need."

"It's no bother, and—"

She slid into the driver's seat of the four-wheel drive, hooked the seat belt and cut across his words by turning the key. "Get in."

He extracted a leather briefcase from the back seat of his sedan before coming around to the passenger side of the four-wheel drive. He barely had the seat belt in place when she let the clutch out with a jerk. She made no effort to evade the gravel road's washboard areas or to slow to soften its potholes.

He didn't grab for the door handle and his hands didn't tighten around the briefcase, but Cambria noted with some satisfaction that his foot braced firmly against the floorboard, exactly where the brake would be if he were driving. She took the turn onto the highway with enough speed to spew the scant gravel and raise a good spray of dust. Pete would be proud of her, she thought, clamping down on a grin.

"You should put that in your brochures," Boone said.

"What?"

"Free roller-coaster rides."

She clamped down harder on the grin. "You don't like my driving, Mr. Dorsey?"

"I'm in awe of your driving, Ms. Weston," he said in perfect deadpan. "And that's something, coming from someone who grew up where moonshiners outdriving the revenuers was such great sport they turned it into stock car racing."

"It's not sport out here, just a way to get around."

"Is that what you were doing this morning out in the truck? Just getting around?"

"In a way. I was dropping off lengths of irrigation pipe for Ted to set up."

"Irrigation pipe?"

"We can't count on nature giving us enough water for the hay and grain we need to get the cattle through the winter. If you were looking for a fancy dude ranch to stay at, you've come to the wrong place. This is not a spa with a few horses and cattle added for atmosphere. This is a working ranch."

She inwardly cringed at her defensiveness. He didn't seem to notice.

"I could help, you know."

"There's no need—"

"I'd like to. I don't know much about irrigation pipe, but I can drive a pickup. Maybe not to your standards, but I can get by."

"We'll see."

"Okay, Cambria. We'll see."

She had the impression she had not heard the last of this.

She drove in silence, Boone Dorsey apparently fully content to observe the countryside without requiring any commentary from her.

"Where'd you see our brochure?" she demanded abruptly.

"What?" He turned to her and the discomfiting suspicion popped into her mind that she'd asked the question partly because she'd wanted to see his face instead of the back of his head.

"You said we should add roller-coaster rides to the brochure. Where'd you see it?"

"I don't know. Must have picked it up somewhere."

She narrowed her eyes and shot him a sidelong look that should have pinned him to the seat. "You couldn't have. We don't have a brochure."

"How do you get bookings?"

"Through the state tourism guide."

"Well, that must have been where I read about your place, then."

All her instincts told her it was a lie. Well, not all her instincts, because some of them were telling her that this was a mighty attractive male of the species.

The last time her instincts had been at war this way had been seven years ago. When she'd first met Tony Sussman.

Then the war had been between her attraction to a high-energy, ambitious, going-places man and some niggling doubts about both his means and his ends. She'd been young enough and hopeful enough to shush her cautionary instincts so thoroughly that they went into hibernation until it was too late to save her.

Now, as they reached the first straggling buildings of Bardville, a car horn beeped a greeting and Cambria absently returned the wave of Sheriff Milano. Her mind was still on the past.

It had taken her four long years, a dose of heartache and a final slap in the face to realize that despite his declarations of love and his marriage proposal, Tony Sussman's interest had been only in trying to sell himself. And he'd been more than willing to go to the highest bidder.

She'd learned her lesson, and this time the bundle of instincts screaming their attraction would just have to lump it. She'd take no chances.

If that made her cynical, as Irene said, then she was cynical.

Cambria pulled into a parking spot that split the difference between Jessa Tarrant's shop and the café, and was only a couple of blocks from the co-op association where she would order the replacement pipe Ted had discovered this morning that he'd need.

"I'll meet you at the café in an hour." Even to her ears, it more resembled a drill sergeant's order than a friendly rendezvous.

Boone stopped her exit by leaning across her body to wrap his right hand around her left forearm as she reached for the door handle.

"I thought we got past yesterday's bad start, Cambria. I apologized, and I could have sworn you accepted. Didn't you?"

His face was too close. She looked out the driver's window without focusing.

"I accepted."

"Then what have you got against me, Cambria?"

She brought her head around to face him, tightening her facial muscles against the probing of his gray eyes, and answered a demand with a demand.

"Why did you come here?"

"Little rest and relaxation, like everybody else."

She shook her head slowly. "You don't belong here."

"I belong here as much as anybody else."

"There's nothing here to interest someone like you."

His eyes flickered with a reaction she couldn't define before the steel closed over them again. He released her arm, but still met her stare for stare.

"How about you?"

It took a heartbeat for her to understand he was saying that *she* interested him.

It took a handful of rapid heartbeats to get the breath to answer. "I don't socialize with guests. Not that way."

"Never?"

"Never. Besides—" She pointedly looked from his expensive shirt to the butter-leather briefcase at his feet. "I don't think a small-time Wyoming rancher's your type."

"You don't know anything about me." He seemed to deliberately smooth his gruff voice. "I'm a country boy, born and bred. I've got that in my blood."

He gave half a grin, inviting her to join in.

Stubbornly she shook her head again. "You don't belong here. You don't...*fit.* I want to know why you came here."

Foolishly, she really thought for a moment that he'd tell her the truth. Then she saw the curtain of evasion come over his eyes and knew he wouldn't.

"Not to do anybody any harm, Cambria." Still watching her, he leaned away and reached behind himself to open his door. A tinge of amusement colored his voice as he added, "So you can retract those porcupine quills."

"I just don't know what gets into Irene sometimes," Cambria grumbled a half hour later to Jessa Tarrant.

Having ordered the pipe and picked up some electrical supplies Ted needed for repairs, Cambria had stopped at Jessa's shop for floor wax and cleanser.

She felt edgy, restless, and if anyone in the world might understand that, it was Jessa Tarrant.

Attending different colleges in Washington, D.C., they'd met at a seminar as juniors and hit it off immediately. That summer they'd both interned on Capitol Hill and shared a tiny studio apartment—the kind of forced intimacy that would make or break a friendship. For them, it was make. While Cambria remained in D.C. over the next few years, Jessa had taken public relations jobs in several other cities before returning to D.C. But whether they lived in the same city or not, the friendship endured through good times and bad.

"Of course you know what got into Irene," Jessa disagreed with a slight smile. "It's what always gets into her—her heart's bigger than her business sense. Making special provisions to take this guest in before you're open, agreeing to give him meals, that's vintage Irene—and that's exactly why you came back here two years ago."

True. The bed-and-breakfast operation, which the Westons had begun to add income, had instead been a money drain under Irene's stewardship. Her warmth and generosity drew plenty of guests, but no profit. Now Cambria ran the business, leaving the hospitality to Irene. And they were finally in the black.

"If I have to keep an eye on this guy, it'll really mess up my schedule for getting the rest of the units in shape," Cambria grumbled.

"Why would you have to keep an eye on him?"

"Oh, you know... Can't just leave a guest with nothing to do."

Jessa's brows rose, and Cambria knew her friend was remembering the number of times Cambria had done just that, saying it was probably the best service Weston Ranch Guest Quarters could offer visitors.

Cambria tipped her head slightly toward the back of the shop. Jessa's eyes followed to where Rita Campbell hummed comfortably as she transferred bug repellent from a box to a shelf. Jessa had hired Rita not quite a month ago to help in the shop, though Cambria suspected the recently divorced fifty-something Rita might be getting more help than she gave. Rita was quite nice, but her presence put a damper on confidences between the two friends.

By implicit agreement, they moved toward the front of the store.

"So what's this guest doing while you're in town?" Jessa pitched her voice low enough that even if Rita quit humming she'd have to strain to hear. "This is Irene's day at the hospital, isn't it?"

Cambria nodded. "He came in with me."

"He— Why?" Cambria couldn't tell if her friend was more surprised that she'd agreed to bring the guest in to Bardville or that he'd agreed to come. Bardville serviced the needs of the community and surrounding ranches, but it held no lure for tourists. "I mean, uh, you should have brought him in the shop. We can always use a customer."

"I think he had other things to do."

Jessa's raised brows asked the question of what things he could have to do in Bardville.

"For someone who says he's here to rest and relax, he seems strung pretty tight," Cambria said. "He brought his briefcase into town."

"Why?"

Cambria shrugged. Glancing out the shop's front window, she said slowly, "If I'm not mistaken, he's making business calls right this moment."

Jessa came to stand beside her. The big front window gave a view across the street to a figure standing at the outdoor public phone bolted to the brick wall of the bank, built when Bardville had been a bustling railroad stop. The railroad had quit half a century ago. The bank remained, though under various names as numerous buyouts demonstrated the financial world's version of the food chain. A previous institution had renovated the building and turned the space between it and Toffeen Pharmacy into a ten-by-ten-foot park. No one knew why the phone had been added, though its position did provide some protection from the wind.

But not enough, apparently, as Boone Dorsey planted a big hand firmly on papers that threatened to flutter out of the open briefcase perched on the small shelf under the phone. His other hand took notes as he cradled the receiver against his shoulder.

"Capable hands," Jessa said slowly. "He's quite attractive."

"I suppose."

"Do you like him?"

"Like him? I don't know anything about him. Besides, he's a guest, a customer."

Jessa brushed that aside with a characteristic quick gesture. "I haven't seen you so...so *ruffled* by a man in a long time."

"There's something about him..."

"Oh."

"No, not, 'oh.' Not that way," she said with perhaps unnecessary vehemence. "There's something that just doesn't ring true. I can't put my finger on it."

She'd told him she didn't socialize with guests, and that should have been the end of it. But her edginess hadn't eased one bit.

"Maybe that's part of it, Cambria. But there's another part. You're attracted to this man," Jessa said stubbornly.

"Hey, are you encouraging me to jump this guy's bones? This stranger? I'd think you of all peo— Oh, God... I'm sorry, Jessa."

Because there was truth to what her friend had said, and because that truth made her uncomfortable, Cambria had tried to deflect it. Only she'd deflected it right into her friend's vulnerability. She hadn't stopped to think about her words' impact until she'd seen Jessa's wince.

"No, it's okay, Cambria. In a way, you're right. In a way, I'd be the last person to advise being pleasant to any stranger, but I'm working on that. And the counseling is helping, a lot. But what are you doing?"

"Me?"

"Yes, you. You haven't opened up to anybody in a long time. I know you were hurt by Tony, but you can't let that stand in the way the rest of your life. I'm not saying this is the guy, but someday...."

Across the street Boone Dorsey hung up, closed the briefcase, then immediately began to dial. Enough numbers to make it clear he'd reeled off a calling-card number and long distance number, both by heart.

Cambria felt as if a gust of wind had blown her off a familiar road onto a strange one. Jessa Tarrant telling her to take a risk? Jessa encouraging her to forget the hurt of the past and open her heart again?

"I don't know what to say, Jessa," she admitted.

"Well, don't make a huge thing of it. I just don't want you to completely close yourself off, especially if it's partly because of my...situation." Jessa slanted a look at her that mingled amusement and a hint of concern. "Besides, you always did have a thing for hands."

"Don't be ridiculous," Cambria said with a smile, relieved at the switch to teasing.

At that moment Boone Dorsey turned and looked directly to where she and Jessa stood, as if he'd felt the weight of their scrutiny. Jessa immediately stepped to the side, where the magazine rack hid her from view. Cambria stood her ground, though her heart pulsed slightly faster. As if the notion of being caught staring embarrassed her, she thought with a twist of her mouth.

They were too far away from each other, and the distortion of the window intruded, yet Cambria had the impression that Boone Dorsey's eyes had locked with hers. And she wished irrationally that she could know if the steel that protected his secrets remained as impregnable.

"Just be careful." Beside her, Jessa sounded worried, her earlier amusement totally evaporated.

"No need," she lied, finally breaking the look by turning to her friend. "He thinks I'm a porcupine."

* * *

"Hey—you still there, Boone?"

"Yeah, I'm here," he automatically said into the mouthpiece, though his eyes remained on Cambria Weston's profile.

"What's happening?"

"Nothing. Nothing's happening."

"Boone..."

He shook his head clear of distraction and turned his back to the woman in the shop window across the street. "Cully, nothing's happening," he repeated.

"Yeah?" Skepticism flooded the word, but a sigh of acceptance followed. "Okay. Finish what you were saying."

"I was finished. I told you everything's fine. I checked in with the office, dealt with a few things by phone that will hold them until I can find a fax outlet somewhere around here." A sound came across the wire that indicated Cully Grainger's lack of interest in Boone's business arrangements. "That's all I have to say. You made me promise I'd call when I got here, and I've called."

"What about what's happening there with the Westons? You haven't said anythi—"

"No, I haven't," Boone snapped. "I promised that, too, and I've never broken my word to you, dammit, Grainger."

"No, you haven't." His friend's voice came back even and cool. "I wasn't questioning your word. I was saying you haven't said anything about his family."

"They're just like you said they were." Boone's mind drifted back to when Cully had first told him about his son. Had it really been just a month ago?

You found him? Is he... okay?

He's fine, Boone. Healthy. Seems like a normal kid.

Where?

Wyoming. A ranch. Nice place, not real fancy. His family takes in guests during the summer.

His family…

Father, mother, sister and the boy. It's a second marriage for the parents. They've been married twenty-four years. The sister's older. Thirty, maybe. She's the father's girl. They seem close. All of them.

Tell me about him.

His name's Pete—Peter Andrew Weston. He'll finish his junior year in high school this June. A few B's, mostly C's. Not real sure about college. He's a regular kid from all accounts, who's had a very regular life. Up till now.

"How do you like them?"

Cully's question brought Boone back to the present. He pushed his wind-whipped hair back from his forehead with his free hand and let out a slow breath. "Fine. I like them fine. They're nice people. All of them."

There was a pause on the line, as if Cully Grainger was delving into his words for more meaning.

"Boone, are you okay about this? I could come—"

"I'm okay."

"You sound edgy."

"I've got cause, don't you think? It's not every day a man finds… Well, you know."

"Yeah, I know." Another of those pauses. "You know, I think you need a kick in the head now and then to shake up some of those strange notions of yours, but if you need somebody around, you know I'd—"

"I know."

"Okay. Well, hang in there, Boone. And give me a call when… well, when it's settled."

"I will."

"Okay. See you."

"Yeah, see you… And, Cully? Thanks."

He wasn't entirely sure his final words were heard before the line went dead.

* * *

The old-fashioned bell tinkled over the door as Boone entered the shop. From the looks the three women gave him, it could have been a blaring alarm.

"Hello. Thought I saw you in here."

Though he addressed the words to Cambria, he smiled first at the older woman at the far end of the second aisle. She smiled back. The younger woman with her back to the magazine rack didn't, maintaining a neutral expression.

He hadn't made a success of his business by being overly sensitive to people preferring he was elsewhere, so he ignored the lukewarm response, as well as Cambria's frown, and raised an eyebrow to her.

Cambria Weston's hazel eyes glittered with annoyance, but she knew her social duty.

"Rita and Jessa, this is Boone Dorsey. He's staying at the Guest Quarters. For now."

He nearly grinned. She didn't bother with subtlety. Her rider said it flat-out—she didn't expect, didn't particularly want, him to stick around.

"Rita Campbell and Jessa Tarrant," Cambria said, completing the introduction.

Boone's interest heightened at hearing the latter name. So the younger woman was the one Irene Weston had mentioned as Cambria's good friend, the one who'd come here from Washington with her. This could be interesting.

They exchanged hellos, Rita's more audible than Jessa's though she was about four yards farther away.

"I've got some things to get," Cambria announced. "If you'd like to go to the café and wait there—"

"I'll wait here for you. It'll give me a chance to look around."

She gave no answer other than a quick frown, then turned away and started down an aisle holding cleaning supplies. "Rita, you have any more of that bathroom cleanser with the bleach in it?"

"Sure, right over here."

Boone watched Cambria a moment before turning to Jessa Tarrant. She immediately showed great interest in straightening the already neat magazines, but not in time to fool him. She'd been watching him, and she knew she'd been caught.

Instinct told him to give her automatic defenses a moment to settle down. He looked around. The wood-and-glass counters came from another era. The phone setup and sleek computer register were strictly modern. Behind the register hung a framed piece of antique quilting next to a photograph of Jessa and the Westons in front of the store.

He picked up a magazine with a picture of baseball's leading hitter on the cover and flipped the pages idly.

"So, Jessa, I understand you and Cambria knew each other in Washington."

"Yes."

"You both decided you wanted a more relaxed life-style, that's why you moved out here?"

"Yes."

Something in her voice snagged his full attention. He wondered what had really brought Cambria back home. "A city like Washington must get intense," he probed.

"It can, I suppose. I liked it. It's a very pretty city, with the monuments and museums and government buildings and a lot of green areas and trees."

"You make it sound real nice. Like maybe you miss it."

"In some ways. But I don't regret coming here. It's my home now, and people have been wonderful, especially the Westons."

He grabbed the opportunity. "They seem like a great family. You always hear how awful teenagers are, but Pete seems like a good kid."

"Pete?" Between the surprise in her voice and the look she flicked toward the back of the store, she gave away that she'd expected him to ask about a different member of the family. He was tempted, real tempted. "He's terrific. A good heart, and getting to have a good head on his shoulders. Now, is there anything—" her gesture indicated the shelves around them "—you need while you're here?"

Boone skimmed the neatly stocked magazine rack, and a surprisingly wide offering of paperbacks next to it. Then he surveyed the scattering of first-aid items, greeting cards, toiletries, basic camping supplies, paper goods, small gifts, cleansers and cleaning tools.

"You have quite a variety."

Jessa Tarrant smiled, the first full smile he'd seen from her. It lifted the faint air of worry that seemed to cling to her features and posture.

"Yes, we do. The official name of the shop's Nearly Everything, though most people just call it Jessa's."

If she weren't Cambria's friend...

Boone pulled up short on that thought—not because of what it said about his reaction to Jessa Tarrant, but what it said about his response to Cambria Weston. That wasn't good. Cambria was definitely off-limits. He'd decided that.

Now he had to remember it.

"I could use a map. Especially one that has this area in detail."

"I've got a county map...somewhere..."

Jessa retrieved the map with an air of triumph from behind the small counter by the door as Cambria came up with a box filled with jars and plastic bottles of cleaning supplies.

"Thanks, Jessa, this'll do great." Tucking the map under one arm, Boone took the box out of Cambria's hands before she could do more than splutter and placed it on the counter. "How much do I owe you?"

"You're not paying for my stuff," Cambria declared.

He raised an eyebrow at her, enjoying the way her softly pointed chin seemed to sharpen. "Okay. But I am paying for the map."

"Oh."

She subsided while Jessa rang up first his purchase, then hers. But when he picked up the box of supplies, Cambria tried to take it from him, though she was still pocketing the change Jessa had handed her.

"I can carry that."

"So can I." He held on. "I swear, I won't steal any of your floor wax or glass cleaner." Before she could give any more answer than a glare, he turned to the other woman. "Thanks for the map, Jessa. And the interesting conversation."

"Conversation?"

Cambria had taken the bait, now he set the hook—quickly, before Jessa Tarrant could ruin it.

"Jessa was telling me about when you and she lived in Washington, D.C, and decided to move out here."

For a slight exaggeration, it got an interesting reaction. Instead of the irritation he half expected from Cambria Weston at the implication that he'd been pumping her friend for information on her, she looked stunned, with an undercurrent of something that seemed split between pleasure and displeasure. But that wasn't half as odd as Jessa Tarrant's stiffening like a child playing Mother May I.

"You were?" Cambria demanded of Jessa. "You told him about—"

"No, I... No."

Boone didn't know what he'd stepped into, but he wasn't about to walk away without at least trying to find out.

"And I was hoping to hear more," he said as if he'd taken no notice of the interplay. "So, why don't you come along with us for lunch, Jessa?"

"Oh..." Jessa Tarrant didn't move a muscle; if anything, she grew stiller. Yet Boone had the impression of a woman backpedaling with all her might. "Thank you, but—"

"Yes!" Cambria interrupted. Her enthusiasm miffed him a bit. She didn't need to be *that* thrilled at having a third party at their lunch. "It'll be good for you to get out, especially with—"

Cambria flicked a look toward Boone that he didn't understand. In fact he didn't understand any of the messages that seemed to be flashing between the two women.

"Sure, you go ahead, Jessa," added Rita, coming up from the back of the store. "It's about time I tried flying solo."

Boone almost felt guilty when Jessa Tarrant remained tense and quiet as she accompanied them on the block's walk to the café, with a brief stop while he put Cambria's supplies in the four-wheel drive.

He did his best to bring Jessa out of that, and to figure out what all this silent conversation between the two women meant. Perhaps because of Cambria's cooperation, he had more success with the first than the second. What really bothered him was the feeling that a lot of those coded messages had to do with him.

Cambria sang along under her breath with the radio's offering about small-town Saturday nights, but she resisted any temptation to push the four-wheel drive toward the ninety miles an hour mentioned in the lyric. She figured she'd give Boone Dorsey a break on the drive back to the ranch.

She even figured he deserved it.

She felt more charitable toward the man by her side than she had from the moment Irene had announced his impending arrival.

That lunch was just what Jessa had needed—a relaxed, no-pressure encounter with an attractive, pleasant man who didn't come on too strong.

Glancing toward the man beside her, she saw mostly his dark hair, with only a narrow slice of his face as he stared out the side window, apparently deep in thought.

"You were very nice at lunch."

He must not have been as deep in thought as she'd guessed, because he turned immediately, catching her look and returning it with a raised eyebrow.

"Nice? You mean, minding my manners? Not talking with my mouth full? Not putting my elbows on the table?"

"Actually, I saw your elbows on the table once or twice."

If the mild teasing of her mock censor surprised him as much as it surprised her, it didn't show. He simply snapped his fingers in apparent disgust. "Thought I'd gotten clean away with that."

She chuckled. Glancing his way again, she saw his answering smile, and the look caught. And held.

She jerked her attention back to the road. This stretch ran straight, smooth, and mostly deserted, but there was a limit to how long a car could safely drive itself. And safety was the issue.

"So," Boone Dorsey asked, slow and easy, "if you're not talking about my manners, what are you talking about?"

Now she wished she'd never spoken.

"It's, uh, it's not easy to be a stranger surrounded by people who know each other real well. I guess the conversation got obscure at times."

He was studying her. She didn't turn, but she was fully aware of those gray eyes probing at her. It made her uncomfortable. Mostly because she didn't want him—or anyone else—to see beyond what she chose to reveal. But partly because, she realized with a flutter of something like shock at the bottom of her stomach, a temptation whispered to just relax all her guards and let those gray eyes touch all the secrets of her soul.

"It was like being a little kid whose parents spelled out all the interesting stuff so he couldn't understand it."

"Like a— Oh." His answer sank in as she pushed aside her unsettling thoughts, and she laughed. "Well, you took it real well."

"For now." He gave a lopsided grin, which matched the tone of mischievous intent. "I'll get even. For that, and for just happening to forget that the library has a fax machine the public can use for a fee."

Jessa had let that slip. When Boone had turned an accusing look on her, Cambria had shrugged and said she'd forgotten about the library's fax.

He clearly didn't believe her.

No skin off her nose. She hadn't mentioned the library fax because this man made her uneasy for reasons she wasn't going to take the time to decipher, and without a fax available there was always a chance he'd decide to move on.

If Wanda Rupert had anything to do with it, he'd definitely move on.

The librarian, who was so inordinately proud of the fax she'd badgered the board into buying, had not taken kindly to Boone Dorsey rearranging the setup to make transmitting more efficient. Even his winning smile when she returned from helping Doris Mooney—frantic with planning her parents' fiftieth wedding anniversary party—find the issue of the *Gazette* with her parents' wedding announcement, had not won over Wanda. She'd left the machine where he'd moved it because it was an improvement, but she hadn't smiled back.

Cambria supposed it was petty, but it rather pleased her that after her entire family, Rita, the waitress in the café and even Jessa had taken to Boone Dorsey, at least one other person hadn't fallen under the spell of his charm.

"Guess you'll be going into town a lot then." With plenty of opportunities to see Jessa.

It would be good for her friend, might help bring her out of her shell, Cambria reminded herself. She had so much to do on the ranch to get ready for the real season that she would have no trouble staying out of Boone Dorsey's path.

She felt that look from him again. Studying her, the way she could imagine him trying to figure out a puzzle.

"Guess I will."

Chapter Three

"What're you doing, Boone?"

Boone, squatting by the stall door, raised his head to find Pete watching him with interest. This boy, so straight and healthy, so open-faced and clear-eyed. His son...

He swallowed, so his answer came out sounding fairly normal. "I noticed this door sticks. Thought I'd take a look."

"Yeah, it's been sticking all winter. Cam said something about having me trim it, but I never got around to it." He gave the screwdriver in Boone's hand a doubtful look. "Don't you need a plane, or a knife or something?"

"I shouldn't. See, if I tighten the screws on this bottom hinge and loosen the ones on the top slightly, that should bring it back into line, and then it shouldn't stick."

Pete followed the procedure with interest. "You want me to hold the door for you?"

"Okay. No, a little higher," Boone adjusted the screws. "Okay, Pete, let it go and let's see how it hangs."

"Hey, it looks pretty good."

Boone frowned at it. "No. It needs more."

"Why? It clears."

"It clears, but it's not straight. Hold the door again. Higher this time."

"Okay, but—"

"What do you think you're doing?" Cambria's demand as she covered the final yards down the open center of the barn stepped on Pete's words, but her frown was all for Boone.

"He fixed the door, Cam. Didn't even have to slice any off. See?" Pete swung the door open.

"Why?"

Boone stood. Having lost the height advantage, Cambria compensated by placing her hands on her hips.

Boone realized he wasn't particularly surprised by her bristling. Maybe he'd figured the pendulum would swing that way again after her softening on the ride home from town. She'd had several hours to regret being cordial. And now she looked at him as if the screwdriver in his hand would turn into a six-shooter any second.

"I noticed this needed doing. It seemed a good way to pass a bit of time."

"I thought you were here to rest, to unwind from stress."

"I was getting a little bored."

She jumped on that as if she'd seen it coming. "Being bored is what you're *supposed* to be. That's how you rest and unwind. Not by being a handyman when you're supposed to be a paying guest."

Oh, yes, Cambria Weston had just defined his spot in her universe nice and neat. Only he didn't intend to stay there.

"Don't see any harm in doing something when I saw it needed being done."

"There's no—"

"If you're looking for something to do," Pete interrupted, "you could come to my team's game tonight. That is, if you like baseball." Boone's eyes swung to the teenager, who shifted his feet under the regard, then shrugged. "I know it doesn't sound too exciting, but we're having a pretty good season and we're playing Sheridan tonight, so it should be a good game. And everybody's coming."

Boone wouldn't have missed it for anything. But some devil in him made him ask Cambria, "Are you coming?"

"Oh, sure," Pete answered for her. "Cam comes to all my games. You can sit together."

The flash of irritation in her eyes left as soon as it had come; he figured it was more for him than Pete. And he was sure of it when she said, with a faint air of triumph, "I promised Jessa I'd sit with her."

"But she always sits—"

Cambria ruthlessly interrupted Pete's protest. "And some other people."

"Too bad. Maybe I'll see you there, then," Boone offered.

He almost laughed out loud when she gave a final mutter that sounded suspiciously like, "Not if I see you first."

Cambria picked up the ringing phone as she passed through the den the next morning. "Weston Ranch."

"Cambria? This is June Reamer. How're the Westons?"

"Everybody's fine. And you? Is your mom feeling better?"

"Much better. Though she said Irene's visits on her volunteer days were so much fun, she almost misses being in the hospital!"

"I'll tell Irene. Maybe she can stop by the house."

"That would be great, but I guess you folks are awfully busy, what with opening early. Why didn't you tell me? I would have recommended you to folks who rent cars."

"We haven't really opened, June."

"But he said... I could swear a man who rented a car the day before yesterday at the airport said he was staying at Weston Ranch. Real nice guy. Nice-looking, too—"

"We haven't opened, not officially, but when this man called and wanted a place to stay, he talked to Irene and—"

A laugh came across the phone line. "Say no more."

"You know, June, as long as you called..." Cambria shifted the receiver closer to her mouth. "I wonder if you have any information on this guy."

She described the car, then had to listen to June's enthusiastic description of the man.

"Yes, that's him," Cambria confirmed shortly.

She wouldn't be interested, she told herself, if Boone didn't insist on insinuating himself into everybody's good graces. If he behaved like a regular guest, pleasant but not too cozy, she could stay out of his path, and he'd stay out of hers—and her family's.

But he didn't.

Instead he charmed everyone in sight. He'd fixed the stall door; he'd sat beside Irene and Ted, taking pictures and cheering mightily at her brother's baseball game, and had been still sitting with Pete on the back steps talking baseball when she'd returned to the ranch after dropping off Jessa. Then this morning, after taking a spot at the breakfast table as if he'd spent his life doing it, he'd gone off to help her father place irrigation pipe.

She supposed she should be grateful. With Ted to give the orders, handling the pipe required no great expertise, and it freed her to get on with the cabins and bunkhouse.

June's voice brought her back to the moment—and the opportunity, perhaps, to get some answers.

"So, what do you want to know? Don't tell me you suspect him of credit card fraud like that couple you caught last summer. This guy was all class."

Cambria bit back the reply that the very best con men were the ones who seemed sincere. Heaven knows she'd learned that. She wouldn't ever be taken in again by a handsome exterior and charming ways.

"I want to fill in the blanks left when Irene registered him." She hoped her stepmother wasn't listening.

"Guess there's no harm in that. Shoot."

"Where's he from?"

"He had a North Carolina driver's license, and listed a business address in Boone, North Carolina."

"Did you check his credit card?"

"Didn't have to. He paid cash."

"Cash?" In Cambria's experience, people driving that kind of car and wearing those kinds of clothes didn't bother much with cash. They were more likely to use credit cards and possibly have an accountant stashed somewhere to write checks when the bills came in.

"Yeah," June added. "He paid for two weeks up-front, then asked about the procedure for keeping the car longer. That *is* sort of unusual. Most folks know exactly how long they're staying because they have to get back to work by a certain day."

Not being typical was no crime, but it sure raised more questions.

"June, what name was on his driver's license?"

"Boone, same as the town he's from. Easy to remember."

"Mr. Boone?"

"No. Boone's the first name," June said, and Cambria felt a little foolish for her suspicions. "Smith's the last name."

"What? What did you say?"

"Don't shout like that. I said his name's Smith. In fact, I joked about it being like that old movie, *Mr. Smith Goes to Washington,* only this Mr. Smith comes to Wyoming. Get it?"

Yeah, Cambria got it. What she didn't get was why this Mr. Smith had come to Wyoming, or why he felt the need to lie about his last name.

She ended the conversation with June, but didn't move from her perch on the arm of the chair by the phone while she put together what she knew.

This man—whatever his real name—didn't fit the mold of their usual guests, that much was certain. He also gave her an odd sense of familiarity. He volunteered nothing about himself, but drew out Irene and Ted and Pete one by one with questions, the same way he had drawn her out in the barn that first day. He was attractive. Charming. *Charming.... Deliberately charming.*

In that moment the vague sense of déjà vu coalesced into a statement: *He reminds me of Tony.*

A simple sentence, fraught with danger signals.

If Irene fretted that Cambria had become cynical, as she had said more than once, Tony Sussman was the reason. Cambria's former fiancé had provided an unforgettable lesson in the dangers of trusting.

She'd already recognized the similarity in her mixed reactions to Boone. Now this smiliarity crystallized into clarity.

There was little physical similarity between this man and her former fiancé. Except perhaps the readiness and warmth of the smile—in Tony's case both polished and practiced tools of his political trade. Otherwise the differences in looks, style and dress would have put Tony in a Brooks Brothers' ad and cast Boone as the Marlboro Man.

But she just might have hit on the real similarity—both were trying to sell something. The charm, humor, smiles, even the hot looks directed at her, all were part of the campaign.

But what did Boone have to sell, and why on earth did he seem to be targeting her family?

An image of Pete sitting on the porch steps with their guest last night, his face eager as he listened to the stranger's words, came into her mind. Her hands curled into themselves.

Maybe she was being paranoid. Maybe she was imagining all this. But if she wasn't... She wasn't taking any chances. This time she wouldn't flinch from finding out what was going on.

Even if it meant spending a lot of time around Boone Dorsey—Boone Smith. A dangerous amount of time.

Cambria put her plan into action when the men came in for lunch.

"Want to take a ride this afternoon?"

Their guest's single raised eyebrow was nearly as blatant an expression of surprise as the looks she got from Ted and Irene.

"A ride?"

His caution irked her. *He* had no reason to be suspicious of *her.* "A ride. On horses. What's the matter, you afraid I'll take you out to the canyon and leave you?"

"Will you?"

"Not until you've paid your bill."

"Cambria!" Irene's reproach eased under Boone's laughter.

"I'll be sure not to pay until I'm safely in the car, ready to leave, and can hand it through the window."

Cambria nodded. Damn, she didn't want to be amused by him. "In the meantime, I thought you'd like a tour, and the best way to see the place is on horseback."

"I'd like that. Unless you need a hand this afternoon, Ted?"

Ted Weston, looking faintly bemused, watched Cambria closely, but he immediately assured the other man. "No, no, you two go ahead and enjoy yourselves."

"Good, then I'll meet you in the barn, Mr. Dorsey." Cambria paused, knowing she'd pulled everyone's attention to her. She packed in plenty of skeptical emphasis as she added, "Or should I call you *Mr. Smith?*"

From the corner of her eye she saw that Irene and Ted looked confused. But most of her attention was focused on Boone. On his face she saw a flash of surprise quickly replaced by wariness, then that, too, was smoothed over.

"You can if you like, but I'd rather you call me Boone."

"Smith is the name you used to rent a car, isn't it?"

"It is my name," he said with mild insistence.

"You told me—us—your name's Dorsey."

"Cambria, have you been checking up on Boone?"

She didn't turn away from studying him to answer Irene. "Maybe somebody should. June Reamer happened to call and happened to mention—"

"A lot of 'happeneds,'" he murmured.

"That his real last name is Smith. At least, that's the way he registered for the car. A car he paid cash for, by the way."

"Dorsey is my name, too—Boone Dorsey Smith. There're so many Smiths in the world, sometimes it's easier to go by Boone Dorsey."

"That's reasonable. But you have no reason to explain to us." Irene reached across the table and patted his hand.

Cambria couldn't shake an impression he was uncomfortable with the whole conversation about his identity. That impression strengthened when he gave her a calculatedly disarming grin and asked, "Is the ride still on?"

"I like to know who I'm riding with."

He met her look with one as direct, but the opaque gray eyes remained capable of hiding many secrets. "I told you, Cambria. Boone Dorsey Smith."

"Cambria..."

She broke her challenging stare at him to meet her stepmother's kind eyes, and couldn't refuse their request for peace.

"I'll meet you in the barn in ten minutes...Boone."

"How come that cabin's over here by itself?" Boone gestured to a ramshackle structure that appeared intent on sinking into the dusty green and golden brown landscape.

They'd been out three hours and had circled around to the main ranch, but hadn't yet crossed the creek that separated this structure from the others. A footbridge crossed the creek a little farther up from where they'd paused to water Jezebel and Snakebit.

"We don't use it. The creek bed changed twenty, thirty years ago and left it alone on this side of the creek. It's not worth it to fix it up, because we'd have to put in a full bridge and special drainage and plumbing, plus putting the electricity and everything over here." She squinted slightly as she studied the structure. "Besides, it's ugly, and the rooms are cramped and dark. I never understood why they built it that way. One of these days we'll tear it down for whatever lumber we can get out of it."

"Okay if I take some pictures?"

She shrugged even as she reined Snakebit to a halt. "If you want to waste the film."

To her mind he'd already wasted a lot of film. She'd taken him out past winter pastures now empty, to more distant pastures where cows with their new calves waited for warmer weather when they'd be taken up the mountains to where higher ground offered better summer grazing.

He'd taken pictures of cows and calves—no prizewinners, just part of the herd. He'd taken pictures of the patterns of fences where pastures intersected, of clouds billowing into a thunderstorm on a distant horizon that could easily be a state away, and of a prairie dog town she'd pointed out. He'd even taken pictures of her demonstrating the most basic of cutting moves on Snakebit.

Wasting film on this old wreck of a cabin fit right in.

She dismounted and dropped Snakebit's reins to the ground far enough from the cabin to keep out of the shots Boone took from astride Jezebel.

He hadn't done a thing she could take exception to. He hadn't asked many more questions than any fairly curious person might in new surroundings. And she hadn't come up with any brilliant ideas of what this stranger could possibly hope to gain from charming the Weston family of Bardville, Wyoming.

Maybe she *was* being paranoid.

Sunlight filtered through cottonwood leaves above him as if for the express purpose of highlighting the strands of gray that filtered through the darkness of his hair.

In profile his face was concentrated, intense. The black slash of his brow stood out above the camera and the strong thrust of his jaw below it. His lips moved, as if he'd muttered something to himself. He had a strong mouth, wide, with the bottom lip slightly fuller than the top.

He shifted his hold on the camera as he turned it for a vertical shot, and Cambria gladly followed that diversion from his mouth. Jessa was right, he did have capable hands. Long-fingered, but in no way delicate. The palms were broad, the knuckles pronounced enough to declare them a workman's. With one blunt-tipped finger, he adjusted the ring on the lens to sharpen the focus. Powerful and deft.

A flutter tickled down her backbone like a localized breeze.

She looked away, focusing beyond the overhanging branches and past the cabin to the ragged bulk of the Big Horn Mountains. Spring had not yet reached the white caps frothing on their crests. Some white would remain intact from last winter to next, on to the one after and beyond. The melting from other crests would keep rivers running and fields greening—with an assist from human diversion and ingenuity—through the summer.

Some might prefer the heaven-piercing grandeur of the Rockies, but she found comfort in the Big Horns' long, uneven line stretching across the western horizon like a painter's thickly laid swipe of color. Many people would find little comfort in the ancient pile of rock and stone, cut by wind and water, inhabited by tenacious plants and tough animals. But she did. They were familiar, a homey anchor that oriented her, gave her a sense of direction as long as they were in sight. She knew how she felt about them, and she knew how they'd treat her. They weren't predictable, but they didn't lie—except to the foolish.

To the person who knew how to look and where to look, they offered a beauty of awesome strength and another of heart-aching delicacy.

A creaking of leather pulled her head around to see Boone Dorsey Smith dismounting. He didn't have the ease of an accomplished horseman, but he swung his right leg over Jezebel's rump and stepped to the ground with the assurance of someone who knew how to use the muscles that bunched and flexed in his thighs.

An image exploded in her head, an image of hands and mouths and thighs and a dark-haired man.

"You know, this has potential."

"What?" She swallowed hard to get the word out, and it sounded like it.

He glanced up from the camera, one side of his mouth raised slightly. Then his gaze sharpened and he straightened, lowering the camera and giving her his full attention.

"Something wrong?"

"No. Of course not."

He watched her, unblinking, alert, yet still relaxed, the trace of a half smile lingering. Like a cat outside a mouse hole, she thought.

She straightened. She was no mouse.

"I just can't figure what you could be thinking possibly has potential." She sounded like herself again.

His eyes stayed on her another moment, then he turned away, examining the structure once more.

"This cabin."

She snorted. "Potential for a junk pile, maybe. Or a bonfire."

"Don't you dare," he muttered, once more occupied with lining up a shot of the cabin. But his tone was intense enough to snag her attention. "That would be a terrible waste."

Before she knew what he was about, he turned the camera on her and clicked off three quick shots. He stopped only when she ducked behind Snakebit.

"Talk about a terrible waste," she grumbled.

"No waste, Cambria." He watched her, but she didn't meet his eyes. Still, she caught the motion of his shrug and knew when he looked away. He added, almost to himself, "I don't waste things. Comes from growing up poor, I guess."

Eyes still on the cabin, he started moving away. She followed. She had questions, and he'd given her an opening—small and to a more distant past than she would have chosen, but an opening nonetheless.

"That was in North Carolina?"

"What?"

"Where you grew up."

"Yeah, North Carolina. In the mountains. Blue Ridge," he added absently as he rotated the zoom lens to close in on a corner of the building that looked to her as uninteresting as a pair of boards forming a corner could be.

She didn't bother trying to discern what he saw in it. She had other corners she wanted to turn.

"So, your parents weren't well-to-do?" Which would mean he'd earned, rather than inherited the expensive clothes, luxury car and fine leather.

"You could say that." Irony loaded his words. "Daddy died owing everybody and his brother, so Mom had two kids and a mostly invalid mother-in-law to support, and not much education. Yeah, you could safely say we weren't well-to-do."

"Oh."

He glanced over his shoulder at her, the half smile in place. "Hey, don't look so tragic, I didn't mean to make you feel bad."

"I don't..." The automatic response faded. She did feel bad. She knew what it was like to have scars, and to have them probed by careless questions. Even if his light tone tried to imply he didn't care, she didn't buy it. Not completely. Irene had a phrase about something being "half kidding, whole earnest." That's how Boone Dorsey Smith sounded.

"It's all old news." If anything, his tone was lighter. "About the only carryover from those days is that I don't much care for being in debt. Not even a credit card's worth."

So he paid for a rental car in cash. Not for any nefarious reasons, but from the remnants of a financially insecure childhood. Now she felt worse.

"You must have worked really hard."

"Yeah, well, I had luck, too. The army did me good. Went in right after high school. Left North Carolina, saw a lot more of the world. It wasn't the life for me—hated the haircuts," he added with a grin. "But it taught me a lot. Never even held a camera until I went in the army."

He regarded the elaborate device in his hands, a thousand dollars of electronic wizardry packed into a handy package. Then his expression shifted. When he spoke again, Cambria had the impression he'd nearly forgotten her.

"But I lost some things, too, when I left for the army.... People."

"Your mother?"

She'd tried to keep her voice soft, but he still started slightly. His eyes met hers in an instant of gray regrets before he looked off toward the mountains she'd stared at not long before.

"Yeah. Gran first, then Mom. My kid sister was finishing high school. I'd just come home, started—uh, started building a life. Maybe if I'd taken more notice, or if I'd taken more of the burden off her before... It was like Mom felt we could take care of ourselves then, so she could quit fighting so hard. She was worn out. Not even fifty years old and she was worn out."

Even while Cambria felt his pain, she pushed aside a slice of envy she had no right to feel. She'd had Irene to fight for her. Nobody could have asked for more.

"I'm sorry."

"Long time ago. Kenzie's the one who bothers me now."

"Kenzie?"

"My kid sister. Haven't seen her in nearly five years. Said she was sick of my trying to run her life." His mouth tilted in self-mockery. "That and dictator might've been the nicest things she said about me."

"I can't imagine not seeing Pete. That must be tough on you." She could see that. She could see the love and hurt and confusion. But only for a moment. Boone Dorsey Smith might open the door on his secrets now and then, but it was a good stout door and he could slam it closed with a smile.

"Hey, I didn't mean to bring in the clouds. Let's say, I see you as being lucky. It must've been great growing up here, with a place like this for home. And having Ted and Irene . . . and Pete."

"Growing up wasn't all easy." Before he could ask the question she saw in his eyes, she hurried on. "I guess no place is ideal, and every kid has problems. The trick is getting past that, learning that sometimes things start out bad, but turn out okay."

He gave her a peculiar look, partly sad, partly hopeful and partly something she couldn't define.

"Yeah, sometimes they do."

Chapter Four

Boone was no monk. He'd seen things in Cambria Weston's eyes. He'd felt it in the air that seemed to shimmer with unspoken connections. And he figured, from what he'd seen of her and from her little speech about not dealing socially with the guests, that she would run in the opposite direction...once he laid to rest her fears he was here to do her family harm.

Until he did that, though, she'd stick to his side, keeping an eye on him and tormenting him with impossibilities.

No, Cambria Weston wasn't hard to read.

But she wasn't easy to fool.

He could tell her the truth of why he'd come—if he wanted to get kicked out faster than a politician voted to raise his own pay.

He'd come here to see his son. To get to know him and to make sure he didn't need for anything. Beyond that...

Well, he'd figure that out once he'd done those other things.

In the meantime he should stay away from his son's adopted sister. He *had* to.

He just wished she'd cooperate.

The evening after their riding tour, Cambria had deftly intervened when Pete had been about to take him up on his offer to help with math homework at the kitchen table. She'd instead settled Boone in the den with a magazine he hadn't wanted to read, with herself on the couch as a most distracting watchdog.

Thursday she'd driven him into town, shown him where to have film developed, then disappeared while he'd made phone calls and given the fax at the library a better workout than it usually had in a month. Leaving town, he'd suggested stopping by the high school and giving Pete a lift home. She'd taken him in the opposite direction to view a historical marker of a none-too-heroic overrunning of an Indian camp.

That night, she'd gotten an assist from Pete. When dinner conversation had turned up the fact that Boone hadn't seen *Field of Dreams,* Pete had been flabbergasted.

"How could you not have seen it?"

"I don't get to movies much," he'd explained mildly. Cambria had given him a probing look, but Pete had been too intent on remedying the appalling lapse in his moviegoing life to be interested in causes.

"Well, you're going to see it right now, because Cam gave me a copy for Christmas."

By the time the movie had ended, with Kevin Costner reconnected with his dead father through a magical game of catch, Boone's emotions had felt so raw, he'd sidestepped Pete's efforts to talk about the history of the players portrayed and retreated to the solitude of his cabin—away from the too watchful eyes of Cambria Weston.

When she'd insisted on driving him into town again on Friday, Boone had bluntly said he'd thought she'd had work to do around the ranch. "I have a few things to pick up" was all she'd said.

Friday night, when he'd hoped to spend time talking with Pete—at best alone, but at least with the whole family—Cambria had organized an outing to an Alfred Hitchcock double feature being shown by the local junior college. At least he hadn't gotten misty-eyed over those films. But after four hours of movies, there'd been no evening left for talk.

There wasn't much she could have done to prevent Irene from including him in a picnic lunch before Pete's afternoon baseball game. But the most he saw Saturday night of Cambria were the threads of light around the drawn curtains in her cabin. Probably because Pete had had a date and Ted and Irene were off to the Mooneys' fiftieth anniversary party.

By Sunday morning Boone was irrationally annoyed at Cambria for avoiding him the night before, after spending the week being irritated at her none-too-subtle maneuvers to keep him away from her family when she could, and when she couldn't, to keep an eye on him.

"Would you like to join us for church services, Boone?" Irene invited at breakfast. "I know young people sometimes don't care to—"

Pete mumbled something around a mouthful of pancakes that sounded like a protest that he was a young person and how come he didn't get a choice.

"And when they get to be adults, they can make that choice for themselves," Irene serenely digressed. "But if you'd like to come along, you're most welcome. We'll leave in half an hour."

Boone would have turned down the invitation, except he saw that Cambria expected him to.

He got an unholy delight at her martyred sigh when he said yes.

She showed up at the appointed time in a simple green dress that reminded him of the freshness of spring flowers—if spring flowers glowered.

"You're coming, Cam?" Ted Weston made no attempt to hide his surprise.

"You know Martin Haines is away for the summer, so Reverend Elaitch is taking his place, don't you?"

Irene's frown didn't ease under Cambria's grim, "I know."

"I didn't think you cared for Reverend Elaitch's, uh, approach," Irene said.

"Reverend Elaitch is a self-satisfied, sanctimonious windbag."

"Cambria!"

Irene's admonishment was lost under Ted's chuckle. He put an arm around Cambria's shoulders and squeezed. "She's right."

Cambria's conspiratorial smile at her father faded when she faced Boone, replaced by a look of pure determination. "But he's not going to stop me from going to church. Not him or anybody."

Boone had a hard time squelching a grin. Served Cambria Weston right for tormenting him all week that she was going to sit through services conducted by a man she didn't like—and accompanied by a man she didn't trust.

She sat next to Boone in the pew, so his senses drank in her subtly spicy scent each time she moved. And he wondered who was tormenting whom. When a latecomer slid in at the end of the row, squeezing out the margin of space, the length of her arm and her hip snugged against him, and through the protective layers of cloth, he absorbed the contact.

He didn't hear a word the Reverend Elaitch said, but he prayed like mad.

His prayers would have astounded the congregation. But they were answered—he made it through the services without making a fool of himself.

Early that afternoon a discussion about the previous day's game ended with Pete wanting to demonstrate a pitch he'd been working on and Boone lowering himself into the nearly forgotten catcher's crouch. He hadn't played ball since the army.

But his muscles remembered, and even as he commented on the pitches Pete threw, Boone's mind was freed to consider another matter.

The past week wasn't all Cambria's doing.

He probably could have found excuses not to spend all that time with her. He hadn't wanted to find excuses. He liked spending time with her. Her tongue had an edge to it, but he didn't mind. Kept him on his toes. He could see her determination not to enjoy being with him, so he enjoyed those moments he surprised a smile out of her, or better yet, a laugh. He liked that a lot. She had thoughts about the land, people, movies, politics, songs, society and preachers. He liked that, too.

He also liked that spicy scent, and the lock of hair she was forever tucking behind her ear, and the precise curve of her back—up to her shoulders and down to her fanny—and the change that lit her when he overcame her reluctance and doubts and earned that smile. Oh, yes, and the way she tested the texture of things with her hands. The quick, light touch to a leather briefcase or wooden fence or dusty horse. Followed by a lingering stroke that seemed slow enough to absorb every nuance of every atom it encountered. Oh, yes, he liked that a lot. It had slipped into his dreams.

"Hey, Cam, did you see that pitch?" Pete called.

"I saw it."

Boone twisted around in time to see Cambria's smile for her brother lapse as she looked at him.

"Boone was telling me I could get better control by changing my hold just a little."

"Was he?"

Pete tugged on his blue baseball cap, the front emblazoned with the yellow letters P.A.W. For Peter Andrew Weston, Pete had said. It was a gift from Ted when they'd been at the state fair in Douglas three years ago. The cap showed wear, but that didn't bother Pete.

"Yeah, and he was right."

Still in his crouch, Boone tossed the ball straight up and let it drop into his hands.

"Was he?" Cambria asked again.

"Happens now and then," Boone muttered. "Sometimes even a blind squirrel finds a nut." He tossed the ball again as Pete rattled on.

The ball didn't come down, and Boone looked up to see Cambria with one hand cradling the stained horsehide. Her other hand brushed lightly across the surface, then stroked across it again, slowly.

Damn.

Where his jeans were stretched by his crouched position, they began to grow snugger by the second.

Was he fooling himself thinking that though Cambria wanted like the devil to be cold, by nature she was the opposite?

"I'm going up—" a jerk of her head indicated the mountains to the west "—to look over the snowmelt this afternoon. I thought you might like to go along."

Boone rested his forearms on his thighs and let his empty hands drop between as if to signal the pitcher.

And watched her eyes follow the move.

"I might at that."

Her cheeks darkened. Their eyes locked for an instant, then she broke the connection.

"Right now, Irene says lunch is ready."

With that she turned and flipped the ball to Pete.

Slowly, Boone straightened.

Did she think she could look at him with that hungry curiosity and speculation and not have him notice? Did she think that turning away, that denying it, would make him blind?

Cambria Weston blew hot and cold, and expected him to only feel the cold.

He didn't think he could.

"The water feeds from here down into that canyon." Cambria pointed and watched Boone follow the gesture with either genuine or expertly feigned interest. "Then across a natural meadow through our near-in pastures and to the creek behind the cabins."

"So that's why you're interested in the snowmelt."

"That's why. Good snowpack can make all the difference in a dry summer, especially if it doesn't all melt at once."

"How's this one doing?"

She shrugged. "Not bad."

He cocked his head to one side and studied her. "So, that's it? You drive up here, walk a couple of miles, then drive back down the mountain?"

That came perilously close to what she'd intended, since her primary purpose had been to interrupt all that male-bonding time he'd been spending with her brother, she reminded herself.

"I want to check some more." She gave a vague wave to a spur of land that jutted between this creek and a smaller one to the south. "Go back to the truck if you're tired."

"I suppose I can make it a few more yards," he said dryly.

She started off, aware of him at her side.

Following deep-sunk tire ruts, she'd driven the truck about half a mile off the highway into the trees, then they'd hiked another mile, out the other side of the trees to where the ground gradually fell away before plummeting into the canyon she'd pointed out.

On the way Boone had asked a lot of questions about the various types of pines. She gave him their names—lodgepole, Engelmann spruce, an occasional white bark pine, plus the more general Rocky Mountain juniper. But when it came to rate of growth and their lumber's durability for building, she'd been stumped after saying lodgepole got its name from Indians using the trunks as framework for their lodges. Other than that, she suggested he visit the district forest service office in Sheridan.

She'd had more success pointing out early blooming lupines and cinquefoils in a protected sunny spot by the highway. Heartier blossoms held sway over ground newly freed from snow—the pink-veined blooms of spring beauty, and in a boggy area, the bright white and yellow of globeflower, even the delicate, nodding heads of the adder's-tongue.

And Boone had listened.

So maybe he wasn't as much like Tony Sussman as she'd once thought. Maybe he was charming. Maybe he was selling something she hadn't figured out yet. Certainly he was worth keeping an eye on, but no way could she extend the similarities to their views of the outdoors.

Tony had considered the deck of a tidy powerboat the only vantage point for observing nature, preferably while sipping a gin and tonic. Nothing too ostentatious, mind you. Just something to entertain a fishing-crazed representative, undersecretary, or other useful connection for an afternoon of prime schmoozing and ego-massaging.

Boone also wasn't like Tony in the way Pete responded to him. The one time her family had met Tony in a visit to Washington—she'd never persuaded him to come to Wyoming—she'd divined in Pete's attitude toward her fiancé a mixture of extreme discomfort and a hint of disdain. Not at all the way he reacted to Boone Dorsey Smith.

Maybe if she'd heeded Pete's instinctive reaction to Tony she could have saved herself a load of grief and disappointment.

She gave her head a mental shake. This was getting all twisted around. If Pete and the rest of her family didn't like Boone, she wouldn't have to worry about the possibility he was out to get something from them and she wouldn't have had to drag him up here.

"How long are you going to keep this up?"

Boone's abrupt question brought Cambria to a halt. He faced her.

"If you don't want to go any farther, we can go back to the truck now." Her offer drew a truncated burst of laughter from him she didn't understand.

"It's not the hike to the truck I'm talking about."

"What *are* you talking about, then?"

"Guard duty. You keeping tabs on me like I'm a foreign spy. What have I done to make you distrust me so much?"

"For starters, you didn't tell us your right name." Was she reminding him or herself of the reasons to be wary?

"I told you—"

"Yeah, you told us." She let him see her disbelief.

"I've got to wonder, Cambria, is it me or is it all men?" His eyes narrowed on her, thick black lashes framing slits of silver. "Maybe all of humanity. Do you find a reason not to trust everybody who's not a resident of Bardville, Wyoming?"

"I've seen your type before, Boone." She ignored the quick, what-type-is-that lift of his brows. "Maybe you don't mean any real harm—"

"Thank you for that vote of confidence."

"But I intend to make sure you don't do any."

"By keeping me busy yourself and out of the way of your family?"

"Yes."

"I'd rather you didn't."

She narrowed her eyes. "Why?"

"Because I don't want to have to work as damn hard as I'll need to if I want to stand any chance of resisting you."

He made no attempt to hide that the blaze in his eyes had been lit by desire. She opened her mouth, closed it, and tried again. "That's not an issue. I told you before, I have a rule—I don't—"

"Get involved with guests. I know. Rules get broken." He leaned forward swiftly, not touching her, yet giving her a sense of being surrounded by him. "And people who play with fire get burned."

Even when he backed off without another word, and they started for the truck with no more discussion and no more examination of the snowpack, she felt the heat.

"There's a dance tonight in town," Cambria abruptly announced at dinner Monday night.

She and Boone had been the only ones around almost all day. Irene had gone shopping, then volunteered at the hospital; Ted had fixed fence on a distant range, and Pete had had a meeting after school, then gone straight to baseball practice. But she hadn't spoken to Boone until now.

She'd stayed out of his way. Not avoiding him, not seeking him out, either. She'd seen him head to town, carrying his briefcase and his laptop computer. She'd been aware, as she'd finished waxing the floor in the cabin on the far side of the bunkhouse, of him sitting on the narrow front porch of his cabin working on his computer—until an afternoon thunderstorm chased him inside. A man who worked that hard on his vacation was probably allergic to dancing.

So why had she asked him?

"So, do you want to go?" she added when her first announcement didn't draw an immediate reply.

Pete gulped a mouthful of potatoes. "Oh, hey, that's the café anniversary, isn't it? They're going to have a live band."

"In the café?" Boone clearly couldn't puzzle out how a band would fit in the tiny café, much less any dancers.

"The café's actually part of the Back Bar, the longest-running business in this county," Ted explained. "One hundred and twelve years old as of today. When the Back Bar was built, Bozeman Road was the main street, but Big Horn Avenue got bigger, so the original owner built the café facing that way and joined the two into a sort of L. Stan Elliston rents out the back room that connects them for meetings and such."

"And parties, like this one. It'll be great. When do we leave, Cam?"

"Not you, Pete. You have school tomorrow. I meant Boone."

Boone raised one eyebrow. "Me?"

"Yes, you. Unless you don't want to go." She hoped that hadn't sounded too much like a challenge.

He gave her a considering look that lasted too long and probed too deep for her comfort. "Oh, I want to go."

"Fine. We'll leave right after supper. It's casual."

After a silent drive into town—perhaps Cambria wasn't in the mood to chat because Boone had finally won the tussle over who would drive, or perhaps she had other things on her mind—she had the sense to leave him high and dry about three seconds after walking through the café and into the cleared back room.

Boone was glad she did, because he was entirely too fascinated by the way the wide neckline of her turquoise blouse slipped toward first one shoulder then the other. No strap ever showed, and that stirred speculation—and other things—that made her leaving him alone definitely the wisest move.

Of course, she had an assist from the fair-haired guy in cowboy dress who snagged her by the arm and drew her onto the dance floor to the strong beat of the small band crammed in the far corner.

She did give Boone a half-apologetic look over her shoulder—a shoulder not quite bared by that turquoise blouse she had tucked into a fine-fitting, above-the-knee, denim skirt—before she swung into the stream of the dance.

"Mr. Dorsey!"

He finished paying for his beer at the table near the door, then looked around.

"Mr. Dorsey!" Only with repetition did he realize the call was aimed at him.

A wave caught his eye and he recognized the older woman from Jessa Tarrant's shop—Rita, that was her name. Rita Campbell. Beyond her, Jessa Tarrant leaned against the wall. He smiled a hello and started toward them. Rita was talking as he came to stand beside her.

"It's good for people to get out, enjoy themselves, right, Jessa?"

Jessa Tarrant responded with a slight smile.

"Sure. Can I get you ladies a drink?"

"No. Thank you."

"Me, either, but that's real nice of you to ask," Rita said. "Oh, they're doing a line dance. C'mon, you two." She edged closer to the dance floor as the space quickly filled with spectators joining lines already forming. "Everybody's going to dance now."

"You go ahead, Rita. You, too, Boone. I'll be fine."

Boone spotted Cambria between the fair-haired man and the portly proprietor of the café, Stan Elliston.

"I'll stay with you, Jessa."

Rita looked from one to the other. "Are you—"

Jessa gave her a gentle push. "Go on."

Boone leaned against the wall next to Jessa. "I'm going to have to get a haircut."

"What? Why?"

"I figure it must be the hair that made Rita worried about leaving you alone with me."

She smiled. "Rita feels responsible. She talked me into coming. I, uh, haven't done much socially lately."

"Me, either."

He knew she was studying his face, and he let her, without returning the look.

"Lately's an understatement. It's about three years."

His mouth twitched. "Six for me—and no, there's nothing wrong with me, physically or otherwise. It's just... I've been busy," he finished lamely.

She digested that in silence for a few moments, then asked, "Do you know how to line dance?"

He smiled. "No, but I'm willing to learn."

They stumbled through three songs, trying to follow more expert dancers. The music slowed to a ballad, and they gladly found spots along the wall. Cambria went right into a dance with the fair-haired cowboy. At least it wasn't a clinch.

"He's in insurance." Jessa said from beside him.

"What?"

"The guy monopolizing Cambria. Kent Kepper. He's in insurance, and Cambria isn't interested in what he's selling."

"Guess she figures there're better investments than insurance." With the ballad still lilting, he leaned in to ask in a conversational tone, "Would you like to dance?"

She looked startled, glanced away, then back, meeting his gaze squarely.

"No. I know I should be flattered and—" The next words came slowly. "I might kick myself tomorrow, but no. Thank you, no. But you should go find someone who will dance with you."

He raised an eyebrow. "Why not you?"

A smile lit her eyes. "Because of the way you look at Cambria. And she's my best friend."

That shook him a little, but he masked it. "So you won't dance with me?"

"Not when you're thinking about how much you'd like to hold her while you're asking me to dance."

He leaned back. "You're pretty sure you know what's going on in my head, aren't you?"

He was rewarded with a warm, approving smile from Cambria Weston's best friend. "Yes."

Cambria watched Jessa and Boone Dorsey Smith talking, and saw the long eye contact and the smiles.

She didn't like it, even if it did keep him occupied and away from her.

He kept secrets, for one thing. And a man who'd flirt with one woman after the way he'd looked at another woman—and reacted to another woman—the way he had just yesterday afternoon... Well, he wasn't to be trusted.

Boone moved away from Jessa. Cambria gave Kent only a brief goodbye before working her way to that side of the room and slipping into the spot Boone had vacated.

"You and Boone looked as if you were getting along fine," she said with a bright smile. "Glad to see you taking some interest in the opposite sex."

Jessa turned her head and gave her a long, openly probing look that made Cambria's smile lock and her shoulders fidget. Sometimes Jessa's observations were too true for comfort.

"Have you told Boone your reasons for coming back here?"

Astonishment unlocked Cambria's muscles. "Why should I? You don't tell people everything about why you left D.C."

"We're not talking about me, we're talking about you. And we're not talking about people, we're talking about one particular man. A man you're trying to keep at a distance because he scares you."

"That's—"

"Have you told him any of your business? Have you told him about your life in Washington, or about Tony, or about growing up, or about your family, or about your mother? No, I know you haven't. You're attracted to him, drawn to him, and you're fighting that like hell, so you're not giving him any piece of yourself."

"I—"

"I saw you do it with Greg Brasson in D.C., after Tony broke your engagement. I could understand it then, the wounds were too raw. But just like you've been telling me, you've got to heal sometime or you'll stay the rest of your life in a cage you've built yourself."

Cambria should have known quoting Irene to Jessa would boomerang eventually.

"He hasn't been exactly open with me, you know. I wouldn't even know his real name if it weren't for June." Even to her own ears, Cambria sounded a shade petulant.

Jessa gave her a level look. "Somebody's got to take the first step, Cambria. And I'll tell you something else you keep telling me—fear can't rule your life or it's not living."

"Good night, Boone."

"Good night."

Cambria took another two steps down the path to her cabin. It wasn't her imagination, he was following her.

"What do you think you're doing?"

"Walking you to your door."

"That's not necessary." She didn't move. "I know the way to my door."

"I figured that. But I feel responsible, since I finally convinced you it was safe to drive with me. Besides, I thought with all the dancing you did you might be so worn out, you'd need a hand."

She grimaced, but didn't object again. She had rather ignored him after inviting him to the party. Though she'd seen him dancing with Rita Campbell, Maureen Elliston, June Reamer and several ladies from the church. Still, maybe she felt a sort of debt.

Fully aware of him right behind her, she walked quickly down the path, then turned at the door and faced Boone.

"Okay, here we are." A high brass fixture dropped a cone of light by the door.

"So I see." He tipped his head slightly and considered her. "Have you had a lot of experience with convicted felons, Cambria?"

"I don't know what you're talking about."

"Ax murderers most likely, or at the very least, someone who beat up old ladies for their last dollar. Been around that type of guy a lot, have you?"

"What are you talking about?"

"I'm talking about the way you look at me. I figure it must be the company you've kept that has you giving me that look—there! That's the look. The narrow-eyed stare that says nobody's going to slip one over on you. Certainly not some country boy from North Carolina."

The cone of light enclosed them, only them, blocking out all the rest of the world. She shifted her weight, and her knee brushed the denim of his jeans.

"Okay, you've made your point."

"Have I?" His voice came low, hypnotic. But which of them was being hypnotized? His eyes traveled over her face as if unlocking secrets with each glance, then finding more behind them. With a look, he made her feel mysterious and exotic. Then he touched her, two fingertips drawn so lightly along her jaw. And she felt the reality of desire.

"What makes you look at me like that?" he asked. "What makes you do things that make Irene worry that you're a sad, cynical woman?"

"I don't—"

"What makes you so prickly, when your skin's so smooth? So incredibly smooth. . . ."

She could have moved away, she simply didn't. "I thought . . . You and Jessa . . ."

"Not Jessa." He reached across the space between them and slid his hand to the back of her neck. "You."

His lips brushed against hers.

His hand tangled in her hair.

He raised his head, breathing in deeply. His dark brows shadowed his eyes from the overhead light, but across the space that separated them she caught a gleam, a heat that echoed the sensation that seemed to burn her lips.

"Damn."

Wonder. Annoyance. Chagrin. Pleasure. They were all in his single word. They were all in her.

The slightest pressure of his fist at her nape brought her mouth back to his. That's all it took, because she didn't resist.

His lips moved over hers, and she sought a deeper contact. Without thought, only with need.

The space between them was gone. His hand, still tangled in her hair, cupped her skull. His other kneaded across her back.

Open-mouthed, he kissed her, seeking entrance. She gave it. Tongue met tongue. And she tumbled into a spinning tunnel of misty gray. But his hunger was sharp and clear. Her head fell back to allow their kisses greater depth. His hand held her steady.

She felt the lurch of his heart under the palm she pressed to his chest. Felt the hard, vital beat of it.

And knew the danger, even as she felt the lure.

His kiss was a rumble of thunder in a darkening sky. It reverberated through her, echoing in her bones and blood. It warned of a greater storm coming. It hinted at lightning that could crackle and flare. That could singe her, make her shudder. And start a fire that would not be put out.

Until it had consumed her.

She broke the kiss with a gasp, for air and for balance, not drawing in enough with the first, nor the second, nor even the third long breath.

She tried to back away, but the door was behind her, Boone in front of her.

"I... I..."

He reached for her. "Dammit, Cambria, you think I don't know?" Gray eyes burned through the shadows.

"No." She pushed at him with the hand on his chest, the palm directly over his heart. He stilled, and in the next pulse under her touch, he stiffened. "No."

Without retreating a step, he gave her space. His arm dropped from her back, opening an escape route. But his eyes stayed on her, not allowing the temptation of immediate flight to take hold.

"I told you, I don't... You're a guest."

"So?"

She became aware of her hands still on him, and snatched them away, one from his chest, the other from the back of his neck. Then she wasn't sure what to do with them, finally tucking them away as she crossed her arms in front of her.

"So, you'll be leaving. I won't do this. I won't..."

What felt like a cramp in her throat nearly swallowed the last word.

"Cambria..."

He leaned toward her.

"No."

And now she did take that escape route. Flight or not, it was the only sane thing to do.

He hadn't taken his hand from her hair, and for an instant the strands caught in his fingers, not hurting, but tugging in a way that reminded he had a hold on her.

Then her hair slipped through.

She didn't look at him as she went in the unlocked door and out of the cone of light.

Chapter Five

"So, how's it going, Boone?"

"Fine."

"Then why do you sound restless as a caged tiger at feeding time? The sister still dogging all your steps?"

"No."

"Ah.... That so?"

Not for the first time in their nearly thirty years of friendship, Boone wished Cully Grainger were half as sleepy as he sounded.

"Yeah, that's so."

It was Wednesday. His second day of coming into town on his own. His second day of seeing Cambria for no more than snippets, mostly at a distance. His second day torn between wondering what in hell had gotten into him to kiss her, and wondering if he'd ever get another chance.

She'd started scrubbing out the bunkhouse, but steadfastly refused his offers of help. Ted was planting a late alfalfa field, with room for only one on the tractor. Irene was visiting a friend and running errands. Pete was in school and busy with practice and friends afterward.

Boone was going nuts.

He couldn't remember the last time he'd spent a day and a half with nothing to do. If this was relaxing, it was hugely overrated.

"Well, you should be getting to know the boy."

"He's in school all day. Has baseball practice most days after. Has his chores and friends...."

Boone had called the office three times yesterday, twice already today. That librarian, Wanda, was growing less and less happy to see him. And he'd started wondering how he could get cellular phone service in Bardville, Wyoming, and how fast he could get a fax hooked up in the cabin—probably after updating the antiquated electrical system. He'd even told the office to send the new drafting software he hadn't bothered to load into his laptop until now.

Hell, he was so bored, he'd delayed opening the developed photos he'd picked up in his morning trip to town, just to have something to look forward to.

"Even so," Cully pressed, "you should know by now if he's happy, healthy, well-adjusted. Those were the things you said you were worried about. The things you said you wanted to see before you stepped into his life or stepped out of it."

"It's not that simple."

In the silence that followed Boone heard a kind of acceptance from his friend. "No. I suppose it's not. So, what are you going to do now?"

"I wish I knew."

A muffled chuckle-snort reached Boone's ear.

"What's the matter with you, Grainger?"

"Just trying to adjust to Porky taking to the air."

"What are you talking about?"

"About pigs flying and Boone Dorsey Smith admitting he doesn't know what to do."

Boone gave a suggestion of what Cully could do, but it was halfhearted.

Through the open cabin window, Boone heard the radio from the bunkhouse where Cambria worked. Pete had joined her about an hour ago. Eleven songs ago she'd turned down another of Boone's offers to help.

Lord, the woman was stubborn.

What did she think he'd do? Ravish her in front of her brother?

Come to think of it, maybe she was smart to keep her distance. Because he had to admit, ravishing her sounded real tempting.

He should be grateful, in fact. He didn't need to let himself get distracted by her when he'd come here to get to know his son. Except, of course, his son was in there with Cambria, where Boone was definitely not welcome.

With a sigh from the gut, he pushed off from where he'd leaned his shoulder on the wall beside the window and went to the square pine table. Photos scattered by restless hands cluttered its surface.

He straightened all the edges, then started through them again.

There were pictures of Pete at that first game Boone had gone to.

His son.

Boone stared at the image of a boy striding toward manhood. Tall and straight, with an easy grin and clear eyes. He looked happy and confident, standing there in his baseball uniform, talking before the game with Irene and Ted... his parents.

Boone quickly flipped to the next photograph, a wide shot of the playing field. He'd loved the game as a kid. Especially playing catcher. Plotting strategy, directing the fielders, calling the pitches that would fool the batter. He'd had some talent, too. The coaches had said so. Even talked about scouts and a future in the pros. But he'd had Gran and Kenzie to watch out for, as well as after-school and summer construction jobs. That hadn't left much time for games.

Had he given Pete his love for baseball? Had Ted and Irene? Or had Pete found it on his own?

Boone shook his head at himself. That was a damn useless line of wondering. How could anybody know? Would it matter if they could?

What mattered was if he could give Pete anything now, or in the future.

Boone turned over pictures from Cambria's horseback tour. Shots of cattle, of prairie dogs, of distant mountains, of fences coming together. Shots of Cambria, sunlight gilding her hair, that enticing curve of her back settled so surely in the saddle, her hand trailing absently along Snakebit's neck.

No sense denying it, he was attracted to this woman. His mouth twisted at that bit of understatement.

But acting on that feeling wasn't going to work, not from his end because of Pete and not from her end because of the shadows he sensed dogging her.

No, she didn't need him trying to seduce her. What she needed was another set of hands helping in that bunkhouse. Only she was too stubborn to even admit it.

Or was she too scared?

Why would she be scared? The question rose up, but he put it aside. What mattered was helping.

The Westons' generosity didn't hide that the house could use some repairs, the barn was shy a couple coats of paint, the four-wheel drive and truck were past due for retirement.

Frowning in thought, Boone flipped through the last pictures. Distant shots of the deserted cabin, then closer ones, followed by a trio of Cambria before she'd ducked away, and finally, closeups of the cabin's construction.

His hand rested on the last shot for a full minute.

When he moved again, he knew what he was going to do—to keep himself sane and hopefully to help the Weston family.

And he didn't think Cambria could stop him.

"What on earth are you doing?"

Boone looked around late Friday afternoon to find Cambria and Pete on horseback not four feet behind him. He'd been so focused he hadn't heard them.

"Trying to salvage this cabin."

"It looks like you're tearing it apart."

"I am." He ripped free the last corner of a strip of tar paper and tossed it onto a rubbish pile already waist high. Snakebit sidled away, but Cambria settled him with a murmur and a touch. Boone made himself look away. Even engrossed by what the past day and a half's work revealed in the cabin, he'd thought too much about Cambria Weston's murmurs and touches. "I'm peeling away the skin so I can see the bones."

"Why?"

"You said you were going to tear it down. I figured if I can dismantle it, save what's good—" he gestured to two other piles, a very small one with three carefully labeled pieces of wood and a slightly larger one that included a fireplace mantel and an interior door "—then reassemble it on the other side of the creek, it could be modernized like the others without the problems you mentioned about plumbing and electricity and a bridge. You'd have another cabin to rent out for not much cost."

"It would still be ugly and cramped," Cambria said. But she tilted her head and squinted at the cabin. She was clearly intrigued. He stifled a victorious smirk. He hadn't felt this good about being featured in the *Wall Street Journal.*

"Not necessarily. The bones show the original design meant it to be half again as big as this. That would widen the front, add another window, change the roofline." He sketched the plan with his hands in the air. "Now the lines are all off—that's what bothers you visually. I can take what's here and use that lumber you've got stored in the barn and make it the way it should be."

"We can't pay you," she said flatly.

"Count it toward working off my board," he offered.

"You're supposed to be here for rest and relaxation."

He shrugged. "Call it therapy. Maybe I should pay you."

"How do we know you know what you're doing?"

"You don't. But what have you got to lose? You were going to tear it down anyway."

Cambria's lips parted—whether to offer another objection or to demand what he needed therapy for, he wasn't sure—but before she could say anything, Pete eased his horse forward and said, "I've seen 'em move houses on flatbeds, but never piece by piece. How will you get this back together if you take it apart?"

"Very carefully." His dry answer drew a chuckle from Pete, but the boy persisted.

"Yeah, but how'll you know where the pieces go?"

Boone heard the interest in Pete's voice, and an idea came to him. "You draw a plan of the building, as best you can tell from the outside, then add details as you take off the shell so you can see the actual structure. Each step, you number every piece you take off and write the number on the corresponding plan. I could use some help, if you're interested."

"Yeah, that'd be—"

"How about baseball practice?" Cambria interrupted. "And your homework? And chores?"

Pete sent a look to Cambria, astride Snakebit with no sign of approval in her face. "I could work it out. Dad would let me take the time from chores to help Boone out, don't you think, Cam? Since it would give us another cabin to rent."

In a stiffly neutral tone Cambria replied, "You'd have to check with your father about that, Pete."

Boone stifled a wince at her words—Pete would be working with *his father.*

"I know he'll say yes. I mean, Boone would be helping us out, so it's only fair."

Yes, only fair that Boone have a chance to spend time with his son, even under the guise of a construction project.

It was also only fair that Pete, his reason for being here, should provide a buffer between Boone and the woman he shouldn't want.

Cambria didn't like it.

Oh, she wasn't foolish enough not to acknowledge that an extra cabin would help, especially if it didn't require much investment. And she wasn't ungracious enough not to recognize his generosity.

But she didn't like it.

"I don't see why not," Irene said, matching socks from the dryer while Cambria leaned against the washing machine.

"He barreled right ahead and started on this project—"

"He knew the cabin was going to be torn down. Why shouldn't he?"

"He could have asked someone, consulted with someone...."

"You mean, with you?" Irene asked mildly.

Cambria grimaced wryly. "Yes, I suppose I do. But it's more—"

"What's worrying you, Cambria?"

"I just don't know how this is going to work out with Pete helping him." Cambria examined her own reaction. "I'm surprised Boone took him up on the offer."

"Why shouldn't he?"

"Boone seems to me to be a man who feels totally responsible for anything he's involved with, and is fiercely determined it will be the best he can make it."

"I'd think you would admire that in a man."

"I do, but—" Too late, Cambria caught the glint in Irene's eyes at that admission. *"But,"* she repeated with emphasis, "it can be taken too far. I've seen this guy in action. Look at how he was with that stall door. All I wanted was not to have to kick it to open or close it. But he had to make it *perfect,* telling Pete to hold it a little higher, and making these fine adjustments. When someone doesn't do something fast enough or well enough for him, he takes over. If you don't believe me, ask Wanda Ruppert at the library. Or Ches at the gas station. Last Thursday when I drove Boone into town and stopped to fill up the four-wheel, Ches was talking away while he wiped the windshield, like he always does, and Boone got out and did it himself because he didn't think Ches was going fast enough or doing it right. He took the squeegee and rag right out of Ches's hands."

"I don't imagine Ches Poole minded a bit."

Cambria drummed her fingers on the washing machine. "No, he didn't. But Pete would. You know how Pete is."

She met Irene's eyes, and read there the recognition that Boone's demanding ways could bruise her brother's teenage pride and confidence.

"What can you do about it, Cambria?" Irene asked softly. "You can't wipe out that Pete offered and Boone said yes, and you can't change either one of them."

"No," she said slowly. "But I can be darn sure to stick around and try to head off any problems."

"Sometimes trying to solve a problem just creates worse ones."

Cambria raised her chin. "Not this time."

Boone was left on his own over the weekend. Saturday, Cambria, Pete and Ted all helped a neighbor vaccinate and brand his spring calves. The next day the neighbor and his hired hand returned the favor at the Weston spread.

Boone had volunteered to help, but Ted had tactfully indicated that the job went faster with experienced hands. So Boone continued dismantling the cabin. It was a considerably more complicated job than straight demolition. As he'd told Pete, he was trying to peel away layers without destroying what lay beneath, both to salvage as much original material as possible and to see what the first builders had intended.

After cleaning up for Sunday supper, Boone crossed the footbridge over the creek to examine the old cabin again. Sometimes coming at it fresh and from a distance showed things you didn't see otherwise.

What he saw instead was Pete, shower-wet hair showing under his P.A.W. baseball cap, and wearing clean clothes.

"Hey, Boone." From that greeting, Pete started on about how much progress Boone had made on the cabin in two days. But Boone couldn't concentrate on the words. In this fresh-scrubbed state, Pete looked like an overgrown child. Boone thought he could catch glimpses of the little boy he'd been.

"So what do you think?"

Boone blinked back to the present, trying to follow Pete's question. "About what?"

"About if seeing Cam's cabin would help you? Are you interested?"

Interested? Yes. *Help him?* Not with what really ailed him.

Boone tried to recall what Pete had been saying while his mind envisioned a baby, a toddler, a boy he would never know.

One of the oldest cabins... original logs... real old homestead...

"Sure. I'm interested."

So Boone found himself standing on the porch where he'd kissed Cambria, while Pete knocked and called out her name.

"What is it, Pete?" She swung open the door, a thin layer of irritation over the affectionate amusement in her voice. "Why're you pounding down the door that—"

She stopped when she saw Boone.

He didn't feel real talkative himself, perhaps because a swell of something as hot as desire, but more complicated than that basic urge, closed off his throat.

She'd just stepped from the shower. Her hair was slicked back from her face, down her neck, to the top of her shoulders, where it dampened her silky robe. Moisture glistened on her face, her throat, and disappeared into the vee of ruby and jade paisley. The robe crossed at her waist under a knotted belt. It reached the top of her knees and past her elbows. And it didn't matter.

Boone felt the same punch to his gut and the same tightening somewhat lower he would have experienced if she'd come to the door naked. He knew she had nothing on under that stretch of shimmery cloth. He could imagine her in the shower moments earlier, water streaming over her shoulders and breasts. He could imagine her unbelting the robe, letting it open, letting him inside...

"C'mon, Boone."

Pete's voice intruded into his fantasy, jerking Boone from that image of a welcoming Cambria to the reality of the woman who was trying like the devil to hide her awareness of him.

If she hadn't tried so hard, maybe he wouldn't have brushed against her as he followed Pete through the open doorway into the cabin. Maybe he wouldn't have brushed the back of his knuckles along the line of her jaw as he passed. Maybe he wouldn't have met her eyes deliberately, and let her see what was in his.

For a narrow slice of time her eyes widened, darkened, and he wondered...

Then she spun away, moving ahead of Pete and stopping him, arms crossed, voice demanding, "What are you up to, Pete?"

"I'm gonna show Boone your cabin. He thinks seeing this one might help him with the one he's taking apart, because it's so old and hasn't been changed a whole lot."

"Oh, he does?" She glared over Pete's shoulder at Boone, defying him, defying the heated look of a moment before.

"It might," he said mildly enough. His voice was a little lower than normal, maybe even a shade harsh, but not enough to alert Pete to the fireworks going on around him. "Of course, if you'd rather I didn't..."

He saw her eyes flare with acknowledgment of the direct challenge.

"Perhaps another time—"

Pete marched right over her delicate sidestepping. "It'll only take a minute, Cam. Get dressed while I show Boone out here. We'll look at the bedroom when you're done."

Oh, no, she wasn't going to strip off the protection of that robe, even to draw on more conventional clothes, not with Boone in her cabin. He saw that resolve in her eyes. He would have grinned if the image of her opening that robe hadn't constricted his muscles again.

"I'll wait." Grimly, she recrossed her arms at her waist.

"Okay," Pete accepted easily. "Dad says this is the original cabin, with the bedroom added later...."

Pete pointed out the features he knew about in the old structure, and Boone tried to listen. He felt as if his attention and senses were divided three ways. First, taking in the wavy glass of an original window, hand-smoothed surfaces of century-old logs, stone fireplace similar to the one in his cabin. Then, observing the plush comfort of the low-slung couch by the fireplace, the barefoot welcoming of soft rugs and the homey gatherings of books and wooden carvings, bowls and boxes on shelves, tables and windowsills. And finally, noting the angular determination of the woman standing in its center.

She sported odd patches of sunburn partway up each arm that he figured resulted from the gap between gloves and sleeves. Another pattern of pink showed inside the neckline of her robe, in keeping with a couple of open buttons on a shirt. He had the strongest urge to kiss each reddened area, to glide his lips over the skin, absorbing the heat.

"The kitchen stuff—" Pete waved to a corner equipped with a small sink, an undercabinet refrigerator, microwave and toaster oven "—and the bathroom got updated when Cam moved back here, but you can probably get an idea of how it was before, if you think that'll help you."

"It might."

On the other hand, Boone thought as he followed Pete into Cambria's bedroom, it just might be the death of him. If not from the dagger look Cambria sent him, then from the fuel added to his already overheated imagination.

The room was not much larger than the bedroom in his cabin. A double-size iron bedstead dominated it. The white spread was plain and soft-looking. A quilt of forest greens with splashes of yellow and red was folded at the foot.

He forced his eyes away, trying to follow Pete's words, without great success.

A double-wide bureau stretched along one wall had a framed mirror over one side, a window over the other. The closet and bathroom were tucked into a corner. A low bookcase by the side of the bed served as a nightstand. One wooden arm and the corner of an upholstered back were all that showed of a chair in the corner, the rest of it obscured by layers of clothes. That and three pairs of shoes discarded at various points around the floor were the only signs of mess—Cambria Weston was a very controlled slob.

She was also a woman who surrounded herself with her family and friends. Framed photos peppered the walls, blanketed the bureau top. A brighter-haired Irene holding the hand of a girl as they walked to a school bus waiting at the end of the ranch road. A pigtailed girl on a pony between Irene and Ted, who held a chubby dark-haired baby on horseback. A Christmas tree behind a smiling family group of mother, father, teenage daughter and solid little boy. Cambria in cap and gown with Ted and Irene beaming pride while Pete, a gawky adolescent, accepted a hug. A montage of Washington, D.C., landmarks, with a younger-looking Jessa among those peopling the shots. Some of the same people in wedding poses and some looking slightly incongruous on the ranch. Another of Jessa smiling hesitantly before her shop bearing a Grand Opening sign. And a poster-size shot of Cambria on Snakebit and Pete on Jezebel with yellow-sparked mountains of fall rising behind them, the quality slightly fuzzy from enlarging, but beneath the teasing smiles, the connection and love as clear as Boone had seen so often in person.

With those photos and that bed before him, Boone knew he shouldn't have come into her bedroom. Probably shouldn't have come into her cabin. Maybe not even into her life.

"Are you two done here?" Cambria demanded from behind him. "I have to get dressed before supper."

"I guess, unless Boone..." Pete looked over at Boone, who shook his head. They headed for the door, preceded by Cambria. "Think this'll help any?"

"Yeah, I do. I think it helps me see things clearer."

Pete looked pleased.

Cambria, however, gave Boone a sharp look, almost as if she knew it had helped him see more clearly what he'd been telling himself from the start—how impossible his desire for her was. No matter how much stronger it grew.

For two days Cambria had started work early preparing the cabins for their end-of-the-month opening so she could join Pete when he returned from school and headed straight for the cabin Boone was rapidly dismantling.

The first day Boone had straightened from where he'd been prying loose a board and given her a long, considering look. She'd glared in return.

For a moment she'd thought he might bring up his abrupt shift in mood of the evening before during his impromptu inspection of her cabin.

His sensual appraisal of her had been so blatant she'd first been stunned, then appalled by the surge of her response, next, concerned Pete would pick up on it, and finally, determined not to show what she couldn't convince herself she didn't feel.

Then Boone Dorsey Smith had walked into her bedroom, taken one look around and walked out in a totally different mood. Distant, grim. She hadn't understood it. She didn't like things she didn't understand.

Which, she'd thought that first day while she'd waited to see if he'd bring up the subject, pretty much summed up her feelings about Boone Dorsey Smith.

Except that he pressed buttons on her libido she hadn't known existed.

But he'd said nothing to her. Not then. Not as they'd worked until dinner. Not the next day as they'd repeated the routine.

He'd talked readily enough to Pete. In fact they'd gone back and forth about baseball until she'd thought she'd scream if she heard ERA one more time.

Her tolerance dropped another notch on that first night when Ted had brought a straw cowboy hat to the supper table and set it in front of Boone.

"Best use that instead of the baseball cap you've been wearing. It'll protect the back of your neck better."

Boone had reached back automatically. "Thanks, but I don't—" He'd broken off with a grimace as his fingers encountered sun-tender skin. "Guess my hair's not long enough or thick enough. Thanks."

"It's too long, if you ask me," Irene had said as she'd set down a bowl of boiled potatoes with an emphatic thump.

"The boy didn't ask you," Ted had interposed mildly.

"If he had, he wouldn't still have it so long," Irene had answered, returning to the refrigerator for sliced tomatoes.

Cambria, filling the water glasses, had caught Pete's delighted grin at not being the object of that particular lecture for once, and the man-to-man wink Ted had sent Boone. His gray eyes, oddly softened by bemusement, had shifted to her.

She'd looked away. He hadn't looked her way again.

This third day since Pete had started helping on the cabin, Cambria noticed that the noise from across the creek seemed muffled. There could have been any number of reasons, none of which mattered to her since Pete hadn't arrived yet.

Only because she'd finished early with the day's chores did she head across the footbridge. The outside of the cabin had the look of a sheared sheep, with the ribs showing clearly now that various layers of covering had been removed.

She soon realized why the sound had been muted; Boone was working inside. With the stairs gone, she braced her hands against the doorframe to take the high, single step to the threshold.

Boone stood on a raised board resting on cement blocks, reaching overhead to take down one of the horizontal crosspieces that tied into the center beam and that had been covered by the long-discarded ceiling material. Nearly a dozen of these long, thick poles already lay in a corner of the room, leaving two others besides the one he battled. With them gone, it opened to the roof rafters.

From Boone's muttered discourse on the piece of wood's parentage and sexual habits, it appeared this crosspiece wouldn't cooperate.

"C'mon, now," he coaxed, at the same time giving a jerk that pulled it loose at the far end. He stretched his right arm out to try to balance the pole across his chest and shoulders, but it had too much momentum and was too heavily weighted to his right. It tipped over his right shoulder and scraped along the back of his arm, drawing an oath and bending him backward in a fight for balance on his narrow platform as the wood crashed to the floor.

Cambria lunged forward, but succeeded only in startling him just when it appeared he might right himself. Instead his back arched, then bowed, then arched again. She caught a flash of his startled look, then he stumbled off the platform and fell heavily against her.

Instinctively wrapping their arms around each other gave them enough combined balance to keep from falling to the floor littered with wood and nail-studded boards, certainly an uncomfortable landing place and possibly dangerous. As it was, they took several awkward steps together that might have resembled a waltz—if the dancers were inebriated bears.

"What in the hell—"

"Let go of me."

He raised his hands in mock surrender as she stepped free.

"No disrespect intended, ma'am," he said in a sarcastic drawl. "Just trying to keep myself from being impaled after you came sneaking up on me."

"Sneaking up on you, why you ungra— You're bleeding."

She looked from the wet, red swipe across her left palm to the stain seeping down the edge of the gaping tear in his right sleeve where she had gripped him.

"Bleeding? What— Oh, hell."

Cambria followed the direction of his gaze to the troublesome pole. A long nail protruded from it, with a scrap of shirt and a reddish mark decorating its tip.

"You idiot." She ignored the tightening in her stomach at the thought of how that must have felt. "Sit down."

"I'm not going to faint from a little bit of blood."

She put her hands on her hips. "If you don't sit down, I'll knock you down."

"Okay, okay." Despite his peeved tone, the corners of his mouth twitched.

He sat on the platform while she rooted through the basket Irene had insisted on refurbishing for him each morning and noon. He no doubt had found the water, cookies and fruit, maybe even the paper napkins. But he hadn't dug to the bottom of it as Cambria did to find the first-aid kit she'd known Irene would include. "Being prepared for life's storms" was what Irene called it.

Opening the plastic box, Cambria straddled the platform to his right.

"Take your shirt off."

He opened his mouth, but apparently thought better of it when he met her look, and satisfied himself with raising his eyebrows. To stop herself from saying anything that might escalate the tension, she pressed her lips tighter. It backfired. The motion drew his gaze immediately to her mouth, where it stayed as his fingers quickly undid his buttons.

Irritated tension wavered into a shimmering awareness. Her hold on the first-aid kit went slack.

She caught it before it slid off her lap, looking up quickly to see if he'd noticed her fumble. He was shrugging his right shoulder free of the shirt, drawing his arm out of the torn sleeve, the line of his collarbone standing out and the muscles and sinew of shoulder and arm bunching and easing in a mesmerizing synchronization.

Almost too late, she realized he'd started to repeat that action with the other shoulder.

"No." All she did was touch the tips of her fingers to his shoulder, but he stopped immediately. She wet her lips. "You didn't manage to get nailed on that side, too, did you?"

"No."

She focused all her attention on the raw gouge down the back of his arm.

"Turn around so I can take care of this."

His eyes rested on her for half a minute before he swung his left leg over the platform so he also straddled it, facing the same direction she did, sitting in front of her.

"Okay?" he asked, glancing back over his shoulder.

"Yeah." She bent his elbow and positioned his upper arm back as nearly horizontal as she could get it. The maneuver drew the skin taut over his right shoulder blade, and brought the muscles into relief except where they disappeared under the shirt that draped the left side of his back. "Now hold still."

"Are you going to use something that'll— Ow! Damn!" She poured a little more of the antiseptic into the wound to rinse it. "That'll sting...." he finished in a fatalistic murmur, then roused himself to complain. "That hurt."

"It's better than you deserve. Trying to manhandle that beam—"

"It's a joist."

"By yourself. What did you think you were doing?"

He grimaced as he twisted to get a look at what she was doing. "Do you know how often you've asked me that question?"

"Not half as often as I could," she answered tartly. "Why didn't you wait for Pete to help you? Or you could have called me."

"Could I?"

She ignored that. "I sure hope you've had a recent tetanus shot, because—"

"I have."

"I'm not partial to nursing anyone with lockjaw."

"Would you nurse me, Cambria?"

"No." But her touch stayed gentle as she blotted the area with clean gauze pads. "Not when it's your own fault for being so determined to do everything yourself."

"I'm not determined to do everything myself."

Was she imagining that his emphasis on the second-to-last word meant there were certain things he'd like to do with someone else and that the sweep of his gaze on her lips narrowed it to her? If she wasn't imagining it, she had a hunk of temptation to put behind her. If she was, it meant her mind was heading in directions she didn't care for.

"Yeah, right."

He twisted farther and peered over his shoulder at her. "What do you mean by that?"

"I mean, if you would resign your position as general manager of the universe, you might have time to relax, even see a movie now and then."

"Hey, I'm here, aren't I? Taking a vacation."

"Yeah, right."

"What does *that* mean?"

"It means you're here, but not on vacation."

Under her fingers the muscle in his arm hardened. She looked up, surprised. She'd thought if anything hurt it would have been the antiseptic. This first-aid cream should soothe. But his hand had bunched into a tight fist. Even his voice was strained when he asked, "What makes you think I'm not here on vacation?"

She snorted, but lightened her stroking to barely smoothing the cream on his skin.

"How can you be on vacation when you're calling your office every other minute? And the minutes in between you're sending off Express Mail. Do you know Jenkins at the post office had to send to Sheridan for more Express Mail envelopes because you've already used up the supply he thought would last the rest of this year? And the few seconds you're giving your office a break, you're hauling irrigation pipe or fixing stall doors or trying to tear down cabins single-handedly."

Her easier touch apparently did the trick because his muscles relaxed some.

"Guess I'm in the habit of doing things myself, being in charge."

"Habits can be broken." She placed a bandage over the gouge to protect it, but not too tightly. "There, you're done."

He swung one leg over the bench so he sat with his side instead of his back to her. He looked straight ahead. "You know what they say about old habits dying hard." Even in profile she could see his one-sided grin. "And that's about the oldest habit I've got."

She'd put that together with what he'd said of his family the first day they'd stopped at this cabin. It sounded as if he'd carried an adult's responsibilities on a child's shoulders. Maybe he needed to learn how to put aside some of that burden.

"Old habits might die hard, but nobody says they're immortal."

He cocked his head and gave her a small grin. "You got something in mind about how I should change, Cambria Weston?"

"Yes, I do."

"That's it? *Yes, I do.* You're not even going to say something like 'it's none of my business, but'?" He was laughing at her, but she didn't mind. Her own grin flickered to life.

"Nope. I was simply going to say it. If you can't listen to good advice because it comes from somebody who has no business giving it, that's your problem."

He laughed. Full out. A wonderful, deep sound that had her smiling—foolishly, she feared—until she caught herself.

"All right, say it." He threw out his arms in a classic gesture of surrender. But when his right hand met her arm, he turned his hand so the act of ending the contact turned into a brief caress. His grin twisted slightly as he added, "I'm at your mercy."

If he hadn't said that, or certainly if he hadn't touched her that way, she wouldn't have felt the uneasy discomfort that made her answering words come out harsh.

"You have to have more patience with people. Let them take the responsibility. Even let them make their own mistakes. Or you'll push them away. Like with your sister." The muscle along his arm bunched again. "I'm sorry." She shook her head, regretting that her stupid discomfort had led her to say something painful. "It really isn't any of my business."

She started to stand, but his hand, warm and large and faintly rough against the curve of her knee, stopped her.

"It's hard.... You know, Cambria, I don't even have a real photograph of her. Only school pictures, nothing that shows how she really is, how she was." She remembered how he'd studied the photo-strewn walls of her bedroom and, earlier, how he'd had regret in his voice when he'd said they'd never held a camera when he was growing up.

"When you've looked after somebody, it's hard to let them go their own way, to let them take the bumps and bruises that come along with mistakes. Especially when you know you could do things for them, make it easier. You feel responsible...." He obviously tried to shake off his seriousness, without complete success. "I guess I shouldn't bellyache. Parents manage it all the time, don't they? Letting go, I mean."

"Some parents don't have any trouble."

Even if she hadn't heard the bitterness in her own words, she would have recognized it from his expression of arrested surprise. She stared at the fallen crosspiece resting at an odd angle, tensing for his questions—until she remembered the best defense was a good offense and launched into speech.

"But that's not the issue here." Ignoring his murmur of "Isn't it?" she straightened her back and put her hands on her hips. "What you can start with is giving your office a break."

"Yeah? How?" He made a tight circle with his palm still resting on her knee. He watched her more closely than she might have liked, but at least he didn't argue. For now.

"First, stop calling them so much. You know how that probably makes them feel?" She didn't wait for an answer. "Like they're not trusted. Like you don't think they can do the job without your looking over their shoulder every second. Quit trying to do everything yourself."

"What makes you think I try to do everything myself?"

She snorted indelicately, ignoring the current of warmth that ran from her knee up her thigh, to an even more responsive territory. "You've got to be kidding. A man who's supposed to be on vacation, who comes a thousand miles for rest and relaxation, who's in daily communication with his office? A man who says he hasn't gone out much in the past six years and—"

"You've been talking to Jessa."

"Can't even find time to see movies. Gee, what could make me think you try to do everything yourself? Not to mention—" she quirked an eyebrow toward the skeleton of the cabin "—I've seen you in action."

"Lord, you sound like Cully."

"Who?"

"Friend of mine."

"Sounds like a wise one if he's telling you to learn to delegate. You'll get more done yourself and you'll be amazed at how much other people are capable of when you stop trying to do it all yourself."

He grimaced toward the ground at his feet. "You and Cully, you don't want much, do you?"

She held silent and, when he turned to her, still with his head partly bowed but his eyes lifted to her face, she held motionless. His look had her heart beating harder and her breath coming shorter. What did he search for so intently when his gaze touched her eyes, her chin, her lips, her hair, before returning to her eyes? What did he find?

"I'll try."

He meant it, and it had cost him. She knew that. On pure instinct her hand covered his where it rested on her knee. His turned immediately to enclose hers in warmth and slight friction.

"That's more than Cully's ever gotten out of me."

Fighting a need to swallow, she echoed his faint smile. He held her hand. That's all. Simply a gesture of accord between two humans. Nothing to speed the heart or slow the brain.

"Next time, will you promise to get Pete to help you?" she pressed.

"Get Pete to help with what?" Pete asked from behind her.

Her hand jerked free of Boone's. The moment ended—a clean break, no infection, no mess.

She was relieved. Definitely. And it didn't bother her in the least that before bending to put the first-aid kit to rights, she'd spotted a shade of something that might have been relief in Boone's expression, too, as he related his mishap to Pete in wry terms.

"Hi."

Cambria had recognized the cadence of Boone's walk crossing the packed earth toward a rental cabin where she was planting a flower box with some of the seedlings Irene had brought back from town earlier that morning. But she'd expected him to keep going to the footbridge to work. She certainly hadn't expected him to come lean on the porch post not three feet away.

He wore a black shirt tucked into comfortably worn jeans, which stretched quite nicely over hips cocked slightly forward. His rolled-back sleeves called attention to the hands he'd tucked into the front pockets.

"What are you doing here?" she asked.

He made a sound, part cluck, part chuckle. "You think that's much improvement on 'what do you think you're doing'?"

Some of her hair slid forward, tickling against her cheek. With her hands coated with dirt, she tried to brush it back with her hunched shoulder, with no luck. He watched the maneuver with apparently detached interest.

"I wasn't trying to impr—"

"Nice to see you, too, Cambria."

Wryness flavored his words. She glanced up, then wished she hadn't.

He propped one shoulder against the log post, with his arms crossed over his chest, loosely, yet enough to tighten the black fabric enticingly. One foot in front of the other drew the denim snugly along his legs' muscular lines.

"I just saw you at breakfast," she mumbled, digging her hands deeper into the soil and peat moss, noticing a smudge of dirt on her knee below her denim cutoffs. The seedling she was planting barely kept its head above ground as she packed it in.

"It seems much longer." He sighed. "Time doesn't fly when you have nothing to do."

"The cabin—"

"The next step's taking down the beam, which is a two-man job, and since I promised a certain pushy dame I wouldn't try to do everything myself, I'm stuck till Pete gets home."

"I thought you were going into town this morning."

"I did. I'm back."

"Oh? So soon?" She added with wicked innocence, "Did your employees finally get smart and not answer the phone?"

"I didn't call." Her hands paused at that. "I thought about what you said the other day. Thought I'd give it a try."

"It has to be more than a token effort," she warned. She tried again to push her wayward hair behind her ear, this time with her forearm, and failed again.

"I know."

His answer sounded distracted enough that she looked up to find him right next to her, reaching for her shoulders. She allowed herself to be turned to face him.

"What are you doing..."

Her demand faded as he raised his hand. His eyes followed his hand's movement as he tucked the errant hair behind her ear, and her eyes stayed on his.

How could such a simple touch, almost impersonal, make her feel this way? The man was dangerous. Decidedly dangerous.

"What am I doing?" he repeated hoarsely, as if to himself. "Something stupid."

His hand continued to the nape of her neck, drawing her to him and tipping her head. It wasn't a rough touch. It didn't need to be. She moved into him, her dirty hands raised shoulder high, like a holdup victim's. A willing one.

Before her eyes fluttered closed, she saw a faint frown drawing down his dark brows, and a fainter smile drawing up his lips. Their mouths met with no fumbling. Firm, warm, moist. She felt the pleasure of his smile against her lips.

He slipped his other arm under her bent elbow and around to the small of her back, drawing her more firmly against him. Leaning into him, with her hands still held away, she let him become her balance.

Open-handed, he stroked her back through the red cotton of her shirt, his palm firm and hot as it slid up to her nape, then down to her derriere. He repeated that several drugging times, then shifted the motion from side to side, the tip of his extended thumb slipping under her elbow and deliberately stroking the bottom outside curve of her breast.

She parted her lips with the enticement of his touch. He deepened the caress until they broke that kiss, pulling in oxygen, while his mouth touched her eyelids, her cheekbones, her temples.

"Cambria..." There was a reluctance in that single spoken word that sent off a warning.

He's holding something back...

Not from his kisses. His tongue swept into her mouth, tasting deeply, and bringing his own taste to her. She answered it.

There was a strange sort of appeal in being held this way, without being able to hold back. A sort of surrender.

No. No, not surrender. She couldn't surrender, wouldn't.

Oh, but his mouth on hers felt so sure. The press of his body against hers felt so good.

No, she couldn't forget. She couldn't ignore the warnings in her head. Not ever again. Not now. But maybe she didn't have to ignore them. Maybe he could quiet them. With answers.

She couldn't surrender, but could a truce be found... a truce negotiated with the truth?

She recognized the risk. Asking showed her desire to know, and that revealed a vulnerability she hadn't risked in a long time.

"Boone?"

His lips trailed the ridge of her jaw, down the side of her throat. His tongue traced a line along her collarbone, then his kisses retraced his path, and beyond, to her ear. He caught her lobe lightly between his teeth as he finally answered with a vague, "Hmm?"

"Boone... Please..." She hated the hint of pleading. She hoped he thought it was a request to stop the tantalizing exploration. Slipping her forearms between their upper bodies, she gained some space—to breathe and think.

"Boone, what really brought you to Wyoming?"

"Maybe you did. Maybe this did." His mumble at her temple fluttered against her skin.

She shivered slightly, but she didn't surrender. "Why did you come here? What aren't you telling me?"

Chapter Six

"I don't know what you're talking about, Cambria."

Within his hold, she transformed. She'd been magical, strong, lithe, pliant and hot. In an instant that vanished. He knew she could do nothing about the heat and pleasured scent clinging to her skin, but one denial from him and her body became so brittlely stiff he thought she might shatter.

He released her. More quickly than the first time he'd kissed her. Because this time he knew he'd caused the break.

But, dammit, how could he tell her he'd come for Pete when the one thing he knew in this whole mess was that his first duty was to figure out the best way to approach his son? He hadn't come anywhere near doing that yet, so how could he tell her?

Besides, he'd heard enough of her views on her family and the outside world to know that if he told her the truth she would circle the emotional wagons with him on the outside.

"I see." Her voice could have frozen boiling water.

Damned if he saw.

Steady and controlled, she returned to the planter. He felt like ripping it out of its holder and smashing it to splinters.

"I don't know why you can't believe me, Cambria, when I say I came here for rest and relaxation."

She didn't pause in her planting, and he didn't suppose for a moment that he had a chance of convincing her anyway.

"Look, I'll help you plant—"

"No."

Now she did look at him, and he wished she hadn't. Looks could cut clear down to the bone.

"I don't need your help. I don't want it."

Cambria pulled the truck into the drive fast enough to have the old suspension complaining audibly. Her eyes hadn't deceived her. There *was* a bunch of strange vehicles clustered at the far end of the semicircle of cabins.

Her first, heart-pounding anxiety eased into puzzlement as she realized they consisted of a cement-mixer truck and a couple of unfamiliar pickups.

Boone, his head lowered in intent survey, stood in the center of a group of men watching two others guide cement into a heavy cardboard tube sunk into a hole in the ground. A scattering of other tubes dotted the area.

Boone looked toward her as she parked the truck by the house, and she thought he grimaced. As she started toward the activity, he backed away from the workers to stand in the shade of a cottonwood.

She headed right for him.

"What do you think—"

"I'm doing," he finished fatalistically. That edged toward accusation as he added, "All we needed was half a day, and you were supposed to be in Sheridan shopping all day with Jessa."

"We finished, and she wanted to get back to let Rita off early." The clerk was in a flutter over a date with Sheriff Milano, and effusively grateful for the extra time to prepare. "You haven't answered. What is going on here?"

"They're setting the piers for the new cabin."

"What?"

"They're setting the piers—"

"I heard you," she snapped. "Under whose orders?"

"Mine."

"Who gave you permission—"

"I did, Cam." Ted Weston's calm voice came from just behind her.

She spun around. "You did? Why?"

"Cabin's got to have something to hold it up."

"That's not—" She snapped her mouth closed, trying to reorient herself to these new circumstances.

One of the men gestured for Boone.

"Go on, Boone," urged Ted.

Boone gave her a final glance, then headed over.

"Dad, how could you let this happen?"

He took off his hat, wiped his brow against a sleeve, then resettled the hat on his white hair. She'd seen him do that several thousand times, whenever he wanted an extra moment before he spoke.

"Like I said, the cabin's got to have something to hold it up. Figured on this happening from the start."

"That's not the issue."

"What is, then?" His eyes, intent on her, contradicted his mildly interested tone.

She shifted her shoulders slightly, then straightened them. "Well, who's going to pay for this? *Him?*"

"I'd say that's between Boone and me."

"But..."

"Cammy, I suppose you think you're fightin' to protect us—the family—but I don't see any need for protectin' in this. But if you're fightin' to protect yourself...well, sometimes you're better off losing than winning those battles. Sometimes what you're fighting to hold off can't harm you near as much as those defenses you put up to hold it off in the first place."

While shock still immobilized her, he patted her arm and walked over to the group of men discussing drying rates and instructions for covering the piers to keep the material moist.

She was only half conscious of saddling Snakebit and riding him out. By the time she returned, cooled him down and tended him, the pounding in her head had subsided and the tendency to fist her hands had eased. Also by that time, the men and construction vehicles had departed and Irene was ringing the bell for dinner.

The talk around the table centered on the cabin to be constructed on the newly poured piers. Everyone had something to say about it, except her. She devoted her attention to her meal. She was finding a great deal of fascination in green peas when Pete made a comment that caught her attention despite herself.

"That layout, the way those—what'd you call them, piers?—are set doesn't look the same as the original cabin had."

"It's not," Boone said. "I, uh, thought I'd change it some. Maybe."

That uncertainty was so unlike Boone that Cambria's gaze left her plate for the first time. But she didn't learn much more because Boone was staring down at his.

The thought that there might be something odd about the construction of the cabin crossed her mind and was dismissed. Not only couldn't she think of any way it could hurt her family, she couldn't believe Boone would try to hurt them.

Her fork clattered against her plate.

"Are you okay, Cam?" Ted asked.

"Yes."

No. She was coming to trust this stranger her family had taken in, without being absolutely certain she should—against her will, against the hard-learned lessons of her past.

May twilight lingered later and longer here in Wyoming than in the Blue Ridge Mountains.

Boone took advantage of that fact after dinner to stop and look over the layout of the piers on the way to his cabin. But his thoughts took another path.

Cambria had to know at some point. And when she did, however she found out, it wouldn't be easy.

He was just glad Ted had come through the way he had this afternoon. A slight frown pulled at the muscles of Boone's face. He'd been sort of surprised the other man had stepped in. Ted had seemed neutral when Boone had mentioned this morning that he'd arranged for the piers to be poured, telling him there'd be no charge because the company wanted to try a new method. Ted accepted that with a shrug, saying Boone knew more about that sort of thing than he did. Boone had studied the man's face, but had seen no hint of added meaning behind that statement.

After Ted had spoken up this afternoon, Cambria had looked mostly confused. But before that... He could still see her face as she'd come toward him. The suspicion. The distrust.

He could still feel the kick in his gut each time she looked at him that way.

Maybe if he'd given her an answer—something, anything—when she'd asked why he'd really come here. She'd wanted to believe him then. She'd wanted to trust him.

He swore under his breath.

He'd fixed that.

Hell, maybe it was for the best.

As soon as he got around her, he forgot the only sane approach was to keep her off-limits. Instead, heated insanity slipped into his bloodstream and burned off every reasoned thought, every promise to himself.

No way around it, he couldn't justify pursuing Cambria until he told her he was Pete's biological father. And that meant telling Pete, too—which he seemed no closer to doing.

He would have thought it would be easier after this time working with Pete. He certainly enjoyed getting to know the boy; Pete's willingness to share his friendship, his dreams, his hopes, humbled Boone.

His mouth lifted slightly. Damned if he didn't also derive very unexpected pleasure at delegating responsibility—taking Cambria's advice—and seeing it handled well by his employees in North Carolina, and especially by Pete.

But the hell of it was, as he got to know Pete, Boone felt even *less* certain how to tell him of their connection. How would Pete react? Pete felt as strongly as Cambria about their family, even if he wasn't as protective. What would being faced with his biological father do to the boy? Pete seemed so stable, was Boone wrong to want to tell him?

Maybe, seeing Pete happy and well-loved, Boone could have walked away…if it hadn't meant walking away from Cambria, too. But how could he stay without telling Pete?

He looked up from an unfocused study of the northernmost pier to find Cambria three yards off, at the edge of the path to her cabin. Their eyes met and held. She took several steps toward him, then stopped.

"I don't understand why you're doing all this." Her gesture indicated the layout for the new cabin, but he suspected she meant much more.

"I'm not a con man, Cambria. I'm not running some scam. I'm doing it because I want to and I'm enjoying it."

"Why?"

"I can't answer that any better than I can answer why looking at you makes me feel the way I do." He reached to touch her hair, but she stepped free of the fleeting touch.

"Don't."

He gave her a twisted smile. "Don't touch you, or don't feel this way?"

Something crossed her eyes, but her voice never wavered. "Either one."

Four feet away, she stopped and faced him. For a long moment she simply stared, as if probing his soul. Then her gaze flicked to the stumpy structures that would support a renewed cabin. "Thank you, Boone."

"Hey, there, I was looking for you." Boone called out the greeting when he spotted Cambria crossing toward his cabin.

It was so good to see her, her hair wind-tousled and sun-glinted beneath a straw cowboy hat that shadowed her face, her jeans snug enough to show curves and her shirt open two buttons from the top to show a narrow vee of slender throat and creamy pulse point. So good it should have scared him. Too good to worry about fear.

"I was looking for you, too."

Despite a reluctance she'd made no effort to hide this past week, he'd felt her moving step by resistant step closer to trusting him. Even though now she sounded grim.

He grinned. "I'm heading into town, you want to go with? We could have lunch at the café. Or better yet, pack a picnic and see that meadow Irene talked about last night."

She didn't return his grin. "No. I just got back from town. Wanda Rupert gave me these to give to you. They came into the library fax about nine-thirty this morning."

She handed him half a dozen sheets of paper. "Somebody forgot the time difference," he muttered as he glanced through them, thinking they might explain Cambria's dour expression. Afraid they might, if a mention of his true interest in the Westons had somehow gotten mixed in.

But they were the usual communications from his office, and no explanation for Cambria's glower.

"Well?" Cambria glared at him, hands on hips.

"Well, what?"

"Aren't you going to try to explain this one away like you did before?"

He gave her a quizzical look. "I might if I knew what I was trying to explain away."

"This." She tapped the top sheet with a stiff finger—right over the company logo of Bodie Smith Enterprises. "We might be in the wilds of Wyoming, but we do get an occasional newspaper and magazine. We have seen articles about Bodie Smith, the sky-rocketing entrepreneur who's doing for log homes what Bill Gates did for computers—I think I have the quote from *Newsweek* pretty close, don't I? Or was it *Time?* Or the *Wall Street Journal?*"

"All right," he acknowledged slowly. "I'm Bodie Smith of Bodie Smith Enterprises, and my business has been real successful. If anything, that should ease your suspicious mind about why I'm in the market for rest and relaxation. So?"

"So? So, my family has taken you in like a long-lost friend, and I've let myself—" Her mouth clamped, refusing to even let the words out. Boone's gut tightened. "You haven't been telling the truth, you've been hiding things. You've—" Her eyes narrowed with a new outrage.

"Damn! How did you arrange for those piers to get poured? Did you tell them who you are?"

"Yeah, I told them, so they'd—"

"Great, just great! And you asked them to keep your little secret from the idiots you're staying with, didn't you? Never mind, I can see the answer in your face. God, they must think us proper fools—"

"Cambria—"

"Boone Dorsey. Boone Dorsey Smith. Bodie Smith—how many other identities do you have you're not telling us about?"

Pete's father. It came into his mind so fast he didn't stand a chance of blocking it completely from his face.

And Cambria Weston wasn't one to miss anything.

"I see."

He snagged her arm as she started to turn away. "No, you don't see, Cambria. None of this has anything to do with what's happening between us."

"Nothing's happening between us."

"You can't shut it out that easily, you can't shut me out that easily. All those names, they're all me."

She shook her head. "I make mistakes, but I don't repeat the same ones."

The day after she'd discovered he was Bodie Smith, Cambria reached the cabin a quarter of an hour before Pete's usual time. Boone glanced up and, seeing the identity of the new arrival, stared openly.

She'd deflected Pete the day before by developing an urgent need to have him drive into Sheridan for shower curtain rings and liners. But she couldn't prevent him from helping with the cabin forever. As long as Pete went, she would, too.

No matter how uncomfortable it made her.

Uncomfortable was exactly how she felt because she'd allowed herself to start to believe in a... a *connection* between her and this man. What a fool she'd been—again. She'd started to trust a man who hadn't shared with her even the most basic information about himself—his complete identity.

It irritated her to realize that even after a long night of self-lectures she couldn't think of him any way other than Boone. Bodie Smith was the public figure, the man the outside world knew, so dealing with him would be safe, predictable. That's how she should think of him.... Fat chance.

Boone Dorsey Smith had lied to her, at least by omission, and hidden things from her—just as her ex-fiancé had. Though even Tony had used his real name from the start.

What else had Boone kept secret?

He sat back on his heels and continued to stare as she started to stack the scrap lumber he'd torn off that morning. Still, his voice made her jump.

"You ready to listen to me yet?"

No, because you're too damn persuasive.

"If there's something you'd rather I do on the cabin than clean up, speak right up," she said.

He came to his feet fast enough to make her have to issue her muscles a sharp order not to step back. "That's not what I meant, and you know it. Dammit, Cambria—" It was the first spurt of hot temper she'd heard from him. It cooled almost immediately into something she thought might prove more dangerous. "All right." He raked his hand through his hair and sighed. "All right, you might not listen, but I'm going to say it anyhow.

"My christened name is Boone Dorsey Smith. That's it. The whole thing. My father was Boone Hewitt Smith, so they called me Boone Dorsey to keep us straight. But Kenzie, my sister, couldn't get her tongue around that when she was learning to talk, and it came out Bodie."

From three feet Cambria tossed a board onto the scrap pile, but its thud didn't drown out his voice or stop his tale.

"The name stuck. Even at school and in the army, everyone called me Bodie. So that's how I started the business, and then I was Bodie everywhere." His dark brows dropped as if trying to recall something. "Except... last month Cully came to my office to tell—for a meeting, and he called me Boone like always. Nowadays he's about the only one who does. And hearing it... I don't know, it sounded strange, but also comfortable. Like coming home after months away. It might be dusty and unused, but it's home."

She had a hard time not answering the hint of question in his voice.

Frustration vibrated in his deep sigh, but he kept going. This man did not give up easily.

"Coming here, finding you in the bedroom, I was... I wasn't really thinking. When you asked my name like that, I don't know, it seemed natural to tell you Boone Dorsey. Maybe I already knew I wanted to be closer to you than having you call me Mr. Smith—" from the corner of her eye, she caught the hint of a wry grin. "Or maybe I didn't want to risk being tied to Bodie Smith Enterprises right off."

All her determination to pay him no attention couldn't stifle a response to that.

"Why? You thought we'd raise the rates? Or sell tickets to the neighbors to see the famous entrepreneur? Let me tell you, you're not that big a draw."

"I just wanted to be liked—or not—for myself. Not for what somebody might've read in a magazine or newspaper. You might not think much of my position, Cambria, but some people do. It was kind of flattering at first for a poor mountain boy from North Carolina. Until you realize a lot of nice people shy away from you, and too many of the ones you don't much like won't take no for an answer."

"The women in your hotel room," she said before she could stop herself.

"The— Oh, yeah. Our great introduction." He grimaced. "There have been women—"

"More than one?" She lifted an eyebrow.

"One at a time," he said dryly, adding under his breath, "Thank God," before going on. "But it's happened more than once. Some executives looking to do business with you still think the way to a man's company is through his...uh, libido. And some women make it a pastime to chase men who've had some success. They're not real subtle, either."

"Poor baby."

That irked him. Really irked him from the darkening of his face. "Look, I'm no saint, but I would like the woman between the sheets with me to want to be there with *me,* not my corporation's year-end profits. Oh, hell—why am I trying to explain this to you? If God dropped a miracle in your lap you'd probably want to know what his angle was."

With that, he attacked a board with a zeal that made the nails screech in protest.

Pete arrived to find two people making enough noise for six and doing the work of half of one.

The next few days took a lot out of Cambria.

She was on hand for every minute Pete helped Boone with the final dismantling of the cabin, while keeping her distance emotionally.

It was like being a swimmer fighting a powerful tide.

She almost got sucked under when they discovered hand-hewn logs on the long south wall. A date carved into one put the original structure at a hundred years old. Boone's interest was contagious. He certainly infected

Pete, as they planned how to remove the logs so they could be kept intact and reused in a place of honor in the rebuilt cabin.

His enthusiasm still bubbled when Irene came by and announced that Pete was accompanying her to the barbershop—now.

"Aw, Mom. I can go tomorrow."

"You've been saying that for a month. We're going now."

"But Boone needs my help. And *his* hair—"

"Is his business. When you're his age, you can let your hair grow if you want. Cambria will stay and make sure to help Boone while you're gone. Won't you, Cambria?"

Irene's sneak attack caught Cambria off guard. Her mind had been split between watching Boone squirm over the talk about his hair and thinking of slipping back to her cabin for a sybaritically indulgent nap before supper.

"I... I don't—"

"Sure, she'll stick around," Boone interrupted with a wicked glance at her. "She'll want to make sure I don't try to do anything by myself."

Irene gave a satisfied nod and led Pete away. Boone started whistling and went to examine the way the logs tied into the rock fireplace. Cambria returned to pulling nails from logs they hoped to reuse.

She sat on a bench in the shade of a cottonwood by what had once been the door of the cabin. The door was long gone. So were all the layers of covering, inside and out, that had been added to these original logs. It had no roof, either.

She attacked a nail that was both bent and wedged in at an angle. She couldn't get the claw end of the hammer around it securely to draw it out. She gave it another half-hearted yank. It stayed put.

The old cabin looked like even less than it had the first day Boone had taken pictures. She couldn't imagine what he saw in it, then or now. Of course, she supposed if anybody could make something out of it, it was Bodie Smith. Among all the laudatory things those articles she'd reread at the library the day before yesterday had said about his business acumen, they'd all mentioned Bodie Smith's incredible knack for designing homes people loved to live in.

She frowned at the memory of Boone's voice at supper after the piers were poured for the cabin's resurrection. His voice saying he thought he might change the design some. Maybe.

Why had he been so uncertain? It hadn't sounded like the Boone Dorsey Smith she'd come to know and it didn't fit the Bodie Smith she'd read about. Why would a man known for his designing be hesitant about changing a ramshackle cabin that would have been pulled down otherwise and that he'd messed with in the first place only to fight off boredom?

"A penny for your thoughts."

She jolted at Boone's voice. She wouldn't give him these thoughts for any price, because they revealed too damn much. Hoping he didn't notice the guilty flush she could feel working up her throat, she yanked at the nail.

"I was thinking unkind thoughts about the original builders who used so many nails in these logs they rival a steel girder. And on top of that—" She grunted as she pressed on the end of the hammer, then gasped when it jerked free of the nail without budging it. "They couldn't even hammer them in straight."

"They didn't."

Boone took the hammer out of her hand. She released it, but narrowed her eyes at him as she asked, "Who didn't what?"

"The original builders didn't use all these nails. These are from people who came along afterward, making *improvements.*"

He gave the side of the nail a couple whacks with the hammer, partially straightening it.

"It must have been pretty awful to start with if the way this place ended up was an improvement."

"The people who came along later could see it needed something, but they didn't know what." He tucked the nail deep into the split in the hammer's claw and tipped it, drawing full benefit from the leverage. "They lost sight of the balance."

Boone gave a slight grunt as the nail came free. Cambria couldn't tell if it was from effort or satisfaction. She held out a hand and he dropped the battered nail into it.

"All right, all right." She looked up, then quickly away from his inviting grin. "What do you mean, they lost sight of the balance?"

He set the hammer on the bench beside her, then sat on the other side of it.

"The problem is, too many people, when they're designing, get too focused on one thing—the inside or the outside—and they lose track of the other." His gaze fastened on the cabin, and Cambria had the idea he didn't see the same woeful sight she did. "You have to look at both at the same time. You can't sacrifice one for the other, or it won't be a satisfying building, or a satisfying home."

"How do you do that? Keep both in mind?"

"By remembering people. The people who're going to live in it and all the people who'll look at it—inside and out. You can't forget either. It's like blowing up a balloon—if you don't put enough inside, it's going to be flat. If you put too much, it'll pop."

"How'd you get started designing, Boone?"

"A job I worked in high school was an addition on this artist's house near a town called Blowing Rock. She said she'd like to have a skylight, but the contractor said it couldn't be done. I got to thinking, and I figured a way. I was having a hard time putting it in words for the contractor and owner. Finally she shoved a pad and pencil in my hand. I don't think I'd drawn since crayon stick figures, but the design just came out, like there was a direct link to the image in my head. I'd never known that could happen—having an image in your head turn into reality like that addition did."

A slow smile spread across his face. "From then on, Miss Knoblauch helped me with the basics of drawing in exchange for odd jobs. She brags her studio's the first Bodie Smith original.

"I worked on my own, a couple classes the high school offered helped, then I picked up a lot in the army. By the time I got out, I started building houses. We figured ways to give people good, solid homes, but cut the costs by using logs and keeping some things standard. Designing came from listening to what folks wanted and finding ways to work that in without sending them to the poorhouse."

Gray eyes glittering, Boone Dorsey Smith was the most excited and at the same time the most relaxed Cambria had seen him. She recognized that condition. She and friends on Capitol Hill, when they helped shoot down a flawed bill or helped put through one they thought would do good, had experienced the same feeling; they'd called it being "juiced."

"It must be wonderful to have a vision in your head, put it on paper, then see it brought to three-dimensional life."

The balloon of his enthusiasm popped as soon as she spoke, and she didn't know why. "Yeah. But that's only a small part of running a business like mine."

"You like the designing best, though, don't you?"

"It's not that simple. Everything has to be overseen. There's hiring, ordering materials, shipping, making sure workmanship stays top quality, keeping on schedule. And there's the matter of supplies. You can't use logs and think there'll be trees forever. You've got an obligation to replant. And let me tell you, reforestation, with all the government rules and regulations, can get damn complicated—"

She waved that away with one hand.

"But the part you like best, the reason you got into this, is designing, right?" She couldn't have said why she pushed him, except she had the feeling he wanted to avoid it. "The matching of people with the homes they'll love."

"You could say that, but—"

"Then it *is* simple. You simply make the time for designing. Let someone else do the rest of it."

"I'm responsible. It's my name on that product, nobody else's."

"None of that's as important as doing what you love. So make time. That's what you should be doing here instead of trying to reclaim this cabin. You should be designing—"

"I can't."

The pain in those two words stopped Cambria cold. "You just need time—"

"No. Time won't help. I don't have it anymore—whatever *it* is." His bitterness brought a dull ache to her throat. "That vision, that ability to blend all the needs and wants into a building, it's gone. I could sit over a piece of paper from here to next week, and nothing would come. Nothing. Believe me, I've tried. I haven't designed anything for more than a year."

Boone's mouth twisted. "I was so busy for so long, trying to get the business off the ground, working night and day, then right back into night again, that I don't even know exactly when I lost it."

Cambria considered being tactful and gentle—for about a second and a half. That wasn't what Boone Dorsey Smith needed. He needed a good shaking.

"If you stopped trying to do everything yourself, stopped trying to personally see to every nail and screw, maybe your ability to design would have a chance to resurface."

"I don't know wha—"

"Oh, give me a break—you don't know what I'm talking about? You're not going to start that again, are you? Trying to deny you oversee every dust ball in every broom closet in your business? We already went through that, even before I knew who you were and what those articles said about you. Besides, you as much as admitted it—*and* said your friend Cully agrees with me."

One side of his mouth lifted.

She watched it suspiciously. "What are you grinning about?"

"Just thinking that 'overseeing every dust ball' sounds a lot like you and Weston Ranch Guest Quarters."

"Maybe," she acknowledged. "But it's not keeping me from doing something I love."

"It's a tough habit to break. Especially..."

His half smile faded. In his eyes Cambria caught glimpses of memories through the gray mists of the past.

"Especially what, Boone?"

"The day we came home from burying Daddy, Gran took me out on the porch. She held me by the shoulders of Daddy's old suit because I didn't have one of my own, and she said I'd better grow broad enough shoulders to fill out that suit, and do it right quick, because I was the man of the family now."

Cambria put her hand lightly over his, a gesture of compassion for a grieving boy loaded with such a burden. Boone caught her fingertips with his thumb, turning the touch into a clasp.

"I tried. God knows, I tried. With Mom working, mostly at the mill, but sometimes picking up whatever she could—cleaning houses, working at the dry cleaners, or one summer picking tobacco down near Greensboro—I looked after Gran and Kenzie. That's all I could do, how I could do my part."

Cambria tried to imagine the boy he'd been, a boy told he must become the "man" of his family. The youngster who'd put aside his childhood to care for an elderly grandmother and younger sister.

No wonder the man tried to do everything. The boy had had to.

"At first, Gran did the cooking, but she got real forgetful, and with that old stove, it wasn't safe. So Kenzie and I made do. Ate a lot of sliced egg sandwiches doing my homework and helping Kenzie with hers."

The ghost of a smile touched the corners of his mouth.

Cambria looked at his face, saw the emotion there, and understood that Boone Dorsey Smith hadn't taken charge only because he'd had to, to help his family survive. He'd taken charge because that's how he'd been taught to show love. By doing things for people.

"Even when Mom was home, she was tired all the time...I pretty much was in charge at home. Until I got old enough to go to work, that's how I could help her, help all of them."

And Cambria wondered if she saw more.

Had he become so accustomed to being valued for what he *did* for people that he didn't consider that he could be loved for what he *was?*

She turned her hand in his, connecting palm to palm. "You had to take charge then, I understand that."

He raised one eyebrow and looked at her askance. "Subtlety, Cambria? It doesn't suit you. I think I prefer your usual straightforward, unvarnished lectures."

"All right." She raised her chin, torn between an urge to grin and a serious desire to make him understand her point.

"You had to take charge then, but you don't have to anymore. Not all the time. Sometimes taking charge *isn't* the best way."

"It is if I want to keep Bodie Smith Enterprises running," he said wryly.

"Oh, yeah? How would you know? Have you tried it any other way? Have you given your employees a chance to show what they can do? No. You've carried everything on your shoulders, trying to do it all. You've spent so much time *doing* for Bodie Smith Enterprises that you've totally lost sight of what you *are*—a designer. That's what got you into that business in the first place."

He opened his mouth, but she held off any rebuttal by raising her free hand and hurrying on. "Look what your way has gotten you, Boone. You come all the way to Wyoming for rest and relaxation, and instead you burn up the phone lines, terrorize small-town Wyoming librarians and run the post office ragged. And it's not only business. Your sister became estranged from you because—"

Horrified, she stopped.

Too late. Letting her mouth run had pushed her to the end of the plank. The water below was dark and cold.

"Boone...I..."

"Kenzie became estranged from me because she said I tried to run her life," he said in a low, tight voice.

"I'm sorry, Boone. I didn't mean..."

"Hey," he said with a smile that made her feel worse than harsh words would have. "I asked for it. I invited the lecture, so I can't complain. And I have a suspicion—"

"Boone."

"That Kenzie would agree with you. The bigger question is..." Her eyes followed the movement as he raised their joined hands, then met his as he drew her hands to his mouth and touched his lips to first one knuckle, then another. "How can I do anything about it?"

* * *

Impatiently hitching the edge of her turquoise blouse back onto her shoulder, Cambria rapped the truck steering wheel in time to the old Randy Travis song on the radio. It was better than pounding on it the way she'd felt like doing the past few miles.

"Did I hear right?" Boone demanded so abruptly she jerked slightly. "Did that singer just say he'd still love his girl if all her hair fell out?"

Cambria bit the inside of her cheek to keep from grinning in relief. It was his first comment since they'd left the co-op, and it had considerably more good humor in it than his previous one.

Boone had been irked when she'd insisted on going into town with him, and more than that when she'd trailed him to the co-op where he'd given Norman a list of lumber. When Cambria had insisted that the lumber go on the ranch's account instead of coming out of his pocket, he'd gotten downright belligerent.

Clearly, the man was entirely too accustomed to getting his own way. After the quick one he'd pulled with the piers—she'd called the construction company and been told there was no charge because they'd tried a new material—she was keeping a close eye on Boone. The Westons didn't need charity, and wouldn't take it. Even if she had to hog-tie Mr. Boone Dorsey "Bodie" Smith. Or outmaneuver him.

It was a good thing Norman had taped closed the bags of nails Boone had requested, or he might have started chewing them.

Well, maybe she'd contributed to his poor mood by telling him, first, that she didn't think much of grown men who always had to get their own way and, second, that just because he'd let his underlings at Bodie Smith Enterprises carry on without him for all of forty-eight hours, he couldn't start bossing her around.

What she hadn't said was that she intended to give him a few lessons in seeing that he didn't have to be *doing* for other people to earn affection. She knew—and it was time he realized—the affection Pete, Irene and Ted had for him had nothing to do with rebuilding the cabin. As for herself... she didn't enter into the situation.

He'd snarled something unintelligible. That was the last thing he'd said to her after he and Norman had loaded the truck and they'd started back to the ranch. Until now.

"That's what he said," she confirmed. "Surely they have country music where you come from. In fact it seems to me Randy Travis is a North Carolina boy."

"Is he? I don't know. I haven't had much time—"

"To listen to music," she finished with him, shaking her head.

The tight line of his mouth eased. The fact that his improved mood seemed to lift a weight off her shoulders was easily explained—nobody liked having someone glowering from two feet away. Besides, she'd gotten used to an easier exchange between them, almost a camaraderie the past couple of days.

"All right, all right. I will ignore all my corporate responsibilities and spend all my time listening to music, learning line dances and watching movies. Anything to make you happy."

That last sentence had Cambria's hands suddenly feeling slick on the steering wheel, and made this seem like a real good time to twist around and look over her opposite shoulder for traffic before the left turn into the ranch road.

"We're going back?" Boone asked. "I thought Irene wanted us to check out some meadow for that party."

She'd nearly forgotten. In her determination not to let Boone leave the ranch by himself, she'd barely heard Irene's request.

"I don't feel like going right now."

"Oh, yeah? Irene asks you to do something, you say sure, then change your mind? Sounds to me suspiciously like a case of a grown woman who always wants to get her way."

Having already made the turn, she applied the brakes hard. Boone braced his arm against the dashboard to stop his momentum, but that didn't dim the glint of his grin.

"All right," she said, fighting an answering grin. "We'll go. Right now." She put the truck in reverse and spurted back out onto the deserted highway. "Even though I happen to know there should be fresh banana-cherry nut bread coming out of Irene's oven right about now."

He laughed out loud. "That's one of the things I love about you, Cambria—you don't do anything halfhearted, not even playing dirty."

Ignoring her instinctive quick-drawn breath at his first phrase, she turned a mock innocent stare at him. "Playing dirty? Why, whatever do you mean?"

"Don't try a fake Southern drawl on this boy, Cambria. I cut my eye teeth on steel magnolias. Now, tell me about this party. Who's coming?"

"Sometimes it seems like everybody in the county. Let's see... of people you've met, Jessa'll be there, and Wanda Rupert, Kent Keller, the Ellistons from the café, June Reamer, along with her mother, the Mooneys, the Pooles, Pete's baseball team, including Coach Lambert. And, the hot gossip is, Sheriff Milano's bringing Rita."

"Sounds like quite a blowout."

"We're so busy during the summer that it's hard to get together with our friends, so a few years ago Irene came up with this idea. Every year, the weekend before we open, we invite all our friends over for a cookout. It's also when some folks bring their horses for our guests to use during the summer. A lot of us'll ride from the house to this meadow just short of Bulwark Canyon. Irene'll bring the four-wheel around with food supplies, so she wants me to check the road and meadow. Sometimes they flood and we need to find someplace else."

Not this year.

The uphill road, an unsubtle climb after the more gradual ascent of the highway, provided a rock-strewn torture test for any suspension system, but it was dry. The high meadow was lush in new grass and fragile wildflowers. They walked to the edge of the creek, which rushed self-importantly over rocks that would stick through its ribs come high summer.

Cambria breathed in the air, spiced with a touch of the mountain noticeably nearer here than at the main ranch.

"This is what we saw from up top, isn't it?"

"Yes." She waited, wary to see where the conversation would go from here.

"So this is your land, too?" Boone shielded his eyes with one hand and slowly surveyed the view. Both his tone and the faint lift of his lips told her he liked what he saw.

No reason that should please her. But it did.

"Yeah. Some of the canyon, too. It's not much use for ranching, but Ted couldn't resist when it came up for sale several years ago. That's part of why they started the bed-and-breakfast operation, to pay that off."

He turned in the direction she'd pointed.

"Can we get back there?"

She hesitated. What did she have to feel vulnerable about showing someone a hunk of land? It was silly. "Yeah. The road's pretty bad, but it goes most of the way."

"Then maybe I should drive."

He made a stab for the keys. She eluded him.

"No way. You'd probably put us in the creek."

"Hey, I grew up driving mountain roads."

While they one-upped each other with tales of harrowing mountain drives, she guided the truck slowly over an increasingly rough track as the scenery shifted rapidly from open meadow to the closing, craggy walls of a canyon cut by eons of water and wear.

"This is as far as the truck goes," she announced. "We can walk up a little more. There's a place to sit, if you want."

He wanted.

She snagged an old blanket from the back of the truck and led the way, stepping from stone to stone that climbed next to the creek like an ancient, jumbled staircase. He remained directly behind her, sometimes choosing a slightly different path, but keeping up.

"This is it, unless you're part mountain goat." Leaving the blanket folded as a narrow strip so it provided more padding, she laid it on a slab of rock that nestled among its more vertical brethren. They sat side by side, not touching.

To their left, the creek tumbled down through a corridor of multicolored rock with a slice of lush meadow visible at its end. To their right, water came rushing at them from the narrow cleft of earth, with fantastically tenacious trees clinging to the sides to grow like gargoyles straining to touch the blue ribbon of sky far above.

"It's a beautiful spot. I can see why you came back from Washington—" He broke off, then slowly turned to her. "No, I can't," he said as if in discovery.

She frowned at him. "Can't what?"

"Can't see why you came here. I can imagine, maybe, but I don't know, and you never talk about it. I know a few folks who left city life for the mountains in North Carolina, and they can't tell you often enough the differences—how long a commute they had, how often they got mugged, how brutal the office politics' back-stabbing was, but you don't do that. Neither does Jessa."

Cambria shifted her weight from one side to the other. "It's her past—if she wants you to know, she'll tell you."

"Okay," he accepted slowly. "Then tell me about *your* past."

"I don't see wh—"

"I've told you about growing up and my family. Hardly fair for you to complain about my holding some things back when you hold everything back. I've told you about my immediate past, about building the company. Now I'm asking about yours. Why did you leave Washington?"

She glanced at him, then back to the harshly textured wall of the canyon. "Disillusionment."

He considered that a moment. "With politics?"

"With people. Irene worries I've become cynical. Maybe I have. Or maybe it's just realistic—being able to accept and be prepared for the fact that most people aren't to be trusted. So, you don't put trust in people easily. And when you do, you keep a sharp eye out for cracks. When those show up, you don't trust that person again."

"No forgiving small slips?"

"No, because those cracks can mean a shaky foundation—you should know that from building."

He met her eyes, his own expression serious. "Some cracks do, but some are cosmetic, the result of settling with age, a building maturing, becoming actually more solid."

She gave a hoot of dry laughter. "Yeah? Believe that of people and I've got some oceanfront property to sell you in Wyoming."

Not returning her laughter, he continued to study her. "Who was he?"

"Who?"

"The guy who was the reason you left Washington."

She picked up a pebble from beside the blanket and tossed it into the stream. Its splash rose straight up, then sank in an instant, absorbed once more into the unceasing movement.

"Cambria..."

Boone's prodding was almost drowned out by Jessa's voice in her head.

Have you told him any of your business? Have you told him about your life in Washington, or about Tony, or about growing up, or about your family, or about your mother? No, I know you haven't. You're attracted to him, drawn to him, and you're fighting that like hell.... You're trying to keep distance from that man because he scares you.

Cambria wasn't scared. She had no reason to be. She had this under control.

"I'd been engaged, but it ended a year before I left D.C., so that wasn't the reason I came back here."

From the sound he made, he didn't buy that—not entirely, anyway—but he let it pass. "Who was he?"

"I told you that wasn't the reason. The B and B operation was losing money instead of making it. I came back to run it, because Irene's about as financially tough as a marshmallow."

"Who was he?"

"God, you're stubborn. Tony Sussman. Okay?"

"What happened?"

She tossed up her hands in disgust. "It was all very boring. We both worked on Capitol Hill. We met. We dated. We got engaged. He broke the engagement. He married someone else. End of story."

Gray eyes probed her face like silver bullets. "I don't think so. That doesn't explain not trusting people. You wouldn't blame somebody for honestly discovering he wasn't in love and finding someone else."

"*Honestly* being the operative word."

"What happened, Cambria?"

The quiet question was the trickle of water that finally burst the damn.

"He was never in love. Not with me, and not with Joanna, the woman he married." She gave a short, rough laugh. "I don't think he was even in lust with either of us. He was in ambition. That was the ruling passion of his life. First he thought I could help his career because I was touted as an up-and-comer on the Hill. But I couldn't hold a candle to the daughter of a powerful senator with all those glittering connections. He even had the gall to tell me when he broke off the engagement, with this earnest voice and clear-eyed expression, that he would never regret our time together."

"Jackass."

On a roll now, she ignored Boone's contribution. "The thing of it was, I had seen hints of it earlier and I'd ignored them. Blindly, stupidly, stubbornly ignored them. I should have known. I'm not some naive innocent who thinks everyone's to be trusted. I had years to judge his character, but I didn't see what he really was. I wouldn't let myself see. So I couldn't blame just him, I had to blame myself, too."

He took her face between his palms, and turned her to face him fully. Instinctively her hands covered his, but she made no effort to pull his away.

"If you made any mistake, Cambria, it was from having a good heart. He's the one who passed up someone incredible. He had you. He had a chance to have a life with you, and he walked away from it. What an ass—" His eyes dropped to her mouth, then slowly rose until she could see into his eyes again. With their faces so close together, the swell of desire that fired his eyes and tightened his expression was like a touch on her skin—and deeper, beneath her skin, where it met an answering swell inside her. "He should never have let you go."

"Boone..."

"I won't, Cambria... I won't..."

Her mind couldn't grapple with what it was he wouldn't do; it was too occupied with what he would... what he did.

His thumbs stroked along her cheekbones as he tilted her face to kiss her. In that first instant his mouth was warm and firm, like his body against hers.

Then it was hot and hungry.

Like her body.

Maybe she'd known this could happen—would happen—from the time they'd come out here. Maybe she'd wanted it to. She knew she wanted to touch him. To learn the texture and resilience of his chest, to feel against her palm and between her fingers the prickle of the wedge of hair she'd glimpsed over the past weeks.

Oh, yes, she wanted. But her rational mind didn't turn off because of that, it simply grew quieter and less insistent than her senses.

"Boone, we shouldn't..."

"Damn right, we shouldn't."

He kissed her, deep, long, involved. A kiss that traveled to mundane spots like the bridge of her nose and the top of her ear, and to more exotic ports like the hollow of her neck, the underside of her chin and the first hint of curve at the top of her breast, but always returned to her mouth, hungry once more.

"I've wondered about this blouse since that night..." he murmured.

Without his finishing, Cambria knew he meant the night of the café party, the first night he'd kissed her. But she was much more interested in what he had wondered.

She quickly found out when he pushed first one side of the wide neckline over the point of her shoulder, then the other. As his hand cleared the material, his lips and tongue trailed along the exposed flesh below her collarbone.

Watching her, he carried her down to the sun-warmed rock. With one spread hand cushioning her head, he slid one leg between hers and half covered her with his chest.

She opened the buttons that stopped her from taking the full pleasure of the touches she'd imagined, and discovered beneath his open shirt a reality much more intense, because her touches fed not only her senses, but his. She found the quick-drawn breath when she stroked, and the fine, involuntary quiver of muscles when she brushed, a surprising reward.

Aching spread, carrying with it a fever. He was unexplained, unexpected. But she knew what was happening, knew where their bodies were leading them.

He'd found the back clasp of her bandeau bra, and she arched to ease his task. When it gave, they both sighed. He caught the end of her sigh in another kiss as he slid aside blouse and bra to touch her bare breast.

Remarkable hands, she thought as the sensation of their roughened surface and restrained power circled the sensitive curves. Patient and thorough, he made her wait until she might have voiced her impatience... if he hadn't kept her mouth occupied. When he touched her nipple, a brush with the side of his thumb over the hardened tip, she jolted and arched against him.

As if the impatience had built as strongly in him, he groaned, low and hoarse, then shifted to take her nipple into his mouth, first dampening it with a swirl of his tongue, then drawing on it deeply, rhythmically.

His movement pressed the blatant ridge under the zipper of his jeans full against her hip.

She clutched at him, tumbling into the sensation, falling deeper when he paid the same service to her other breast, and greedily she wanted even more.

When he kissed her mouth again, she felt the erotic rub of her dampened nipples against his bare chest, and skimmed her hands down his bare back, over his loosened belt and below, pressing him to her lower body.

He released her mouth and backed away a little. She closed the space by kissing him. It was a while before they came up for air again and he spoke.

"Are you..." She lost some of what he said as he dropped a brief kiss on her lips. But she heard the end of it. "Birth control pill?"

Reality ripped her haze of sensation. "No. I'm not on the pill. Don't you have any... anything?"

Boone stilled, too. Then he jerked out a rough curse. "No. I never thought... I wasn't expecting this kind of complication. I should have done something, but I can't seem to keep things straight when I'm around you."

He groaned, with an ache that reached deep inside her. She slid her hand down his side, over his hip, then forward.

"I could—"

"No." He caught her wrist. "You were right at the start. We shouldn't do this." He jackknifed to a sitting position, putting his elbows on his bent knees. "Just give me a minute."

He let loose another curse, then exhaled through his nose.

"I didn't expect you, Cambria. And I sure as hell didn't expect how you make me feel."

She couldn't argue with him. Not without arguing with herself, too.

She wanted this man. Wanted the feel of his body against hers, inside hers.

But she still didn't know if she should trust him.

She sat up and adjusted her clothes to cover herself.

"I'll wait in the truck," Cambria said.

She'd rehooked her bra and had the neckline of her shirt as high as she could get it when he joined her in a few minutes. Reaching across from the passenger seat, he brushed the back of his fingers down her cheek. She didn't look at him. She didn't pull away.

"I'm sorry, Cambria."

"No need. It wasn't all your doing."

"I mean about turning down your offer. Just the thought... It was a near-run thing...."

She swallowed, feeling the rough desire in his voice as if it were a touch.

"But I want to be with you. Inside you. I'll make sure next time there's no reason to stop."

She turned the ignition key, still without looking at him. She knew better.

"You'll be gone before there can be a next time."

Chapter Seven

"Cambria, as long as you're heading out, could you take these clean towels to Boone's cabin?"

Irene's request stopped Cambria in midstretch. She and Ted had been going over financial figures after dinner, while Irene folded laundry. Pete and Boone had headed out together right after finishing Irene's apple pie and clearing the table. Cambria had wondered where they were going off to, but hadn't been about to ask.

Besides, her mind had been divided between mulling over Pete's studiedly casual comments at dinner that he wasn't entirely sure he wanted to go to college next year, and wondering exactly how the Weston coffers would stretch to tuition, room and board, if he did.

"Irene, I don't think—"

"His car's gone."

"Oh."

She couldn't think of any reason to refuse with the cabin empty. But she didn't particularly care for Irene's knowing smile, or the look that passed between her and Ted.

Cambria frowned over that as she crossed the moonlight-washed porch of the darkened west cabin.

Partially juggling the double armload of towels, she rapped perfunctorily on the door. Irene was right—the spot in front of the cabin where the rental car usually sat was conspicuously empty. She let herself into the cabin.

The lack of artificial light didn't bother her. She'd cleaned these cabins often enough to walk through any of them blindfolded, and with the moonlight filtering in, she easily passed through the outside room and into the bedroom, heading for the bathroom.

Halfway across the bedroom she jolted to a stop with an audible gasp.

"What are you doing here?"

A low chuckle reached her from the bed before Boone Dorsey Smith unclasped his hands from behind his head and lazily propped himself up on one elbow.

"Shouldn't I be asking you that?"

She hitched an arm to indicate the towels.

He sat up and swung his legs over the edge of the bed. When he stood and came toward her, Cambria made herself remain where she was. She had no reason to think he'd do anything...other than take the towels from her.

"Thanks." Two strides took him to the bathroom, an instant to put the towels down, then two strides back. That gave her a head start. "Hey, where're you going? Stick around awhile, keep me company."

Once she left the dim bedroom behind, curiosity slowed her exit.

"What are you doing sitting in the dark?"

"No—" he stepped between her and the lamp she'd been reaching for "—don't turn the lights on."

"Then I'm leav— No, wait, you're trying to distract me from the point, aren't you?" Hands on hips, she considered him. "What's going on? And where's your car?"

Even in the splintered moonlight she saw his slow grin. "Pete's got it."

"Pete!"

"Let's go sit outside. It's a nice night."

She let him guide her out the door and take the pile of towels for her cabin from her, setting them on the camp table next to a rocking chair on the porch. "Boone..."

He held his hands up in classic sign language for innocence. "You have nothing to fear from me."

Without touching, they moved to sit side by side on the single step from the small porch to the path. Cambria thought she heard a murmur from him that sounded suspiciously like "For now." But when she studied his face, it revealed nothing.

"Nice night, isn't it?" he offered.

"You think a nice night's going to make me forget that Pete has your car? Your *expensive* car?"

"He's got a big date tonight."

"But he said he was going to the library—"

"He did go to the library. He took Lauren."

"Lauren?" A memory hit her of Pete's talking in the most casual manner possible, to a fair-haired girl at his past two baseball games.

"Yeah. Lauren. I think it's serious," he said with absolute solemnity. "She makes him laugh and she doesn't giggle."

"Mmm. Potent combination."

"That's right, and he wanted to impress her, so..."

"So you loaned him your rental car. That's nice of you."

He shrugged. "He's got school tomorrow, so he shouldn't be too late."

"And you don't mind sitting in the dark waiting for him?"

He shrugged again. "He's a good kid."

She smiled, while part of her wondered how she could feel so at ease with Boone yet so unnervingly aware of him. "Yeah, he is."

The man beside her gave off a tension she'd felt from him before, most recently at dinner not three hours earlier. "You think he meant what he said about not going to college?" he asked abruptly.

"I hope not. But there's time before that becomes an issue—as long as nobody pushes him into making an absolute statement too soon."

"I didn't say a word."

She laughed. "No, you didn't. And it was a close call between you and Ted which of you would have burst first if Irene hadn't changed the subject."

"I like that," he objected. "I bit my tongue until it bled, to follow your advice, keeping my mouth shut even though I think... Well, as you said, it doesn't matter what I think."

"I didn't say that. It's how you let people know what you think that can make all the difference—especially with someone like Pete. If you push him too hard, he gets his back up and then he gets so stubborn there's no budging him, even if he wants to be budged. You should understand that. It sounds like your sister might be the same kind of person."

He looked out toward where the moon hung low and jack-o'-lantern big on the horizion.

"Yeah, she is."

She sensed his tension, heard it in his voice. She'd blundered into his vulnerability, bringing up his sister. She subsided into silence, but after a moment he broke it.

"Will it be pushing too hard if I ask you a question? Kind of personal."

Her heart started beating more heavily. "Depends on the question."

"How come you mostly call your parents Ted and Irene?"

A breath slid out of her. She hadn't expected that.

For the second time this evening Boone Dorsey Smith had surprised her.

She'd seen at dinner how much he'd wanted to jump into the discussion and tell Pete he damn well should go to college. But he hadn't, as hard as she knew that was for him, given his personality and his background.

"Pete doesn't," he went on. "And it sort of surprises me that you do. I know Irene's your stepmother, but Ted's your fath—"

"Ted's my stepfather," she heard herself saying. She raised her hands, palms up. "I don't know officially what that would make Irene. But it doesn't change how I feel about her."

"I can see that."

Maybe it was his sincerity. Or his patience. Or the restraint he showed with Pete.

Or a less explicable urge inside her to share with him.

"My father—or maybe I should say, the male who provided sperm to my conception—" Boone flinched slightly at the ironic twist in her voice. If he felt sorry for her, it was wasted. She'd never felt the man's absence. "My so-called father left before I was born. My mother got notice of his death about a year later. I don't even know if it caused a ripple in her life. She'd already met Ted. I can't remember him ever not being there."

She smiled, though she blinked against a burn in her eyes.

"Angie Lee married Ted, and he adopted me. I'll always be grateful for that. Because it meant when she took off, nobody could take me away from him. He gave me a name and love and a home and a family."

"She left you?"

"Yeah, she left us. Both of us. Walked out on her husband, leaving a four-year-old for him to raise on his own. She left because she had to find herself, because she was driven to experience life to the fullest and that, of course, required the drama of a big city."

"Ted told you that?"

"No, not in those words. He made it sound much better, but I read between the lines. And there were enough people around here who knew Angie Lee to fill in the gaps."

"It must have been tough for you, not having your mother."

She turned and faced him, to let him see the truth of what she said. "It really wasn't. Dad...Ted was always wonderful. And when Irene came into our lives..." She smiled, no burn in her eyes this time. "I couldn't have had a better mother. No one could. She should have had a dozen kids, but nature doesn't seem to take that into account. I was fourteen when they asked me how I'd feel about having a little brother or sister. And then we had Pete. We might seem an odd patchwork family to some people, with no link of blood among us. But patchworks can be beautiful, and blood doesn't make a family."

She could see things behind his eyes, but couldn't separate them, distill them into words. It was like trying to make the remembered fragments of a dream fit together into the whole it had been when you slept.

"Have you seen your mother?"

"No. I told you, I have all the family I need."

"I know, but—"

"It all happened a very long time ago. I've never missed her and never wanted any part of her. That's something I learned a long time ago—the past is over and done with, there's no going back."

"It might be a long time ago, but that doesn't make it impossible. There are groups you can register with. If she's been looking for you—"

"Looking for me? You haven't been listening, Boone. She knows where I am, because Ted and I are in the same place we were when she left. But that doesn't make any difference. I don't want to see her."

"You might feel different if you connect again. First, you register with those groups, then you advertise. I'll put you together with somebody who's good at finding people. You tell Cully what you remember about your mother, the last address you had for her—"

She jolted off the step, spinning to face him.

"Stop it. Right now. Stop trying to arrange my life the way you think it should be. Your high-handedness might be acceptable—barely—when it comes to renovating cabins, but you have no right to apply those tactics to my life." She was aware of headlights coming up the road, then sweeping across the dark bunkhouse as they turned toward the cabin, but it didn't slow her any. "If I wanted to find Angie Lee, I would have been perfectly capable of pursuing it myself. But I don't want to find her. All that woman would do would be to disrupt this family—*my* family. I won't let *anybody* do that. And I sure won't go *looking* for it."

"You can't know that's what would happen. I think if you—"

"You don't get it, Boone. I don't *care* what you think. Is that clear enough for you? If it's not, I'll say it plainer—butt out. I didn't tell you this because I'm a child looking for you to be the grown-up taking charge and 'fixing' things for me. I told you because— Because... Come to think of it, I don't know why the hell I told you."

Pete got out of the rental car just in time to watch his sister stalk away without a word.

He looked at Boone with one raised eyebrow as he came around the front of the car. "What's the matter with her?"

Boone didn't move, and he didn't answer right away. He'd never had a conversation turn so wrong so fast. Especially not one that had mattered to him so much. Except maybe with his sister Kenzie.

One minute they'd been talking, easy and friendly, then Cambria had started opening up to him in a way he'd sometimes doubted she ever would. And then she was firing up like a quick-fused stick of dynamite.

Had he really struck the match?

He hadn't meant to. He'd wanted to help. He'd wanted to step in between her and the hurt of her past. He'd wanted to make it better.

Was that so wrong? Was that what Cambria meant when she said he tried to take over? When Kenzie said he tried to run her life?

He drew in a long breath, then blew it out in a stream of frustration.

"If you asked her," he finally said to Pete, still standing a yard and a half away, watching him, "she'd probably say I'm what's the matter with her."

Pete gave Boone a long, level look, obviously assessing whether whatever had irked his sister was something that required a brother taking her side. In the end, he grinned and tossed the keys to Boone, who caught them one-handed. "Nice catch. Females do get some strange ideas, don't they?"

"Yeah, they do."

"I mean, Cam's great, but there are just some things you can't talk to her about."

"True." More true than Pete knew.

"Yeah, a lot of things. Like... like the future."

Boone didn't make the mistake of looking at Pete—that would only make the boy, already shuffling his feet on the packed earth in front of the step, more self-conscious—but

Boone did pull some of his thoughts from what had just happened with Cambria to Pete's overly casual tone.

"That so?"

"Yeah. She sees things one way, and she's full-speed ahead with it. But sometimes there are others factors mixing in. She can get like she's wearing blinders, seeing only what she's set her sights on, and going straight toward that."

"But you have other ideas?"

"Sometimes. Take me going to college. Cam thinks I should go right after graduation, and that's it as far as she's concerned."

"And you don't want to go to college?"

"Sometimes wanting isn't the only thing that matters."

A wistfulness in Pete's voice stirred a memory Boone had not thought of for nearly twenty years, of passing the ball field where the high school team was preparing to play for the district baseball title, wanting with all his heart to be part of it and having to walk away, heading to his part-time job.

He didn't want his son to feel that way. He didn't want him to have a memory of regrets twenty years later, especially not about something a sight more important than a ball game.

"It's not the only thing. But it's a big thing, Pete. First you decide if you want something, then you can figure ways to go about getting it."

"If you're talking about scholarships, I've thought of that. That's how Cam went through school mostly. But I don't have the grades she did or the test scores. Maybe something'll come through with baseball, but I'm not counting on it. I thought maybe the army..." Pete turned earnest eyes on him. "You were in the army, weren't you?"

"Yeah."

Pete yawned, but still had questions. "You got a lot out of it, didn't you?"

Another swift kick toward maturity for a kid who'd been born old, that's what he'd got.

Boone didn't want Pete to have to grow up that fast. He wanted him to have challenging professors and mind-boggling libraries and late-night debates on the creation of the universe and Saturday football games and Friday night pizza parties.

"It didn't kill me, if that's what you mean." With Pete momentarily taken aback, Boone pressed his point. "You've got to remember that going into the army is about preparing to kill and being prepared to die, if that's what it comes down to."

"But if we're not at war..."

"You can't go into the army expecting peace. That's not the bargain you make. You sign up knowing there could be war, then if it stays peace, you luck out."

"Well, there haven't been too many wars lately." Boone opened his mouth to prick the optimism of youth, but Pete was going on. "And they have money to help you get through college afterward."

"So you would like to go to college."

"Eventually, sure."

Pete's offhand tone didn't fool Boone. The boy wanted college, but he wouldn't let himself set his heart on it because he was worried about his family sacrificing for him.

"Maybe something'll come up," Boone offered, the urge to do more, to take care of things for Pete, held in check by the memory of Cambria's angry accusation minutes before that he was trying to take charge.

"Yeah, maybe." Another yawn gave the words even less credence than Pete's tone. "I'm going to turn in. See you tomorrow, Boone."

"Good night, Pete."

Boone didn't move from the step, watching the lanky figure cross the open area to the house where the back porch light had been left burning to welcome him.

His son would have the money for college. He'd see to that. Some way. Any way. No matter what Cambria said.

Maybe she was right about his learning to just give love without trying to take over, but this situation surely called for him to *do* something.

As his eyes slid to the cabin tucked deep under the cottonwoods with a faint light showing through the bedroom curtains, Boone rubbed his palms over his bristled chin.

What was he going to do about telling her he was Pete's father?

He was damned if he didn't, damned if he did.

For them to have a chance at what was brewing between them, he had to be honest with her. Both so she could trust him and so he could know she *should* trust him.

But how could he? He'd known from that first day that it would surely complicate matters between the two of them. Now he feared that telling her he'd come here to find his son might do much worse.

Cambria Weston would fight like a tiger to protect her family from anything she perceived as a threat to it, including her own mother—and him. And the hell of it was, he *was* a threat to the family she'd known for sixteen years—because he wanted to claim Pete as his son.

A dream drove Boone out of bed, out of the cabin, back to his seat on the step under the black, vast, lonely sky.

In daylight the unending vault of blue sky gave a man a sense of lung-filling space, no boundaries, no limits. But at night it could make him long for the thick-hanging branches of the wooded slopes of his native Blue Ridge Mountains, whose nooks and crannies could shelter an army of hermits. The Wyoming night sky felt like an eternity without refuge. Nowhere to hide from the goblins of dreams.

One side of his mouth lifted in self-derision. Wouldn't be so bad if his dream had been about goblins. But it hadn't been a figment. It had been a memory. Accurate in every last, damning detail.

Four months ago Hank Morton had stopped by his office; it was a surprise visit from a friend Boone hadn't seen since high school. A pleasant hour of reminiscences, cut short by one seemingly innocuous comment as they'd caught each other up on their lives of the past sixteen-plus years.

That first Christmas after graduation, with Marlene finally herself again after having the baby....

Only it wasn't innocuous, because Hank's cousin Marlene had been Boone's high school girlfriend. And she'd had a baby sometime in the six months between his leaving for the army and the next Christmas.

If Boone had had any doubt that the baby was his, it ended when horror had spread across Hank's face as he realized what he'd let slip. The man had scrambled out of the office as if the president of Bodie Smith Enterprises were the devil himself.

Maybe that's how he'd looked, too, as he'd tried to grab his old friend by the collar, demanding to know where the baby was, where Marlene was—to know everything. Hank had told him nothing more. When Boone had calmed down, he wasn't surprised—family loyalty ran strong in their mountains.

But so did friendship. And when he'd called Cully and said he'd needed to find Marlene, Cully hadn't hesitated. Three days later he'd called with Marlene's married name and an address in a comfortable suburb of Memphis.

Boone had meant to be unemotional. He'd meant to be reasonable. He hadn't known Marlene wouldn't want to tell him. He hadn't known he'd confront her with an anger and hurt that tore at him.

"Why the hell didn't you tell me, Marlene? I would have helped you."

She'd sat, tense but composed, in the center of a sofa upholstered in splashes of red flowers. No one else was in her house; she'd seen to that before she'd agreed to see him. "You couldn't do anything that my family wasn't doing for me."

"I would have—"

"You would have taken over like you always did, Bodie. You would have insisted we get married and keep the baby. I was just a kid, but I knew that would have been a disaster. Certainly for me, probably for the baby, too. Even for you."

"If you hadn't wanted to marry me, all you would have had to say was no."

Marlene's laugh had held no humor. "If I could have said no to you, I wouldn't have been in that situation." Her words had stopped his pacing like a lance through the heart. She'd immediately leaned forward to touch his arm. "No, that's not fair. I wanted you as much as you wanted me—maybe more. I wanted to know what it was all about. I just got a more complete lesson on the consequences than I'd bargained for."

Behind the dry smile, beyond the emotions swirling through him, Boone had glimpsed the recognition that Marlene had become a clear-eyed woman who didn't flinch from being honest with herself.

"But I couldn't have stood up to being married to you, Bodie. Certainly not then, maybe not now—and I wanted our baby to have his own life. A good life."

"How about you, Marlene? Have you had a good life?" he'd asked on impulse.

She'd smiled. "Yes. I have a wonderful husband—and, yes, he does know about what happened—and a terrific family."

"How about our baby? Did you know the people who adopted him?"

"No, but I know they're good people. He has a good life."

He'd stopped his renewed pacing. "You've seen him?"

"No. I've thought sometimes... But it wouldn't be fair to try to divide him between two mothers, two lives. All good parents have to let their children go sometime so they can be complete people on their own. I had to let him go—completely—from the start. It wasn't easy, but I know I did right."

"Marlene—"

"I don't know where he is. I wouldn't tell you if I did."

In the silence, he'd weighed her dignity, her conviction, and grudgingly accepted them. But that didn't mean her decision was right for him. He had to make his own destiny.

Don't do it, Bodie, her soft plea whispered in his mind, from the past and from the dream. *Leave him alone. Leave the boy to his own life. The best thing you can do for him is to let him go. Let him go....*

"I can't," he said aloud, though only the night heard his harsh whisper. "He's my son. I have to take care of him. I can't let him go."

Maybe not even to reach for Cambria.

"Cully? What the—" Boone looked around quickly, relieved to see no one else paid any attention to the stranger standing by the door of his cabin.

Amid the swirl of activity centered on the barn and main house, maybe one more arrival wouldn't be noted. At nearly six-foot-four, Cully Grainger's lanky figure was hard to overlook, but his jeans, plain shirt and running shoes were in keeping with what everyone else wore for the Westons' annual cookout. And his unobtrusive rental car was lost in a welter of horse trailers, trucks and four-wheel drives littering the grounds.

With another scan of the area, Boone ushered his old friend into his cabin and out of sight.

"Getting ready for a party?" Cully asked with a jerk of his head in the direction of the barn.

"Sort of. What are you doing here?"

"Glad to see you, too, old buddy," Cully said wryly.

"I just don't want you putting your foot in it."

"Me? Known coast to coast for my tact?"

"Yeah, that's why you've left your bridges in flames on your past two jobs."

Cully's smile tightened into a grimace. "They were jackasses. I just told them so before I left."

"Well, I don't want you telling people here things before you leave."

Cully's eyebrows rose. "You trying to rush me out of here, Boone? What have you been up to?"

"Things have gotten complicated."

"Must have. I thought you'd be back by now. So did some of your associates. Your assistant, Phil Mickelson, remembered my visit and got in touch with me. He says he hasn't heard from you in five days and you missed a deadline for the final okay on an ad layout. He seemed to think death, amnesia, or kidnapping were the only possible explanations for those lapses."

Boone rubbed a finger along his lower lip. "Forgot all about the ad layout. I'll get in touch with Phil. He and Hannah in advertising should be able to make that decision."

Cully gave him a long, considering look, then wandered to the window. He stood angled to one side, so he could see out but wouldn't be spotted easily from outside. "Sounds as if you've dropped a few of those strings."

"What are you talking about?"

"All those strings you insist on holding. Every string in your life."

Boone didn't bother to dispute him.

Cully seemed to take the silence as permission to go on. "Question is if you've let loose some of the strings only to pick up new ones?"

Cully tipped his head to indicate something beyond the window. Boone moved next to him and saw Cambria and Jessa leaving the path from Cambria's cabin and stopping to look at the activity before them.

"Some of the new strings complicatin' your life?" Cully asked.

Cambria and Jessa both laughed then, and started off on diverging paths—Cambria to the barn, Jessa to the house.

Cambria waded into a group preparing to unload two horses from a trailer that someone else wanted moved before the unloading. Even from this distance, he saw the disputing parties turn to her, prepared to let her decision stand.

"So, it's one string," Cully said. "A brown-haired string with a stubborn jaw and a great rear end."

Boone realized Cully had followed the direction of his gaze, which had automatically gone to Cambria.

He swore. A single, short, disgusted syllable of frustration.

Cully's eyebrows rose. "What's the big complication with that? Females haven't exactly run from you in horror in the past."

"Her name's Cambria Weston. She's Pete Weston's sister."

Cully's eyebrows shot higher. "Holy—" The curse slid into a low whistle. "You pick 'em, Smith. You sure do pick 'em." He leaned a shoulder against the wall and considered Boone. "You told her?"

"No. Not yet."

"'Not yet.'" Cully repeated the words as if testing their flavor. "The month's almost up."

"I know, dammit. But I want to do it right. If I don't... It's not just Pete. It's the whole family."

"And her?"

"And her."

"Well, like I said, I can't remember females running the opposite direction from you when you took time to get your nose off the grindstone and look back at them. 'Specially not now. You're a successful man, Boone." The faintest whisper of envy came through those words, and for the first time Boone wondered how his friend felt about the meteoric rise of Bodie Smith Enterprises. "All the world says so."

"Am I? Guess that depends on your definition of success," he muttered, an image of Ted Weston's weathered, smile-creased face coming to mind. "And what exactly did I do that got the world so hot and bothered, anyhow?"

"Well, first, you built a better mousetrap. And second, you stood out in front of the world and said you believed in it. Both pretty rare."

"Then how come I feel like I'm the mouse that's caught in this trap?"

An instant's regret clutched at him at making the admission. He'd always been the one to handle things, to take care of things.... But this was Cully.

His oldest friend gave him a rueful, commiserating smile.

"Because you, my friend, make one hell of a good mousetrap."

Ted and Pete had left with the first group of riders. The four-wheel drive was loaded and ready for Irene and Jessa to drive out, and the chaos of vehicles, horses and people had settled into mere confusion. Cambria took a deep breath and pushed her hair back from her face.

That's when she spotted Irene talking to the tall stranger, with Jessa sitting silently in the four-wheel drive, and Boone looking as if he wished the guy would disappear.

"So of course you'll come out and have a meal with us," Irene said as Cambria walked up. "A friend of Boone's can't come all this way and not have something to eat."

"Thank you, ma'am, but I have a flight I have to catch."

"Oh, our local airport?" Irene asked with her gentlest smile.

"Yes'm, then a connecting flight from Denver."

"Then you have plenty of time, because June Reamer, who handles the car rentals there, said she didn't have to be back to work until after eight because the only remaining flight today is eight-thirty."

Cambria thought Boone groaned, but that might have been the breeze through the cottonwood leaves.

"Say 'thank you,' Cully, and give it up," Boone muttered.

"Oh? This is the famous Cully Grainger, is it?" Cambria stepped forward with a hand outstretched. This time she knew she heard a groan.

But Boone performed the necessary introductions, and Cambria shook hands with the tall man whose mouth seemed to flirt constantly with a grin and whose eyes strafed her. His blue-green gaze barely seemed to touch her, yet she felt examined, cataloged and permanently memorized. She rocked back slightly, and a tinge of apology crept into his grin. Then he slid on sunglasses, and she could have put the whole thing down to imagination if she'd been another kind of woman.

"Do you ride, Cully?"

"I can get by."

"Good, then you can join Boone and me on the trail. Unless you'd rather drive with Irene and Jessa?"

Boone and Jessa both glared at her, but Cully Grainger, after a faintly bemused glance at Irene, said, "Thanks, I'll take my chances on the trail."

It wasn't the easiest thing in the world to question somebody when you were riding single file. Especially not with the object of the questions consistently managing to get between the questioner and the questionee.

Cambria was sufficiently frustrated by the time they got to the meadow to let Boone spirit his old friend away from her almost immediately. She'd bide her time.

Chapter Eight

"Dad and Cambria and a bunch of the guys are going to hike a ways up the canyon, you want to come?"

Pete divided the question between Boone and Cully, whom he'd just met.

"The guys?" Boone asked.

"The guys on the team."

"No, thanks, Pete. We'll stick around here," Boone said quickly, unwilling to examine the illogical surge of relief that the "bunch of guys" accompanying Cambria to that canyon were nearly a decade and a half younger than she. But that fact—plus the fact that she'd have Ted's escort—allowed him to concentrate on other problems. There were plenty of people around the creekside camp they'd created in the meadow that he could divert Cully's attention to, minimizing potentially dangerous contact between him and the Westons.

"Speak for yourself," Cully contradicted. "I wouldn't mind stretching my legs. See you later, Boone."

Boone snagged his friend's arm as he started to follow Pete. "Cully—"

The other man didn't quail beneath the wealth of warning in that single word. "Boone, quit bird-dogging me. I'm not going to spill any of your beans."

There wasn't much Boone could do but let Cully go. He debated following, saying he'd changed his mind. But what good would that do? He couldn't stop Cambria from asking questions and he couldn't make Cully any more close-mouthed than he already was, which, come to think of it, was pretty damned close-mouthed. He'd only show how uncomfortable it made him to have the two of them within speaking distance, which would rouse even more of Cambria's suspicions.

Besides, he thought as he caught sight of Jessa Tarrant sitting alone on a rock a little way upstream, he could better spend his time asking his own questions.

"This seat taken?"

Jessa gave a faint smile. "Help yourself." She scooted over, leaving him more room on the flat stone. "But let me warn you, the springs are shot."

"See what you mean." He shifted, trying for a more comfortable accommodation between himself and the rock. "But the view's great. Want some?" He held out one of the bunches of grapes he'd snagged before heading her way.

"Thanks." She ate one. "If you were looking for a great view, you should have gone with Cambria and your friend and the others. The canyon's great."

"Yeah, it is."

Something must have come through in his voice because she gave him a searching look. "You've seen it?"

"Yeah." Before she could do more than open her mouth, he added the first thing that came to mind. "But I'd had my fill listening to Cambria try to grill Cully on the ride up."

"Are you surprised?"

"No. I just wish I knew why she thinks she has to be so suspicious of me. Why she won't open up. Why it's one step forward and two back with us."

He shut his mouth with a snap. For somebody who'd meant to ask questions, he talked too damned much.

After a thoughtful silence, Jessa spoke softly. "I'd say the answer's the same to all of those. Cambria doesn't trust very easily."

He slanted a look at Cambria's best friend. "Why?"

She shook her head. "You wouldn't think much of your friend if he told your secrets, would you?" she asked, as if she'd tapped into Boone's thoughts. "But I can tell you about one thing that hasn't helped."

The faint surprise he'd heard in her voice at the party was back. He waited, watching her shred the grape stalk with quick, jerky motions.

"I had a—a situation back in D.C. Cambria and I shared an apartment at the time and she went through a lot of it with me."

He might not want to hear the answer, but Boone had to ask. "What kind of situation?"

Jessa Tarrant looked at him, then at the sky and creek, finally settling on her own hands. She dropped the splintered grape stalk and tightly laced her fingers.

"I was stalked. I guess most people would say I was the victim of a stalking, but I hate that—*victim.*"

"Damn. Did he—"

"He never got close enough to do me any real physical harm—Cambria was a big reason for that. She took it seriously from the start. Even before I did. Long before the authorities did. I used to tease her about not trusting anybody, about being so suspicious. Not anymore. I never even went out with this guy, and he destroyed my life. My work, my home, my friends—I could never get free of him."

"Couldn't they catch him?"

"They finally did, and he's in jail, though not on stalking charges. At the time the law didn't deal with this sort of situation."

"So you came out here for a fresh start."

"Yes. Cambria helped me find the shop and a place to live. She helped me feel safe again, and then she started badgering me to reach beyond where I feel safe." Jessa looked up for the first time, staring into his eyes, gauging him. "She's a remarkable person."

He swallowed, not wanting to show too much, knowing if he showed too little he'd lose this potential ally in a heartbeat. He met her eyes.

"Yeah, she is."

"She doesn't trust easily, but when she does, she's the most loyal, most giving friend or—" she quirked an eyebrow at him and gave the next phrase a faintly ironic, questioning tone "*significant other* that anybody could hope for. And once she trusts, if the trust is broken, it hurts her so deeply that she finds it very hard to ever forgive."

Boone Dorsey Smith recognized a warning when he heard one, even cloaked in the reserved accents of Jessa Tarrant.

The twitch at the corner of Cully Grainger's mouth might have been from suppressing a grin, and heaven only knew what lurked in those laser eyes now hidden behind mirrored sunglasses. Cambria didn't care. She'd run out of time.

The group had already explored the lower part of the canyon and started the return trip to the meadow. Up to this point, Cully Grainger had managed to avoid Cambria's subtle efforts to isolate him. So, to hell with subtlety.

She snagged his arm when he would have passed her, and held on while several others went by on the narrow path, until they were the only ones left.

"Something I can help you with?" His mouth gave that twitch and his sunglasses pointed in the direction of her hand on his arm.

She let go, but she didn't relent. "Yes. You can answer some questions. What brought you to Bardville?"

"I was in the neighborhood."

"Oh, really." She packed a full load of skepticism into that.

He appeared totally undaunted. "Near enough. I was checking something out for someone just over the Montana border."

"Checking out what?"

"I believe the appropriate phrase here is, 'I am not at liberty to say.'" His mouth definitely quirked this time.

"I understand you've known Boone a long time."

"Most all his life." He started down the path, and she kept pace.

"So you knew him when his father was alive."

"Yep."

"Having his father die and having to help his mother when he was so young must have really changed him."

The mirrored sunglasses were trained on her. If she hadn't been so intent on what he had to say, she might have found it unnerving. "Not changed so much, as made his tendencies hard habits."

"What do you mean?"

"Even before his pa died, Boone took on things, taking care of things more than the rest of us. My aunt Philly used to say Bodie collected responsibilities the way some kids collected baseball cards."

"It helped get his family through."

As soon as the words became sound, she wanted to kick herself. What was *she* doing defending Boone? Especially to his longtime friend? She should be filling in the gaps Boone had left.

"That it did. But the man doesn't know when to quit. Doesn't know when it's time to let somebody else carry the responsibility."

"You mean, with his job."

He paused a moment, finding the right footing on a water-splashed rock as they reached nearly level ground. "Yeah."

"I agree. He's working too hard, trying to do everything himself. Nobody can carry that sort of burden forever. Something's got to give."

Though she couldn't see his eyes, she had the sense he was measuring her. "You told him that?"

"Yes. He says you've told him the same thing."

"Does he now?" he murmured.

"Not that he seems to listen to either of us."

"Hasn't listened much to me ever. Maybe being here will change some of that."

Cambria wasn't sure she wanted to know what he meant by that. It didn't matter anyhow. They were getting too far off what she wanted to know, and they were nearly to where a group milled around, taking burgers off the grill and filling their plates from Irene's bounty spread out on folding tables.

"Why do you think he's staying here so long?"

Cully Grainger chuckled, a rumbling sort of mirth that barely disturbed the lines of his face. "You looked in a mirror lately? Better yet, have you seen a reflection of yourself from his eyes? A man doesn't walk away from that easy."

Cambria felt a flush, hot and tingly, rising through her body. Its most disturbing aspect was how damn good it felt.

Before she had to think of something to say, she caught sight of Boone striding toward them. Apparently Cully did, too.

He stepped in front of her, his back to Boone, masking her from Boone's view. With one hand, he held her upper arm, keeping her in place; with the other, he raised his glasses and studied her through narrowed eyes.

"What do you—"

He interrupted as if he hadn't heard. "Boone's the best man I know. If I was in hell and had one chance to get out, he'd be the man I'd call on." He dropped the glasses into place and his mouth gave that twitch again. "He also needs to be hit upside the head now and then. You look to me to be just the woman to do it."

With that, he released her arm, turned on his heel and intercepted Boone, still five yards away, steering him toward where Ted held plates out to both of them.

Cambria had the feeling she was missing something...but what? She had no answer. But the feeling didn't fade as Boone maneuvered Cully away from her until the shadows lengthened and everyone started back to the main house. If anything, it grew stronger as she watched Boone say goodbye to his longtime friend, standing by the open door of Cully's beige rental car, their faces serious, their handshake firm enough to edge toward pain.

"I see you in the boy, Boone."

Boone closed his eyes for half a minute. "I wasn't sure if I really saw it or if I wanted it so badly I made it so. But that makes it more complicated. What if they see—"

"They'd have to be looking," Cully said. "It's the eyebrows, the shape of the head. His coloring's different, and that makes it harder to see. But what's the difference—you're going to tell them, aren't you?"

"Yeah. When the time's right."

"Not as easy as you thought it'd be?" Cully asked.

"I didn't think it would be easy, but you're right, it's even harder than I thought. Harder to know what to do. Harder to—I don't know what to call it—intrude? But a hell of a lot harder to think about just stepping away."

"From him or her?"

"I don't know."

Cully cleared his throat. "You want me to approach the family, Boone? It might be easier, coming from a less interested party."

"No," he said slowly. "It'll take care of itself."

"Now, how did I know you were going to say that?" Cully asked with resignation.

They started a campfire in a circle of stones in front of the bunkhouse. In a week there would be strangers here. But for tonight it was a circle of friends and family, telling stories, laughing with one another.

Cambria looked across to where Boone sat listening to something Pete said from beside him.

Somewhere inside her she accepted that he belonged in this circle.

She could see Boone as a young boy, gawky and thin, then older as he started to fill out—so clearly it was as if she'd been there. She could see him as the boy described by him and by Cully. And she could see the man he'd become. The man Cully Grainger said was the best he knew.

"You've really made progress with the new cabin," Jessa said from beside her.

Cambria smiled as her eyes went to the shadowy form beginning to rise on the concrete piers. It would be about fifty percent bigger than the structure that had stood on the far side of the creek, and though she couldn't envision the finished product the way she suspected Boone could when he narrowed his eyes and his face grew dreamy, she had faith it would be a vast improvement. She'd already figured that if reservations stayed at last year's level, they could make their money back on it by the end of this season.

"Boone and Pete have made progress. I'm the unskilled labor on this project."

"He's quite talented, isn't he?"

Cambria had told Jessa one night over a plate of nachos and margaritas about discovering that their bed-and-breakfast guest was Bodie Smith. Cambria had still been steaming, but Jessa, while she shared her surprise, did not participate in her outrage. When Cambria cooled off, Jessa had speculated about what sort of pressures would bear down on a man in Bodie Smith's position. Her calm voice had Cambria squirming in very short order, because Boone Dorsey Smith had already given her insights to that by his honesty about his childhood.

"Don't you think so?"

Jessa's voice startled Cambria out of her reverie.

"What?"

"That Boone's talented."

Cambria sidestepped that. Just as she wouldn't tell Boone about Jessa's past, she wouldn't discuss his problems designing with anyone else. "Must be to have such a successful business."

"That doesn't rely on talent."

Before Cambria could formulate an answer to that, Jessa made an announcement that turned the conversation in a totally different direction.

"I told him about what happened in Washington."

"You told... Boone?" She turned to stare at the friend sitting beside her. Jessa looked as calm as she sounded. "Why?"

"Because you didn't."

"It's not my decision to tell your business. But I don't understand—"

"I wanted him to understand you better."

"Me? That makes no sense."

Jessa shrugged, a faint smile lifting her lips. "It does to me. I also told him because I trust him." She looked Cambria directly in the eyes. "Do you?"

Cambria looked away, her gaze locking with the man across from her, who was staring at her. They were illuminated by sparks, separated by fire.

"I don't know. I wish I did."

It wasn't until she was in bed that night that she wondered if her own words had meant that she wished she knew if she trusted Boone Dorsey Smith, or she wished she trusted him.

A brisk, warm breeze made Monday morning perfect for hanging out the bedding for the cabins that would hold their first guests come Friday, when Memorial Day weekend kicked off the official opening of the Weston Ranch Guest Quarters.

Irene stored the bedding each winter in the cedar closet Ted had built years ago in the attic. Cambria tried arguing each year that since people paid good money for cedar air fresheners, the scent should please them just fine in the cabins' quilts, blankets and coverlets. Irene replied each year that if the guests wanted cedar they could buy it, but the Weston Ranch gave them something never caught in a bottle—the wind-scoured, sun-blessed, sage-tinged clean scent of Wyoming.

Cambria had started right after breakfast, but the task was taking longer than she remembered. Maybe because the sight of Boone, hard at work on the new cabin across the open circle, posed such a distraction.

She wished he'd put his shirt back on. Or maybe she didn't. She wished they'd made love last week in the canyon, and she was relieved they hadn't. He made her laugh; he made her angry. She admired his responsibility, determination and discipline, then lost all patience when she saw how they had hurt him. She dreaded his leaving, but she looked toward it as her salvation.

She didn't have one thought or feeling about this man that couldn't be turned on its head and still be true. Jessa had been right from the start. She was deeply attracted to him, in a combustible chemical sort of reaction she couldn't deny or explain away. She was also drawn to him on a level that had to do with mind and character and the integrity in a pair of level gray eyes.

Boone Dorsey Smith ruffled her. More than that, he scared her.

Cambria was putting out the last quilt on the double row of clothesline when she saw Sheriff Milano's car turn onto the road. Holding aside a blanket billowing like a sail, she gave him a wave. He waved back and stopped the car well short of the house. When he got out, he started toward her, only pausing for a brief wave of hello at Irene, who'd come out on the porch at the sound of the unexpected arrival. Cambria tailored her path to meet him.

"Well, Sheriff, how are you this morning? Sorry I didn't get a chance to talk to you Saturday, but you seemed pretty occupied."

Dark color flagged the sheriff's naturally ruddy cheeks at her oblique reference to his interest in Rita Campbell. Cambria expected a teasing answer in return, or at the least, an admonition to not be starting on him. Instead, with a solemn face and an unusually solemn tone, the sheriff said, "I had a right nice time, always do at the Weston cookout."

"Glad to hear that," Cambria said slowly, trying to gauge this unusual mood in a man she'd known all her life.

Instinctively she glanced toward the rising cabin across the way. Boone had been watching. As soon as she looked up, he started toward her. From the corner of her eye, she saw that Irene had already left the porch, heading this way.

"Uh, Cambria, I got something I need to tell you."

A weight of anxiety pressed against her chest. "Yes?"

"You'll be getting official word a bit later, but I thought I'd come by and tell you personal."

She felt as she had once when, rear-ended by a drunk driver, her car went airborne over a ditch before landing on an embankment. In those brief seconds she had felt weightless, suspended. For that beat of time she had been uninjured, unbruised, yet fully conscious that pain would come as soon as she landed.

"Just tell me."

"Angie Lee's dead. She died last week in Los Angeles. It was cancer. I—"

"What is it?" Irene demanded, still several yards away. "Oh, God... Is it Pete?"

"No, Mama." Cambria met Irene, putting her arms around the white-faced older woman and holding on. "Pete's fine."

Sheriff Milano cleared his throat. "It's Angie Lee, Irene. I was just telling Cambria, she died last week in Los Angeles."

Irene's hold changed, from taking support to giving it. But Cambria didn't need that. She straightened away and met Boone's worried look over Irene's shoulder.

"What's wrong?"

"Nothing's wrong, Boone. We're okay. You can go on back to work."

Irene, keeping one arm around Cambria's waist, reached out her other hand to cup Boone's arm. "You stay right here, Boone. Sheriff Milano came to tell us that Cambria's mother has passed away. Poor soul."

"It's no concern of mine." The harsh words left Cambria's throat feeling ragged and sore.

"Oh, Cambria."

Irene's hold on her tightened as if she needed consoling, and Boone's brow creased in worry.

"It's not," she insisted.

Sheriff Milano cleared his throat. "Matter of fact, it is, Cambria. That's the other thing I came to tell you."

"Her dying doesn't change the past and it doesn't change that she's no concern of—"

"You're her sole heir. I got a letter from a lawyer here that says so. And I guess you're going to have to be deciding what to do about her things and such."

He handed over a sealed, crisply thick envelope with her name typed in the precise center. Cambria accepted it, but made no move to open it.

"But how did you get it, Tom?" Irene asked.

"This lawyer fellow called our office yesterday trying to find out if we knew where you might be. Seems the last address Angie Lee had for you was Washington, D.C.—" Cambria gave an involuntary jerk at the news that Angie Lee had bothered to keep track of her at all, much less as recently as her life in Washington. "When a letter they sent there came back Addressee Unknown, he got associates to check. 'Course they didn't find any sign of you. Not having any fancy *associates* in our corner of the world, he decided to scope out the lay of the land. I talked to him yesterday and said when the official letter got here I'd bring it to you personal. Damned if he didn't get it here overnight."

"That was nice of you, Tom. Real nice. I know Ted would appreciate it, too."

"It only seemed right. It's a shame..." He let that trail off without specifying what was a shame. "Lawyer said Angie Lee got sick suddenlike, and when she went to a doctor, the cancer was too far gone for them to do anything more than make her comfortable."

"Poor soul," Irene repeated with genuine sympathy.

Cambria pulled from her and faced off against the three people watching her, each with a mix of wariness and worry.

"How can you waste your sympathy on her like that? You knew her. You knew she never cared for anyone but herself. She thought of herself first, last and always. Dying doesn't change that. And it doesn't change that I don't want to have anything to do with her."

"Cambria..."

She brushed past Boone, knocking away his hand when he would have touched her, and headed for her cabin. She knew someone would follow her; Irene most likely. And Irene's calm good sense would coax the poison out of Cambria's system bit by bit as it had many times over the years.

But this would be the last time, because Angie Lee was dead.

And first, Cambria needed some time alone.

"Give her some time." Irene's hand on his arm stopped Boone's instinctive move to follow Cambria.

He listened while the sheriff and Irene talked quietly, a few commonplace memories of the woman who'd borne Cambria easing into the everyday doings of their community and ending with Irene's thanking Tom Milano again for coming by personally.

Boone stood beside Irene as they watched the sheriff drive off in a slow-growing tail of dust. He nodded when she said, "I'm going to find Ted," then watched her head off in the four-wheel drive to the range her husband was working. He went to his cabin to wash up, then he went to find Cambria.

She sat on a sun-bleached picnic table bench in the shade of the cottonwood behind her cabin, not far from the creek. Leaning forward with her forearms on her thighs, she used her thumbnail to peel an orange with slow, meticulous attention. The pages of the opened lawyer's letter sat loose atop the envelope on the bench, as if waiting for a breeze to spirit them away.

He picked them up as he sat beside her, not near enough to touch, not willing to admit he was afraid to touch her.

Without lifting her head from her task, she said, "Go ahead and read it if you're interested."

"I don't—"

"Go ahead. Read it."

He looked at her bent head for a long moment, reading one message from the straight line of her back, the levelness of her shoulders and the studied movements of her hands. But he heard something else in those rough-voiced words that sounded again and again in his head. He smoothed the sheets and started to read. When he'd finished, he folded the pages together and returned them to their envelope.

The dry, legal phrases that had followed a stilted expression of sympathy had calmed him, put him back on a familiar ground.

He drew in a deep breath.

"I can imagine how you feel, Cambria. You must—"

"You have no idea how I feel."

"I've pushed people away in my life, too. My sister. Friends. Employees. My high school sweetheart."

He swallowed on that one, pausing long enough that she shot him a dour grin that sliced his breath in two even as she returned her attention to her orange.

"Is that supposed to have special significance, Boone? Did you think I'd be jealous of your youthful liaisons?"

"No. Who is not the point. The point is that I did it. I pushed people out of my life. I didn't know I'd done it, but I see it now. Being here has helped me see that."

"Good for you. But that has nothing to do with Angie Lee dying. If you're thinking I'm feeling bad for pushing her out of my life, you have it totally wrong, Boone. She walked out of my life. And she never looked back. She did me one good turn in my lifetime and that was leaving me with Ted. For that I say thanks, even though I suspect it was pure lack of interest on her part rather than any concern for me. There's no reason to pretend I'm sad about her dying."

"She left you everything she had. Her house—"

"She left me nothing. Nothing I want. I don't want her house—*this* is my home. Ted and Irene and Pete are my family. They are what counts in my life. Nothing else."

She was your mother. Just as I'm Pete's father. He had the sense not to say that. "She left you a beautiful name."

"A beautiful name..." Her thumbnail dug deep into the flesh of the orange. Juice welled up over her nail, then dripped to the ground between her feet. She didn't seem to notice. "I went to see it once, you know, when I was about twenty and... Well, I suppose I was curious, so I went to see this place I was named after. Has anybody told you about Cambria, Wyoming?"

"Yeah, remember?" He reached to stroke her hair. She drew back, no more than half an inch, but his hand stilled immediately. He brought it to the bench between them, wrapping his fingers around the edge. "Irene told me the day I arrived, it's the name of an old mining town."

She shook her head. "Not even a town. More a scratch on the side of a hill early this century. Now it's nothing. When the mine went dry, folks just up and left. They walked away, left their houses, their furniture, even the dishes on the table. Are you starting to get an image here? Coal-mining. Dusty and dirty. Nothing worth taking along. Deserted. That's what my mother named me after, that's the legacy she left me. Maybe she had a premonition."

He had to do something. Something to help her deal with this, with the emotions she might not admit, maybe even the ones she wouldn't let herself feel. But he didn't know what. And that clawed at him worse than anything. So he did what he'd always done.

"Don't worry about any of this, Cambria. I'll take care of everything. It says there's a house she owned that's yours now. And all the contents. I've got connections in L.A. I can find a good real estate broker there. Someone who can take care of all the details for you. Find an auctioneer to deal with the furniture and stuff. I'll call this lawyer in the morning and see about—"

"Shut up."

She didn't say it loud, but it stopped him.

"Cambr—"

"I don't want you doing things for me. I don't want you organizing things. I don't want you to make any phone calls or send any faxes or shoulder any responsibilities for me. I don't need your help. Is that clear?"

He looked at her pale, strained face and knew she did need help, even if it wasn't with dealing with lawyers and auctioneers and real estate brokers. It was obvious there wasn't anything he could *do* for her. That's what scared him. He didn't know how to be what she needed.

"That's clear. I'll leave you alone then."

"Fine."

He stood. "If you change your mind..."

"I won't."

The moon, nearly full, valiantly spread thin, silver light across an infinity of sky.

Boone had gone into Bardville for dinner at the café, figuring Cambria would surely be more comfortable alone with her family considering the way he'd messed up this afternoon.

It was near midnight. He hadn't seen a light in her cabin all night. When he couldn't take the wondering anymore, he went over and quietly opened the cabin door to listen; he heard only the silence of emptiness.

He went looking for her.

He almost missed her among the shadows under the cottonwoods. She sat on a large rock by the wooden footbridge. Her forehead rested against her arm, which was supported along the edge of the bridge. She might be staring at the water below through the triangle formed by her arm and body, or she might have her eyes closed—he couldn't tell.

He knew she heard his approach, but she didn't move.

He sat beside her, the ground cool and faintly damp through the tough fabric of his jeans. He didn't touch her.

They sat there for a time he never thought to measure. He watched the glints of light from water running over a sprinkling of submerged rocks, and remembered when he'd been very young. A time with his parents and his grandmother and his younger sister and growing up on the mountain with Cully. And he wished he could take Cambria back to that safe, magical time, to protect her always from pain and disappointment.

"I'm not crying."

Beneath the huskiness her voice held a healthy dose of belligerence.

"I know that."

"I'm not grieving."

"Okay."

"I have no cause to grieve, so I have no need for your sympathy."

"That's not why I'm here."

"I don't need your damn organizational skills."

"That's not why I'm here, either."

For a moment he thought that would be the end of it. Then she shifted, straightening slowly, as if she'd grown stiff from holding the same position. Not until she sat completely straight did she turn to look at him. In the faint light her eyes looked dark and shadowy, like a forest path that wavered and glinted as branches moved—tossed by benign breezes or the stirring of a coming storm? Impossible to tell.

"Why are you here?"

Swinging his shoulders around, he faced her as squarely as he could.

He was here to give her what she'd said she didn't want. Consolation. Caring. Solace.

He was here to give it to her in a way he'd never known. A way he hoped he could learn for her.

He brushed his fingertips along the line of her cheekbone, then to the fragile indentation at her temple, and finally along the arch of her brow.

He was careful to take his hand away before he bent his head to her. He would not hold her, not by even such a light touch, if she did not want this kiss.

He didn't hurt her, but the kiss was not gentle. His mouth was firm and hot on hers. He wanted, and his lips told hers that.

An instant, that's all. But for that instant she held utterly still and he felt as if his soul had stilled as well.

A slight, sighing gasp escaped her, slid from her mouth, over his and out into the night. Then she brought her mouth back to his.

Tilting their heads broadened the kiss. Another move, and it deepened. Tongues, teeth, lips sought and gave. Still, he didn't touch her anywhere else. They leaned into each other for kisses that left them gasping, then greedily returned for more. He sank into the heat of it, the waves washing over his head. Another second...

"Cambria." He lifted his chin when she would have stilled his mouth with another kiss. She placed her lips to his Adam's apple. "Damn. I'll go crazy if I can't hold you, but if I hold you... This is only leading one place—"

She was rising, taking his hand and drawing him to stand beside her.

Feeling slightly dazed, he stood. "What are you doing?"

"That's my line, remember?"

"But—"

She tugged on his hand, leading him away from the creek. "Inside."

"What?"

"That's where this is leading."

She smiled, and he followed her toward what he wanted. But inside her bedroom, the faint light of moon and stars glinted through the sheer curtains to cast a shadowy glow on the pictures of her family, reminding him of who she was and who he was. *Damn.*

"Cambria, I don't... I don't know if this is the right thing to do."

"For you?"

"For you."

She took his face between her palms. "I know that I want to be between the sheets with you, Boone Dorsey Smith, and it has nothing to do with your financial assets." A wicked little grin played at the corners of her lips, a contrast to the heaviness of her eyes. "Though certain other assets do interest me."

He might have denied his own wanting, but not hers.

Sitting on the edge of the bed, he grasped her waist and drew her between his legs. She started unbuttoning his shirt. Under the loose material of her blouse, he sculpted up her ribs to the underside of her breasts. Cambria moved in closer to reach the lower buttons of his shirt.

Boone couldn't begin to count the number of times he'd taken a shirt off in his life. Old, worn, sometimes dirty shirts in the old days; new, luxurious, indulgent shirts more than occcasionally now; and almost every variation in between.

Not one of those had felt like this, with Cambria's palms sliding along his skin as she spread her hands across his chest, over his shoulders, then down his arms. The fabric followed, aided by the shifting of his shoulders. Cambria unbuttoned his right cuff with infuriating and enticing exactitude, and tugged it over his hand.

By the time she started on the left cuff, his patience was fraying. He returned his freed hand to her jeans, trying to unsnap them one-handed, without success but with the pleasing side effect of tucking his hand against her warm, smooth abdomen.

As soon as she released his other hand from his shirt, he made quick work of her snap. Resting her hands on his shoulders and leaning forward, she placed an open-mouthed kiss at the indentation of his breastbone. He wanted to never move again, to absorb the smooth, moist heat of her caress on his skin until it reached into his bones and touched his soul.

But his body pushed him now, demanding and urging.

Unzipping her jeans allowed them to slip partly down her hips, snagging low and gapping in a most inviting way. He slid his hands inside that opening, over her hips and down to the edge of her panties.

Deprived of her kisses when Cambria straightened, he had the compensation of the small sound that came from the back of her throat as he dipped his fingers under the edge of her panties, and deeper. Smooth, smooth skin. A crisp tickle over her mound. Moist heat beckoning his touch.

His thumbs stroked, and she moaned, eyes closed, head dropped back.

He stroked deeper, dipping inside her, and she shuddered, her hands clenching his bare shoulders and drawing an answering shudder from him.

"Cambria..."

Her eyes fluttered open.

He wanted to give to her, to care for her, to provide her solace. To take her out of this moment, this pain, and into pleasure. All that, he wanted to do for her, with touches and kisses and patient, building caresses. He wanted to brush her skin, and have the touch melt into bone and blood until it whispered at the core of her.

But she wouldn't allow it. Not completely.

She slid her hands down his chest in tormenting tandem, then unbuttoned and unzipped his jeans with blessedly less deliberation than she'd taken with his shirt. When she slid her hand inside and cupped him, a light pressure against his aching length, he knew his patience had reached its limit.

He unhooked her bra and skimmed both it and her shirt over her head. Pausing only to pull a condom from the pocket, he also shucked his jeans and briefs in one move. She was still kicking free of her jeans and panties as he laid back and pulled her on top of him.

He hadn't known breathing could be so erotic. Each rise and fall pushed her breasts against his chest in a contrast of sensations from the hardened tips surrounded by softness. Each rise and fall fanned shudderingly against the skin at the side of his neck. Each rise and fall brought the faintest scent of her, the scent that matched the taste he'd found with his lips and tongue.

Hands roamed, explored, tormented, met, left for new worlds to conquer, returned to the old, and started anew.

He marveled at the texture of her back, sleek and smooth. He gritted his teeth at the sweep of her bent knee across the apex of his thighs. He garbled a moaned curse deep in his throat when her open-mouthed kiss to his nipple slid to the most delicate of sucking motions.

Grasping her rib cage, he held her away, gaining much-needed sanity, though less control than he might have hoped for.

"I've got to..."

Her look followed the slight rustle as his groping hand found the condom packet forgotten among the covers.

"You could wait a little..."

The space he'd created between their bodies conspired with her questing hand to make him forfeit nearly all his sanity.

He circled her wrist, but didn't have the strength to pull her hand away.

Her voice dipped to a whisper. "You're so soft."

A single moan of tormented laughter was all he managed. "If I were any harder, I'd explode."

"I meant the outside." She sounded flustered, a shade defensive.

It stopped him from mentioning that the last thing a man wanted to hear in these circumstances was a woman marvelling at how soft he was. It also made him feel oddly protective of her. "I know you did, Cambria."

Any lingering defensiveness dissipated in her fascinated interest in the maneuvers required to transfer the content of the packet to where it would do the most good. He was sweating and pulsing with a fabulous ache by the time he spread his hands wide on her back and drew her down for a long, deep kiss.

Still, he would have had her set the pace. He let her know that. Instead, she used her hold on him to tug him as she rolled to her side. He followed, but primitive instinct drove him to do more, and he completed the roll with her firmly under him. She wriggled, he slid, and the contact between their slick, fever-hot bodies was complete.

"Cambria..." He rolled his hips, bringing his heat and hardness to the entrance of her body, easing so slightly inside, letting her know how she made him feel, but giving her choices of how and when.

She skimmed her hands down his back to his buttocks, where her palms pressed while her hips rocked, slicing away choices until only *here* and *now* remained.

He probed her deeper, straining to resist the urge to pound into her. She shifted, tilting her hips, and he slid in more. Her lips parted on an indrawn breath. Her hands tightened on him, drawing him into her. He thrust. Withdrew slightly, then thrust again. And again.

"Boone... Boone," she whispered. Her hands roamed, curving over the hills at either side of the valley of his spine. Gentle strokes, as if he needed soothing.

This was supposed to be for her, to give to her...

He shifted his weight to one arm and moved to slide the other hand between their bodies, but she caught his wrist.

"Don't take over, Boone."

Forcing his hips to near stillness, he dropped his forehead to hers. "I don't know how much longer I can keep it slow for you." At least he'd give her honesty in this. "It's been so damn long, and you're so...you feel so good."

She shifted and found his mouth. Her tongue slid inside and her hips lifted slightly, two fleeting, delicate motions that set off a volcano.

His hips drove against hers. "Damn, Cambria—"

"It's okay, Boone. It's—" She gasped and her hands tightened on him.

She hadn't pushed him over the edge, she'd shoved him off a cliff. And he had no chance of stepping back to level ground. He was free-falling, with only her to hold on to. Only the sensation of her beneath him, around him. Only the smell of her skin and their passion. Only the sound of her short, panting sighs.

Impact was staggering, shattering, muscle-convulsing, body-draining. He threw back his head and shuddered with it, bright patterns of colors exploding behind his closed eyelids.

He collapsed, only one conscious thought slicing through. He'd wanted to give to her. Instead she'd given to him.

Chapter Nine

All right, so maybe she'd rushed him a little.

Maybe, somewhere in the deepest corner of her mind, Cambria had wanted to hold on to the part of herself she would give up if she came apart in his arms.

Maybe she hadn't quite been ready to trust him with that, with the knowledge that he could give her a climax.

That was no reason for Boone to be so ruthless.

She'd been asleep, content in his arms with the quilt haphazardly drawn over their cooling bodies. But not so deeply asleep that she hadn't heard him go into the bathroom, hadn't felt the mattress dip under his return, hadn't turned into the warmth of his chest. And drifted off again.

She woke to a mercilessly soft stroking. Her body throbbed with sensation, beating to a pulse he'd set and would not release. Her senses rushed toward the completion that she'd denied them and that his touches promised.

She knew it was too late, still she reached to touch him, to try to regain some of the control. He caught her hands and pinned them gently above her head with one hand while he held her body with his weight.

"Not this time, Cambria. This time, I'm taking over." He let her see his wolfish smile before he lowered his head to take her nipple in his mouth.

It was the kind of exquisite torture that could leave a woman screaming. Lips, hands, hips, teeth, chest, tongue, legs—all were his instruments. He never hurt her, but he wasn't gentle. He demanded—that she accept the pleasure he gave her, that she acknowledge she wanted a satisfaction beyond the pleasure.

He brought her near release, but held her back as he fit his hips between her thighs and drew her legs around him.

"Cambria, open your eyes."

She did. And she kept them open as he drove deep into her. She kept them open even as her body arched to meet him. Even as the rolling shudder of satisfaction carried her away from sanity, followed by a second, deeper tremor. Even as she came apart as completely as she had feared.

She shut her eyes only when the weight and width of Boone, still joined to her, collapsed on her like a human blanket of comfort. That's when the tears slipped free. Stupid, inexplicable tears. But Boone asked for no explanation. He shifted her to within his arms and kissed her salted cheeks until they dried.

She slept then. From pure, sated, physical exhaustion.

But in that period before dawn when dark retreats but light isn't strong enough to hold full sway, Cambria slipped out of bed, drawing on her robe. She opened the second drawer of the bureau as quietly as she could, bending to search its shadowed interior for underwear.

Boone rolled to the side of the bed, but before she could turn to see if he was awake or simply stirring in his sleep, the brush of his fingertips on the back of her right calf made her gasp.

His voice behind her was rough and slow. "If I ever meet this jackass Toby—"

"Tony," she murmured automatically.

"I'll be damn tempted to slap him on the back and thank him for being such an ass. For not knowing what he had in you. So you came back to Wyoming, where I could find you."

His touch slid higher, across the delicate skin at the back of her knee. It tickled a little, but she couldn't move away from the sensation. Not for anything.

She heard the whisper of the mattress, and knew he sat directly behind her. His left hand rested at her hip, then followed the curve of her bottom, gliding over her robe, heating the material caught between their skin until it seemed to liquefy.

His right hand slid higher up her leg, under the hem of the robe, then echoed the caress of its brethren, but with no material intruding.

"Close the drawer, Cambria." His voice was low, ragged.

When she bent lower to comply, his hands flexed against her. Her breath caught at the sensation and her head came up, meeting her own heavy-lidded reflection in the mirror over the far end of the bureau. The image surprised her. She hadn't known she could look this way...like a woman who could get lost in sensation.

She recognized a faint rustling of foil, but she paid no heed until a stirring behind told her Boone had stood, even before his image joined hers in the mirror.

He was behind her. Around her, his hands reached the belt knot. He slipped it open without his fingers even brushing against her through the robe. The belt dropped to the floor and the robe opened a shadowed gap. Boone leaned over her shoulder, kissed the lobe of her ear, then tugged it slightly with his teeth.

He traced the side of her throat with his tongue, then raised his head just enough to meet her eyes in the mirror. At some level she saw his reaction to her more clearly now, through the mirror, than the first two times they'd made love. The light was brighter, or her eyes were clearer, or his desire was stronger... or she was more willing to see.

She leaned against him, arching her back, letting the robe's opening gap wider and deliberately, delicately, snuggling her hips against him. He grasped her hips and made the contact blatant. Her eyes shot open at the sensation, through the silk of her robe, of a man, hot and hard, pulsing against her.

"You're..."

The mirror reflected his slightly strained smile.

"Hard? Hell, yes. I told you it had been a long time. The down side was a short fuse that first time. The up side—" he rocked against her, drawing a gasp "—is having a lot of reserves built up."

His hands at her hips gathered handfuls of robe, drawing it up in quick, uneven spurts over her skin until it bunched at her waist, and he pressed against her, full and hot.

"Just looking at you, Cambria..." His mouth was low at the side of her throat, pushing against the material of her robe to explore the slope to her shoulder. She shifted, letting the covering drop onto her arm, then repeated the action on the other side.

He reached around to cup her breasts in his hands, circling the aureoles lightly, then stroking firmly across the tips with the pad of his thumbs. With sensation shuddering through her, her head fell back to his shoulder as the rhythm of his hands on her breasts and their hips swaying together caught and meshed.

He trailed a hand down the center of her body, then slipped a fingertip to the entrance, teasing lightly.

"I've thought of touching you like this, Cambria. From the first time I saw you."

His rough admission should have shocked her. She turned to put her lips to the side of his neck, pressing her teeth against his skin when his teasing touch turned into a deeper invasion. She was near the edge.

"I want you... inside..."

"The bed? Or..."

"Now."

His second's hesitation brought her to the edge of reconsideration, but then he moved and there was no regret. She braced her arms on the bureau and let her head drop forward as he guided himself into her. A shuddering wave crashed over her, quick and so sharp she cried out with it.

Then she nearly cried.

So fast.... She hadn't meant it to end so soon.

"I'm sorry... Boone, I..."

He stopped her words by rolling his hips against her, into her. And she knew it was far from ended.

She knew he watched her in the mirror. She raised her head, wanting to see his hands on her, her body flushed. Most of all, to see the fierce satisfaction in his face.

Sensation built, echoing off nerve endings, streaking to her core. She gasped with the stretching, deep sensation of his thrusts. And cried out a second time at the sight of his reflected face in its stark, possessive grimace as his climax collided with the full, pulsing reality of him inside her.

She never knew how he got them to the bed, but that was where she came to a sense of herself again. And she knew, absolutely, that she had not settled herself on the mattress, between the sheets, head on a pillow. Left on her own, she would have collapsed on the floor between the bed and bureau and stayed there indefinitely.

She didn't sleep. Perhaps she was too shaken.

She'd had good sex before. She wished that was what this was, even as she faced the reality that it was nothing that unthreatening. The first time they'd made love—well, they'd probably been edging toward that from his first day here when they'd brushed against each other in the barn. But the second time couldn't be written off as sex or curiosity. She had given a part of herself, a vulnerability, to him. No denying that. And this third time...well, she wouldn't think about that right now.

Instead she raised her head and watched him sleep, studying his face, wondering at herself. And at him.

Even when she knew she was avoiding one issue, Cambria could be honest with herself in another area. Especially in retrospect. She knew her protective skin of wariness, even cyncism, could grate on men's egos. Some turned away, some grew defensive, some got nasty, some waged a campaign of cloying kindness. Boone simply accepted.

She touched her fingers lightly to his chin, craving even more contact than body wrapped around body, and he turned his head toward her in his sleep.

She smiled, ignoring further temptation so that he could sleep.

Acceptance.... Yes, he'd given her that. But not as a burden to bear or a flaw to overlook. He seemed to take her prickly exterior as part of her and almost enjoy it. From the start, he had taken her tart retorts in good humor, often giving as good as he got.

Maybe that's why he'd scared her—because instead of being driven away by her barriers, he'd embraced them wholeheartedly. How could a woman resist that? She couldn't.

She couldn't.

Cambria dropped her head to the pillow, a puff of amazement escaping her lips.

She couldn't resist. She hadn't resisted. She wouldn't resist.

The thought she'd pushed away, deciding not to think about it, had circled around and caught her anyhow.

Oh, dear lord, she was falling in love with Boone Dorsey Smith.

Boone didn't have a moment alone with Cambria all that interminable day.

At least not after they'd made love in the shower before she'd practically shoved him out of her cabin so he wouldn't be spotted by her early rising family.

But he saw her—from the start of the day, when she came into the kitchen where he ate Irene's breakfast offering as if he'd been starved for a month, to several sightings as she and Irene hung curtains and did other chores in the guest cabins that would receive their first occupants this weekend. Then for a couple hours while she and Pete joined him in working on the cabin. Through picnic supper at the ball park before Pete's game that went into extra innings.

Each time he saw her, the same two emotions surfaced—a primitive possessiveness and a grim determination to tell her the whole truth.

When he noticed her move with a certain gingerliness, a pang of remorse brought a quick frown. But when she returned a faint smile and a shake of her head, he was reassured enough that his worry slid away under a surge of something less civilized. Call him a Neanderthal, but that private sign of their lovemaking the night before gave him a kind of smug satisfaction. As long as she wasn't really hurting.

He supposed, he thought during the tenth inning of the baseball game, it was the feeling a man might have seeing the woman he loved pregnant with his child.

He sat up so abruptly that Ted jerked his head around to him.

"Did you see something? You think they're going to try a double steal?" Ted asked anxiously.

Boone looked at the field, where the opposing team mounted a threat, without really seeing it. "No. No. It was...uh, a crick in my back."

More like in his conscience.

He loved Cambria Weston. Damnation.

Loved her. Wanted to marry her. Wanted to have children with her.

Children like the son he'd come here to find. The son who was part of the family she held so dear.

He had to tell her.

He owed her—he owed all of the Westons—honesty.

Boone rubbed the back of his neck.

It would never have been easy. Not when he was an absolute stranger. Not after the Westons had taken him into the family. Not now that he and Cambria had made love.

Angie Lee's death added another twist to the knot.

Ted and Irene and Pete are my family. They are what counts in my life. Nothing else.

Nothing else...

He wanted to count in her life. He wanted it so badly it scared him. Scared him enough to want to delay telling her and risking that she'd push him away. Scared him enough to know that delay would only make it worse.

He wouldn't touch Cambria again until he'd told her the whole truth.

It was stupid to feel shy after the things they'd done last night—and this morning—but that was how Cambria felt as she opened the door and let Boone into her darkened cabin. They'd made no plans, hadn't said anything to each other that wasn't in front of her family and friends. She'd turned off the outside light and everything inside except one soft light in the bedroom . . . in case. In case he should come and in case anybody was looking from the main house.

She'd waited until, finally, feeling stupid to be sitting in the near dark fully clothed, she'd taken off her jeans and shirt. When the soft knock came, she threw on her robe and fought a hammering heart to answer it.

"Cambria, we have to talk."

The taut lines of Boone's face and the abrupt words as soon as he'd entered set anxiety thrumming through her.

She gave him one wary look. "I don't want to talk."

"God, I don't, either," he said grimly. "But we have to."

"Don't start about Angie Lee again, Boone. It's past. There's no changing what she did. There's no changing that she's dead." She stepped to him, slowly running her hands up either side of his shirt placket. She felt his response in the tightening of the muscles under her touch. "I've told you, I don't want—"

He stopped her by clasping both her hands between his. "This has to be said, Cambria."

Her emotional system had taken several heavy jolts in less than twenty-four hours. First the shock of her mother's death and will. Then the leap-from-the-high-dive excitement, thrill and fear of taking Boone Dorsey Smith into her bed, and the even more bone-melting, soul-rattling lovemaking once they got there. Finally the recognition that had dawned on her along with this day that she was falling in love with him.

She felt raw. Certainly not prepared to hear anything like what his grim tone threatened.

Not now. Not yet.

She curled her hands within his grip, the nails drawing lines through the material of his shirt. A fine shudder gripped him. Desire changed his eyes to slate.

"Cambria..."

Stepping in close, she tipped her hips against his. He released her hands and gripped her shoulders. He breathed out through his mouth.

With her hands freed, she began undoing his buttons, revealing his chest. It surprised her to find how much that affected her. She had explored his body through the intimate hours of last night, with touch and taste, but as her fingers reacquainted themselves with the sensations of the webbing of muscles and the wedge-shaped sprinkling of hair, she found this renewed connection pulsing a molten languor through her. She kissed the spot where his throat met his jaw, then pressed her teeth lightly there before touching the tip of her tongue to the spot.

His arms tightened around her.

"Listen..."

No. Whatever it was, she didn't want to hear it. Not now. Not yet. Too much had happened too fast.

"Boone... I want you."

Restraint had beaded sweat on his forehead, the dip between chin and bottom lip.

"I want you, too." He dropped his head back. She couldn't see his expression, but she could feel the tautness in his body. He straightened. "Aren't you sore... too sore?"

"Not too sore."

Her heartbeat sounded in her own ears four times. Before the fifth, the rumble of a muttered oath had barely echoed into being when Boone's mouth crashed down on hers.

She stepped into the whirlwind. No, she leapt into it, met it, fed it, gloried in it. Let it rip her from her moorings and toss her higher than she'd known she could go.

And then she gloried in it as thoroughly when it gentled, slowed, drew out to a breeze that drifted over her as softly as Boone's hand stroking down into the hollow of her back, then up the flare of her hips.

"You have a great fanny."

She smiled into his shoulder. "Please, no detailing of body parts. I just want you to remember the whole is greater than the sum of the parts."

"I love the parts because they're part of the whole."

"Smooth talker."

"Not when it counts."

She caught an undercurrent in his answer that renewed her earlier wariness. With a noncommittal "Mmm," she purposely burrowed deeper into the pillow and promptly fell asleep, like a baby who'd had all its needs met, or like an adult whose emotions and mind had shut down from overload.

They woke with dawn spilling warm air through the light curtains, their bodies already humming with the current of the spooned position they'd assumed in their sleep.

"It's going to be a scorcher today."

Boone ran his hand from her shoulder down her side, to her waist and over her hip before answering.

"It already is."

Cambria gave the driver of the gravel truck a smile that had him blinking at her in masculine appreciation as she signed the receipt for the load he'd just delivered. The road was drivable because she'd had him pour his load out along its length rather than drop it in one heap. But it would take dusty hours with a hand rake to get it to look good.

Instead of starting now, she headed to the cabin where Boone and Pete were preparing the tops of the walls to hold a roof.

She couldn't fool even herself any longer that she worked on the cabin to protect Pete's teenage ego from Boone's demanding ways. Oh, he'd been impatient with Pete at times. But never nasty, and always instructive.

No, she returned to the cabin—with a side trip to the house for a pitcher of lemonade and cups—for her own sake.

"Just in time," Pete yelled as soon as he spotted her. "I was about to go in and get ready for practice. Now I won't die of thirst between here and the house."

"Florence Nightingale with a pitcher!" Boone hailed her from the platform he and Pete stood on while they worked. Both were shirtless. Tan and sweat gilded their shoulders and chests, one broad and muscled, one still filling out from a boy's thinness.

"I think that was Molly Pitcher," she said with a grin.

"I don't care if you're Clara Barton or Richard Burton, just give me some lemonade," her brother demanded.

She filled a plastic cup and handed it up, but her eyes were on Boone. His answering look remembered the past two nights' sultry heat and promised encores that could boil a thermometer.

Boone hunched his shoulder to wipe his sweating forehead, then ran a hand through his hair. "You know, Irene might have something with all this talk about getting a haircut. If this heatwave continues—" he gave Cambria a significant look as he took a filled cup from her "—I'll have to get a crew cut to try to stay cool."

Grinning, she turned to Pete. "See, Mom was right about getting your hair cut."

"Maybe it's a little cooler because it's not on the back of my neck. But if Mom would let me grow my hair, I'd look really—"

"You'd look just like Boone, and no self-respecting mother around here would let you date her daughter."

Boone's smile at her teasing gibe seemed a bit thin, but Pete laughed.

"Yeah, but the girls would all go crazy for me." Pete split a sly glance between his sister and Boone.

"All right, all right. I don't know how my personal life got mixed up in this discussion of Pete's hairstyle, but let's keep to the important stuff." Boone thrust out his cup toward Cambria. "More lemonade."

"Me, too."

Laughing, she filled both cups to the brim, emptying the pitcher.

"Looks like I better get a refill." But she made no move to leave, caught by the sight in front of her. Boy and man, side by side, with the same hip-tilted stance, each turned three-quarter profile toward her.

They raised their cups simultaneously, an unconscious synchronization as they closed their eyes under heavy brows and tilted their heads back to pour the cooling liquid down identically working throats. The sinking sun was behind her, glaring strong into their faces, washing out color and leaving only structure.

Identically working throats. Her own thought circled in her head. *Identically... Look just like Boone... just like Boone...*

She remembered Boone and Pete in front of the campfire Saturday night, and her own certain vision of what Boone had looked like as a boy. It had been so clear because she had seen it...watching Pete grow up.

A hundred clues from a score of days surfaced as if they'd been lying in wait for this precise moment. Her early sense of déjà vu. Boone's intense interest in the family. Her lingering sense of familiarity sidetracked when she'd likened him to Tony. His patience with Pete. Her uneasiness. His evasiveness. All those, and the rest of the hundreds of glimpses and nuances and shadings of voice and one-sided grins and distinctive eyebrows, realigned themselves, forming a pattern, a likelihood. Then clicking firmly into place... and she *knew*.

Oh, God.

For one stark instant of weakness she wished with all that was in her to be transported back just a few minutes, before she knew, before two cornerstones of her life had taken such a devastating blow—the security of her family and her relationship with Boone. And that in itself was too frightening to even consider now—that Boone had so quickly become a cornerstone of her life.

How could he have kept this from her? That agonized demand quickly made room for another. *What did he want?*

She might wish she hadn't seen, but she had. She might feel a turmoil inside of regrets and wishes. But what she had to do was very clear: look out for her family. That was what was important. That was what counted. That was what would get her through this.

She had to think of them. Of Pete and Ted and Irene. Family.

That had been her security from the time she'd first experienced such a concept. Preserving and protecting that family was her instinct—her *need*.

"You better get to practice, Pete," Boone advised in his easy drawl. "And I better get back—"

The pitcher crashed against a cement block left on the ground, shattering in a splash of glass fragments on the hard ground beside her.

"Cambria, are you okay? Did you get cut?"

She heard Boone's questions. They sounded tinny and distant against the roaring in her ears. She gave no response, but he must have satisfied himself with a look that she wasn't cut because he didn't ask again. He moved quickly to just outside the circle of broken glass.

"Cambria, what happened?" Pete demanded.

"I... It slipped."

"Be careful, those shards can go right through your shoes," Boone said. "I'll get a board you can step on. Don't move."

She couldn't bring herself to respond to Boone's caution.

Pete's brow creased as he considered her. "You want me to get something to put the glass in? And maybe some gloves? Or I could—"

"No. No, you go on ahead to practice, Pete." She tried to make it firm, but her voice might have edged toward urgent.

Pete's brow remained creased as he looked from her to where Boone checked the thickness and length of boards on a nearby stack.

"Go on ahead, Pete," Boone said.

Pete did.

And her numbness sank under its own weight in a crest of anger and hurt that had her quaking.

"This isn't quite long enough, but the others are either too thin or too warped." He laid down the board. It stopped two feet short of her. "Here, take my hand and step on this." He came out on the board and extended his hand. "Then we'll—"

"Don't touch me."

His head jerked at her tone. "Cambria? What is it?"

"Back up. Out of my way."

He hesitated, then complied. Steadying herself with her left hand against the building, she stretched her legs to span the area littered with glass to reach the board. She crossed it, then took several steps away from the cabin and Boone before his quiet voice stopped her.

"Are you going to tell me what this is all about?"

She spun around to face him. "Why don't you tell me what it's all about?"

"I don't know what you're talking about." Tension undercut his patience.

"I'm talking about you and why you came here."

She wasn't imagining it. He flinched at that.

She wrapped her arms around her waist, trying to hold in the pain. "I can't believe I didn't see it when it was staring me in the face." She gave a mirthless choke of laughter. "Right in the face. God, I even thought you looked familiar." She went ramrod straight. "I want to hear you say it. Why did you come here?"

"I think you know why."

"Say it. *Say it.*"

"Pete's my son."

Even expecting it, she recoiled from the words.

"God, what a fool I've been," she murmured. "You were lying all along. Even before you came here. Did you get a kick out of that? Did you—"

"That wasn't how it was. Cambria, listen to me—"

"Listen to you? I was a fool to ever listen to you. To ever trust you. But I won't be a fool anymore. I want you out of here. Clear your things out of the cabin, get off Weston land."

He gave no sign of hearing her. "If you won't listen to anything else, listen to this, Cambria. I would never purposely hurt you or any of your family."

"Get out."

"Cambria—"

"I said, get out. And you stay away from Pete."

"I have a right to—"

"You don't have any rights. None. Pete's the one with rights. He had the right to be happy and stable and loved. You can't come waltzing in here after staying away his whole life and try—"

"I didn't know, Cambria." That stopped her for a moment. "I didn't know until three months ago that I even had a son. As soon as I found out, I started looking. This isn't like your mother walking out on you—"

"I didn't say anything about that."

"You didn't have to. It's pretty obvious what you're thinking. And feeling."

"You don't have any damn idea what I'm thinking or feeling. This doesn't have anything to do with me. It has to do with Pete. And what's right for him. And for Mama and Dad. For our *family.* Pete doesn't need you, he doesn't want you. So just get out of our lives. You've done it all for nothing. Coming here, using me, staying—"

"No." The force of that single word stopped her again. They stared at each other through three heavy heartbeats. When he spoke again, he said the words slow and deep, giving each full emphasis. "I never used you. What happened between us was between *us*. Only us."

"I don't believe you." She *couldn't* believe him. "You once accused me of looking at you like an ax murderer, like somebody who'd beat old ladies and steal their last dollar. I wasn't that far off the mark, was I?"

"That's not fair."

"Isn't it? You come in here, prepared to turn a boy's life upside down—why? So you can feel better? So you can feel satisfied you finally did the right thing? Or fill some emptiness in yourself? That's about as low as it gets, Boone, using a kid to make yourself feel better."

Under the tan, his skin had turned gray. Lines dug deep grooves into the skin at the corners of his eyes and his mouth.

"I'll leave the ranch, but I'm not leaving Bardville. I'm going to stay nearby. I'll still be around. I'll be right on your doorstep. So what will you tell everyone? Ted and Irene? Pete? You'll have to tell them the truth."

Before she could stop it, a vision of her telling her brother sliced into her. Her second thought brought nearly as much pain. What would this do to Irene and Ted?

She had to protect them. Her pain was like a blow to the soul, nearly doubling her over. But she had brought it on herself—she had allowed herself to trust without cause, she had allowed herself to love without complete trust. But her family... they were the innocent victims in this. And she would not let them suffer.

"You'll have to tell them the truth," Boone repeated.

"There's another kind of truth. I'll tell them we've fought, and you're leaving because of that."

"A lovers' quarrel?"

"Yes." She bit it off.

"I do love you, Cambria."

She hadn't known he could be so cruel. "Get out. Within the hour. Before Pete comes home."

She didn't look at him as she started to leave.

"Cambria."

She stopped, but didn't turn around. Angry and hurt as she was, she didn't want to see his pain anymore. His familiar voice came from behind her, the sort of words that could haunt a lifetime. "Lovers' quarrels are rarely the end of the story."

Chapter Ten

Bardville boasted no motels. Boone got a room in a place this side of Sheridan with no pool, no cable and no room service. The vintage fifties strip of identical rooms did offer a bed, shower, desk, chair, phone and electrical outlet. That was all he needed to get back to work.

He threw his bags on the bed and set up and turned on his computer and fax in the first fifteen minutes after renting the room. He sat at the desk and pulled the phone toward him. But he pressed no buttons. He didn't know how long he sat like that, leaning his arms on the desk with the phone between them as if he were a dog with a bone. The blank-faced machinery around him hummed with energy but no purpose.

All he could see was Cambria, hazel eyes wide with shock, face pale, arms wrapped around her middle as if she were cold . . . or sick to her stomach.

He'd done that to her.

Finally, a pair of headlights sweeping through the window broke his trance. It was nearly midnight.

Not bothering to change out of his clothes, he pushed his bags to one side and dropped onto the mattress, staring at the ceiling. Not thinking and not feeling. Just staring.

He must have slept, because the sunlight woke him—that and the insistent reminder from his stomach that he hadn't eaten for nearly twenty-four hours. Like the computer and fax machine, his body consumed energy and demanded a source for more, even if his mind wasn't working.

Absently he supplied it at the tiny cement-block café across the highway.

He returned to his room, intending—if that wasn't too strong a term for his state of automatic movements—to slip behind the mask of work to make sure he continued to not think or feel.

Instead he sat at the desk, doodling aimlessly on the backs of envelopes until a knock jerked the pencil across the paper in a harsh, startled line.

Probably the maid.

He flicked aside the curtain on his way to the door, then fumbled with the lock with suddenly clumsy fingers. The knob slipped from his hand so the door flung open with unnecessary force.

Irene Weston didn't seem to notice, smiling warmly as she walked in.

"Afternoon, Boone. How're you?"

"Irene? What are you doing here?"

"You have five nights left you've already paid for. I'm here to tell you to come back."

"It's not that simple." He dragged one hand through his hair. He felt as if he'd been saying that a lot lately. "Cambria—"

"Cambria runs the bed-and-breakfast business, but she's not the only member of this family with a say-so," Irene pronounced calmly. "May I sit down?"

"Of course." He pulled the desk chair around for her, and perched on the edge of the bed.

"Ah, I see you've been working."

Irene wasn't looking at the computer and fax. She'd picked up the envelope with his doodles and studied it. When she laid it down, a corner of his mind noted with some astonishment that the aimless lines had taken the forms of buildings. A different version of the new cabin, a stylized barn, a rough sketch of a house of stone and log and glass.

But most of his consciousness addressed a very different matter. He tried desperately to figure out what this visit meant. Had Cambria told Irene he was Pete's biological father?

"Did she... did Cambria tell you where I was going? Does she know you're here, asking me to come back?"

"No. No need to tell her, and no need to ask her for information. I have my sources in this county." A hint of humor edged into Irene's face. "And a few other counties, besides."

He tried to make sense of it, but he felt as if his brain had filled with dust and tumbleweed. "Somebody told you where I was?"

"I asked around," she amended placidly. "I thought, considering how Cambria doesn't always think through everything she says, that you could likely do with someone to talk to."

"But I could have gone back to North Carolina—"

She gave him a chiding look, though her voice remained gentle. "I don't think so. I don't know you near as well as I know Cambria, but you didn't seem to me to be one to turn tail so easily. Especially not when it's something important to you. And Cambria is important to you, isn't she?''

It was barely a question, and Boone's head was spinning with trying to figure out how much Irene knew and what she guessed. But his answer came automatically. ''Yes, she is.''

''I'm glad.'' Irene smiled at him, and for the first time in twenty-four hours a bit of hope curled loose inside Boone. ''Love isn't easy, especially not with someone as careful of her fences as Cambria. But behind the barbed wire, she has a heart that's made for joy.''

She leaned over and patted his knee. ''Ted gave me a plaque once with a saying about the best kind of love being one that gives the person you love—a spouse, a child—'' Did he imagine that her expression tightened slightly on that word? ''—a friend, even a parent—both wings and roots. The roots for security and the wings for freedom.

''I like that, but I like even better what my mama used to tell me, about a good marriage being like a trapeze act. Sometimes one partner is the catcher and the other's the leaper, then sometimes roles swap. For it to work, each partner has to be willing at times to let go of the bar and take that leap of faith toward the other. And at all times both have to realize that it takes both of them working together—neither can leap the abyss alone.''

He didn't need it spelled out that she meant Cambria and him—especially her wariness about trusting someone else and his stubbornness in trying to take charge of things by himself.

''I don't know if—''

''I know.'' Irene patted his knee again. ''The first step is to come back. Come back, Boone.''

''Cambria won't be happy if I go back.''

''She's not happy now. I've never seen her less happy. Come back, Boone. This isn't the way to solve things.

There's only so long a soul can pretend a situation doesn't exist."

"But—"

"Come back, Boone. Nothing's ever solved by hiding from the truth."

He studied her—the kind, soft eyes, the fading ginger hair, the arms made to deliver solid hugs. He couldn't have said what made him so sure, but he was. Irene Weston knew why Cambria had told him to leave. She knew who he was.

"Are you sure, Irene?"

She looked a little pale, but she answered without hesitation. "I'm sure. We both are, Ted and I."

"Before the first guests come tomorrow, Irene, we'll need to—"

With a hand pressing at the small of her aching back, Cambria stopped—talking, breathing, moving, even thinking—as if a master control had been switched off. And the one pressing the button was Boone Dorsey Smith, who sat at the kitchen table with Ted and Irene, where she'd never expected to see him again.

She'd survived the past twenty-four hours by refusing to think or feel. All yesterday afternoon she'd smoothed the gravel in the drive, working at a pace that left her drained and sore. It hadn't been enough to make her sleep. After curtly telling her family that Boone had been recalled to North Carolina on business and letting them infer that things had gone wrong between the two of them, she'd skipped dinner and sat on the bench behind her cabin most of the night, staring at the darkness, seeing nothing ahead of her.

This morning she'd eaten like an automaton, refusing to meet Irene's worried looks. When Ted had asked if she'd help him seed a barley field, she'd turned him down flat; it was an excuse to get her aside to talk to her, and she couldn't take that right now. Pete had revived enough from his funk at Boone's departure to laugh a little and say it was a good thing, since Cambria didn't look in any shape to operate heavy machinery.

Instead she'd launched a back-straining marathon of bed-making. She'd made every bed in the bunkhouse and in every cabin. Including the one in the westernmost cabin, where the sheets still carried the faint scent of the man she'd been falling in love with.

That man now sat before her, looking her full in the face. Why couldn't he be back in North Carolina, with a thousand miles between them, instead of sitting here, waiting for her to rip into him again? He'd had his chance. The damned idiot had walked back in front of the firing squad and wouldn't even use a blindfold.

"What are you doing here? I told you—"

"I asked him to come back, Cambria," announced Irene.

"Mama, don't interfere in this. He has to leave. Right away."

"Now, Cambria—"

"I mean it—"

"I know you do, dear. But I think you're wrong."

"And I agree with her." Without any other motion, Cambria slowly turned her head toward Ted as he spoke. "He's our guest. No matter what problems there are between the two of you, he's our guest—Irene's and mine."

"There are reasons . . . other reasons."

"We know."

She shook her head at Irene's calm certainty. "You can't know. It's not just between him and me. It's . . . it's other things."

"It's that he's Pete's birth father."

In that first instant Cambria was too stunned to do anything more than meet Boone's eyes. If she'd had a chance to consider how to hone her look, it might have been a glare of accusation. But a glance would have convinced even the most skeptical that he was as puzzled as she was.

Cambria swung around to Ted. He looked no more surprised than Irene had sounded.

"I don't understand."

Irene reached for Cambria's hand, hanging limply by her side. She gave it a squeeze, then tugged on it slightly, nodding for Cambria to sit in the empty chair beside her.

"We know, dear. We were just going to have a little talk with Boone here. I think you should join us."

Cambria sat. Because Irene wanted that, because her legs didn't seem terribly reliable at the moment, or because it was the only logical thing to do, she didn't bother to sort out.

"We wondered those first couple days after Boone arrived, but it didn't take too long before we were certain," Ted said with the same intonation he used to talk about the weather. Not uninterested—no rancher or farmer could ever be uninterested in the weather—but with an acceptance that he couldn't change it. He could only prepare for it, enjoy its best and stand up to its worst.

"How..."

"Irene mentioned it first." Ted nodded to his wife for her to explain.

"I saw a resemblance. I wondered... then I went back through old pictures of Pete. When I looked for it, I could see a... a *look* about the two of them. Plus, I knew Pete's biological mother came from North Carolina. They told us that, and that she and the father were both eighteen and in good health. That's all we knew."

"But after Boone came, we did some research on him," Ted continued. "And that pretty much confirmed it in our minds."

"But you never said anything."

"You mean to you, Cambria?" Ted shook his head. "No. It seemed like the two of you should work out what you wanted to be telling each other, and what secrets you weren't telling each other."

Boone's eyes flicked to her, and she knew he'd recognized that her father's words pertained to her as well as him.

"Pete..."

Ted shook his head. "No, we never said anything to him. If Boone didn't want to tell him, there was no point. And if he did... well, that would wait until we got to that bridge."

"How could you be so nice to him, then? How could you take him in and treat him like part of our family when you knew who he was and what he wanted?"

Irene's calm never wavered. She even smiled a little. "How could we not be nice to him when we knew that he'd helped give life to part of our family? As to knowing what he wants—" She looked at Boone, sitting across the table from her. "I don't believe that even *he* knows what he wants."

Boone, clearly stunned, had sat motionless while they'd talked about him as if he weren't there, but now he roused himself and looked from Irene to Ted, then back to Irene, sparing only the merest glance at Cambria.

"I don't want to take him away from you. I swear that. Maybe before I came here I thought... But once I saw him... I wouldn't take him away from you, not any of you."

"You couldn't." Irene's pronouncement almost sounded as if it held a note of sympathy for Boone under its certainty.

Cambria shook her head, hard—none of that misguided sympathy Irene sprinkled around like fairy dust would stick to her. She would keep clear sight of what was really going on here. "This is insane. He has no claim on

Pete. Donating a few sperm isn't what makes a father." She rounded on Ted. "You tell them. You're the only one here who knows about really being a father."

"And you're the one who taught me." He put a weathered, gnarled hand atop hers, calming, slowing her as he had for as long as she could remember. "The day I married Angie Lee, you marched up to me and you looked me right in the eyes and said, 'Who are you?' And I said, 'I'm your daddy.'" Cambria's eyes filled so quickly she couldn't stop one tear from spilling down. "It wasn't blood or birth that made that so. What made it so was you and me, in our hearts."

"Then tell them, tell him—"

"It's not you and me this time, Cammy. It's them. Pete and Boone. They're the only ones who can decide who Boone'll be in Pete's life."

She was shaking her head before Ted finished. "No. No. He has to leave, Dad. He can't just show up here sixteen years later and start making demands."

"I'm not making any demands."

Cambria swung on him. "You want Pete!"

"I'm his father. I want to help him. I *can* help him. I can't change not being around the first sixteen years, but I can offer Pete things—money for college for one thing."

Cambria knew Irene and Ted exchanged a look, but she couldn't interpret it. It might have been that it was coded in the closed communication of long-married couples, or it might have been that she was too strongly focused on Boone to divert her full attention.

"Isn't that just like you, Boone Dorsey Smith." From her first word his eyes narrowed and darkened, sensing the coming attack. But she didn't relent. "You walk in here and start trying to take charge, to order everyone's life around. As usual. You're going to move right in and do the things for *your son* that you think need to be done. You've decided he should go to college, so that's it. Off he goes.

On your schedule, of course. Is that the way you treated our sister, too? No wonder she doesn't want to see you anymore."

Boone flinched, but before anyone else could react, the screen door flew open and Pete came barreling in.

"What's— Hey, Boone, you're back! That's great! That's..." Pete's headlong pace slowed, then stopped several feet short of Boone. His outstretched hand dropped to his side. "What's going on?"

At first the only answer was silence that must have shouted at him that the discussion had involved him. Then, as always, Irene stepped in. "Boone would like to talk to you, Pete. Maybe the two of you can go for a walk, down by the creek."

The boy gripped the back of the empty chair in front of him, his knuckles straining white. His face matched their paleness except for a streak of dark color on each cheek. It made his eyebrows stand out darkly, emphasizing his resemblance to Boone. "No."

"Pete," said Ted quietly. "There are some things the man needs to say to you."

"Okay, he can say them. But say them here, in front of everybody. There's nothing I want to hear that you all can't hear." He looked around a little desperately. "You're my family."

Cambria reached out to clasp Pete's hand, even as Ted nodded reassurance and Irene said, "Of course we're your family," the same way she would have said the sun would rise.

With that backing, Pete faced Boone, chin raised, and demanded, "So say what you've got to say."

Even feeling the fine tremor of Pete's hand under hers, Cambria felt her heart constrict at the strain in Boone's face, and the pain and fear she caught flickering in the gray depths of his eyes, so similar to the ones that challenged him now.

The voice that had made her laugh, that had persuaded her to trust, that had whispered passion to her, that had gasped her name and that had spoken of loving her, cracked slightly, but got the words out.

"I'm your father, Pete."

Chapter Eleven

"You're not my father. I have a father. He's the only father I'll ever want."

Feelings rushed over Cambria like a dam-break flood. Colliding, fighting each other, sinking and rising. *Relief.* That Irene was right; Boone couldn't take Pete from them. *Pleasure.* That Ted had those fiercely honest words to remember if he ever wondered what he meant to his son. *Pride.* That a young brother, who could so easily have been swayed by the romantic vision of a long-lost father, instead valued steady, calm love so wisely. *Pain.* That Boone's sure hope had been rejected. *Regret.* That Boone could not have been simply a guest she'd fallen in love with.

"I know you have a father, Pete." Boone tried to make eye contact; Pete focused somewhere over his left shoulder. "I know you love him very much, the same way you love all your family. I guess I should have said I'm your biological father. I just—"

"So you've been lying to us all this time. Pretending you wanted to be my friend. Liking baseball and all that. That was all lying." Pete's mouth twisted as if with a bitter taste.

"No. When I came here I wasn't sure how to go about all this. I'd just found out..." He took a quick, heavy breath. "Let me tell you from the start, Pete. There was a girl I dated in high school, right before I left for the army. I didn't know she was pregnant when I left, and I never knew she'd had a baby—our baby...you. I didn't know until a few months ago, when an old friend let something slip about his cousin—my girlfriend. When I went to talk to Marl—"

"Don't tell me!" Pete backed away. Cambria held her breath, afraid that he might bolt. But he didn't. "I don't want to know her name. Don't tell me her name. Don't tell me any more." He looked from Irene to Ted. "You said it was up to me if I wanted to go looking for my birth parents, right? All along you've said that. So it should be up to me if I don't want to know, either, shouldn't it? Shouldn't that be my choice? Well, I don't want to know. I don't want any parents other than the ones I've got. I don't want any other family."

Boone leaned forward. "Pete, I wouldn't ever... I know I couldn't take Ted's place in your life. I don't want to. I swear that. But part of me helped make you, and there are things I can do for you—"

"Leave me alone. You can do that for me."

Boone winced, but he didn't look away from Pete. "There are ways I can help you. I owe you that. Doors I can open. I can help you pay for college, or—"

"No!" Pete's face went red and mottled under his tan. Even clenched into fists, his hands betrayed a tremor. "No, you can't. We don't want your charity."

"You're my son. It's not—"

"That's for families to do. I'm Peter Andrew Weston—that's who I am. I have a family and you're not part of it. You came in here and pretended to be our friend, pretended to like us just for us, but you were lying. A fake and a liar—that's all you are. We're a family—a *family*—and we don't need anybody like you around. Go away and leave us alone. Just leave us the hell alone."

Pete spun around and slammed out the door. It crashed against the outside of the building on the backswing, swung closed so hard it gave another *whack* against the frame, then connected again and again, each thud less violent as it slowly reverberated to a rest.

Irene broke the frozen tableau. She gave a great sigh, then reached across the table and took Boone's hand in hers. She held his hand for several moments, while his eyes slowly closed.

When she released Boone's hand and stood, Ted rose with her. While she headed down the hall to their bedroom, Ted hesitated. With a jerky motion, he put a hand on Boone's shoulder and squeezed. Boone's facial muscles tightened and he gave a slight nod of acknowledgment.

Then Ted followed Irene, and only Cambria and Boone were left.

She didn't know what to say. She didn't even know what to feel. The undammed emotions still swept through her, twisting themselves together, pitting themselves against one another. So opposite and so strong.

Boone's eyes opened slowly. He pushed back his chair, then levered himself up with his palms on the table. Even walking slowly, he'd nearly passed her chair when she finally pushed out some words—paltry, inadequate, but at least something.

"I'm sorry, Boone."

He stopped next to her, still looking straight ahead. "No need. You warned me. You called this one right, didn't you? Totally right."

As he continued out, she could only repeat, "I'm sorry."

"Yeah, me, too."

At midnight Cambria took a last glance at the light in Boone's cabin that had gone on twenty minutes before, turned off her lamp and went to bed.

At one, the light in the westernmost cabin still burned, and she gave up the notion of sleep.

Pete had gone to practice as usual, then called and said he'd eat dinner with a teammate's family. When he returned home, he retreated immediately to his room, mumbling something about a lot of studying.

No one had seen anything of Boone. He hadn't come to dinner, and Cambria, Ted and Irene ate a nearly silent meal. Maybe too much had been said too fast, and they needed time to assimilate it. When they gathered in the den before a television set none of them heeded, Cambria supposed an instinct for human contact drew them together.

Boone had had none of that contact. The man who'd been raised to believe he had to do things for people to earn their love sat alone in his cabin, having been told he could do nothing.

It surprised Cambria to realize that though she wasn't finished with her anger at Boone, it didn't stop her other feelings for him. The only one she allowed herself to acknowledge as she crossed the darkness between their cabins, however, was concern.

She considered knocking, but instead pushed open the door and called his name softly.

There was no answer, though she heard movement from the bedroom.

She went to that open doorway and found Boone transferring a folded shirt from a drawer to a suitcase opened across the arms of a big chair.

He glanced up, unsurprised.

His elevated brows asked why she had come. She didn't choose to answer. She wasn't sure she could, anyhow.

He exhaled through his nose, accepting her presence. A jerk of his head toward the bed indicated she might as well sit... if she was going to stay.

She sat.

"I shouldn't have bothered to unpack this afternoon when Irene brought me back," he said, resuming his chore. "Would have saved a lot of time."

He hadn't been packing in the eight hours between the time he'd left the kitchen and his light had gone on. If Cambria had to guess, she'd say he'd sat somewhere without noticing that bright sunlight turned to twilight, then faded to night, while the grooves around his mouth sank deeper and the lines at the corners of his eyes, which had gradually disappeared since his arrival three and a half weeks ago, returned.

She didn't mention any of that. She hooked her heels over the bed-frame rail, cupped her hands around her bent knees, and went directly to the point.

"I'm sorry, Boone. I said some harsh things. About your sister, I—"

"It was harsh, but it was true." He didn't look at her, continuing to pack with steady, automatic motions.

"Maybe it was. But it wasn't fair to throw in your face the mistakes you'd made in the past when you're trying so hard to change."

"Close only counts in horseshoes, and I don't know if trying counts in anything."

"Boone..." What could she say to make this easier for him? What did she want to say? He was hurting, but he'd also inflicted hurt. She took a deep breath and said what came to mind. "You don't have to leave."

"Staying's not going to help anything. Or anybody. Even Irene and Ted, generous as they are, can't feel real comfortable having me around after this. I don't want that. And you..."

He flicked a look at her that she didn't meet. He went on. "Pete probably wants me around even less than you." His expression grew distant. "You know, with all the things I should have been feeling, I found myself looking at Pete this afternoon and seeing that cut-through-steel directness, and I couldn't stop trying to sort out if it reminded me more of Kenzie, Irene, or you." He blinked, and his eyes focused once more. "It doesn't really matter, does it? I don't see him coming around to thinking better of me anytime soon, do you?"

"He can be stubborn," she admitted.

Boone's mouth twisted. "Well, at least there you'll agree he takes after me."

"He's nicer than you are, because he hasn't had as many hard knocks."

His expression eased, almost achieving a smile. "Subtle as always, huh, Cambria? But you're right, he is nicer. I'm glad. And grateful he hasn't had hard knocks." He grimaced. "Except the knock I just gave him."

"Why didn't you tell us you were Pete's biological father? Why didn't you tell me?"

"I wanted to. Almost from first seeing you." He added the black shirt he'd worn the day he'd kissed her by the flower box to the growing pile in the suitcase. "I had this strange urge to ask you how I should handle it. Because you seemed to see right into me, to see the gap between what I've done and what I want to do—with the company, with people.... Cully says I need a kick in the head to shake up some of my notions. You sure did that for me."

"Then why didn't you tell me?"

Boone said simply, "It didn't affect only me. It was Pete, too. And I didn't feel free to tell anyone before I told him. That's what I'd planned—to tell Pete first, then the two of us would figure how to go from there. But I fell for you and that got all tangled up with everything else. I knew I should tell you before we made love—" He gave a self-mocking parody of his grin. "But I wasn't thinking about being fair or open with you, I was thinking about what you did to me. I tried to tell you, the night before last, but... I didn't try hard enough. When you confronted me yesterday, I couldn't lie to you and—" He shrugged. "And everything came apart."

Cambria was taken aback. She'd used very similar words not so long ago in explaining to Jessa that she hadn't told Boone about Jessa's situation because it wasn't her secret to share. It bled away more of her anger, weakening her guard on her other emotions.

"I love you, Boone."

Heat immediately burned at her cheeks. Not at what she'd told him, but at how she'd done it. She'd made it sound like a confession, a dark secret, unwillingly admitted, tinged with anger.

And she'd said it to his back. The bureau mirror showed his face, but with his head down to look into the open drawer, shadows and his lowered eyelids masked any hint of his emotions. Only his stillness betrayed he'd heard her.

Then he took another shirt from the drawer, the final one, apparently, because he slid the drawer shut with his hip before placing the shirt in the suitcase.

"I love you, too, Cambria." Though matter-of-fact, his voice sounded husky, its usual smooth edges roughened, almost raw. "I told you that."

"I know, but..." His calm forced an urgency on her. "Will you stop that damn packing, Boone Dorsey Smith?" His hand dropped short of the drawer handle he'd reached for. In the mirror, she saw his eyes squeeze shut. When she spoke again, her voice softened. "Please, Boone. Please come sit with me."

He hesitated, then he did as she asked. They didn't look at each other, but she felt immeasurably comforted when he took her left hand from her knee and clasped it in his.

"Okay, Cambria. I'm sitting. What else have you got to say?"

She blew out one breath, then pulled in another. His hands tightened around hers as she spoke.

"You are not responsible for Pete. Yes, your genes are in him. But the people responsible for raising him, for making sure he brushed his teeth and played nice with his friends, are his mom and dad. And the person who's responsible for who he's going to be from now on is him. You wouldn't be doing him any favors by trying to take over that responsibility from him, even if he'd let you, which he wouldn't."

With her free hand she pushed her hair behind her ear. She risked a glance at his face. He appeared to stare at the juncture of the floor and wall.

"All you can do for Pete now, Boone, is to love him. If he'll let you."

He slowly turned to face her. She drew in another deep breath. She might as well get all the poison out at once. It would either cure them or kill them.

"That's all you can do for me, too, Boone. You can't change my past. You can't change my feelings about Angie Lee. You can't heal all the hurts. I'm responsible for dealing with those—or not dealing with them. All you can do is love me. You know how Irene talks about life's storms? Well, I want someone to stand beside me during those, not to stand in front of me."

Silence weighted the seconds, dragging them longer.

"I don't know if I can."

It hurt her, no denying that. But what brought even more pain was the look of battered hurt in Boone's eyes. A lifetime of doing things one way warred with this new notion.

"I've tried, Cambria. God, I've tried. But nobody knows better than you about my failures. Between you and Kenzie and Cully, well, I see what you're getting at, but I don't know... When you told me about your mother walking out, and then she died, the first thing I did was try to take over. And with Pete... I messed that up just about every way there is."

She touched his cheek. His eyelids dropped and he turned into the touch. Then they were reaching for each other, mouths meeting in a hunger for closeness and forgiveness, taking greedily, giving generously.

So generously that the desperation eased. Without releasing his hold on her completely, Boone threw the pillows to the headboard and shifted around to prop his back against them, drawing Cambria with him, within the crook of his arm, while she wrapped her arms around his waist, their outstretched legs tangled together.

He stroked her hair.

"I do love you, Cambria. I want you to know that. Really know it." He kissed her temple, softening the words to come. "But that isn't really where you have doubts, is it?"

"No." It came out a whisper.

He rolled his head to look at her. "You need me to stand beside you instead of in front of you? Well, I need things, too. I need you to trust me. Not accepting everything I ever do, but trusting me on a basic level, including my secrets.

Every human being has secrets. That doesn't mean they're evil. Every human being makes slips. Can you accept the secrets and forgive the slips? Can you trust me like that?"

He gave her no chance to answer. Smiling rather sadly, he kissed the bridge of her nose. "Do you think we can learn all those things?"

"I don't know." Her tightened throat allowed only a whisper.

Boone's arm brought her to him. As he lowered his mouth to hers, he said, "Neither do I."

From the doorway, Boone looked back at Cambria, asleep. In his bed. In the disorder of sheets, pillows and blankets they had created together, making love as if their physical passion and the bonds it expressed would prove that what they had between them could surmount what they didn't have.

He wanted to remember her like this.

He had to leave. That's what he'd told her in the letter propped on the bureau. A second letter was addressed to Pete.

He'd written them in an unthinking stream when he'd risen from the bed, as soon as he'd been certain Cambria had fallen deeply asleep. He hadn't read over what he'd written, but had sealed each letter as soon as he'd finished, and put them on the bureau for Cambria to find.

Then he'd finished packing and loaded the rental car. The suitcases and clothes and computer and fax seemed such paltry belongings. What he left behind was so much more precious.

But he couldn't stay, and he didn't deserve to take the love and affection he'd been given.

He'd come here to find a son who didn't want him as a father. He'd tried to reconcile himself to that, to reorder his thinking, to adjust his heart. He hadn't succeeded.

Unless he did, he couldn't be around the Westons without causing all concerned pain. He wouldn't do that to them even if their generosity allowed it.

So where did that leave him and Cambria?

Together, maybe they could work on the changes they'd talked about a few hours ago. If he asked, Cambria might go with him, separate from her family. But how could he ask that? She needed them and they needed her. He wouldn't ask her to make that sacrifice.

Mostly because he loved her. But a small, selfish part of him also knew that if he asked her to come with him and she said no, his heart might not survive.

He didn't kiss her goodbye. Not because he feared she would wake, but because he feared he wouldn't go if he touched her again.

There shouldn't have been any time. Not a moment to think or remember or hurt.

The cabins were filled nearly every night. Ranch work demanded as much effort as ever. Irene took on the organizing of a benefit bake sale to send the high school band to Denver to perform at halftime of a Broncos game in the fall. And Pete, besides helping both her and Ted, divided his time between baseball and Lauren.

But Cambria thought and remembered and hurt. And she suspected that Pete, though steadfastly refusing to read the letter Boone left, or to acknowledge any interest in Boone Dorsey Smith, did the same. She saw shadows in the clear eyes under the dark eyebrows so much like those of the man who had helped conceive him, then had become his friend.

She became more convinced of that the noontime she walked into the kitchen to find Irene and Ted staring across the table at Pete with surprised concern.

"You're not going?" Ted asked, obviously trying to clarify something he'd just heard.

"Nah. It's dumb."

"But Coach Lambert's going to rent a big-screen TV to show you all a movie, then have a stereo set up so you can dance. All your friends will be there with their dates."

"I see those people all the time. It's boring."

Cambria knew they were talking about a big team party the baseball coach was throwing. Pete had talked about it all season. Now he didn't want to go.

"But, Pete—"

"I said I didn't want to go. What's the big deal?"

He pushed back from the table and left before Cambria could draw a breath.

Irene's gaze went from the door that had closed behind her son to the plate with food still on it, and her eyes filled. Ted put a hand on her shoulder.

"I know," Irene said with a slightly wavering smile. "Everything will be all right. I know."

"That's right. Pete'll be just fine." Ted's voice was the rock of calm and love that had been Cambria's anchor. "He's got a good head on his shoulders, and a strong heart. Give him some time."

Pete did have a good head and a strong heart. But Cambria doubted this would all smooth away with time.

"I still don't understand why you needed me to come along," Pete grumbled an hour later from the passenger seat as the truck bounced slowly over the dirt track to timbered acreage up the mountain.

"Because you have a strong back for hefting logs into the truck once I chain-saw the fallen trees to firewood size," Cambria said.

"Why are we getting firewood now, anyway? It's the middle of summer."

"Better to do it now than when it's freezing. Besides, it gives the wood time to cure."

"Did you have to pick the hottest day of the summer?"

Before she could burst the bubble of his exaggeration, Pete flipped on the radio, set to Bardville's only station.

"So come out and support our boys Saturday at their game at Tippett Field. But before that, Coach Lambert is giving his players a chance to let loose—not too loose, boys!—at a party Wednesday night. There'll be a cookout to start and a dance to finish, with a showing of a movie sure to inspire a baseball team—*Field of Dreams*—on a special, wide-screen TV donated for the occasion by—"

Cambria turned off the radio. Pete sat frozen, hands on his knees, staring straight ahead through the windshield.

She gave Pete another quarter of a mile to see if he would say what needed saying on his own. He didn't.

"You need to decide, Pete."

"I decided. I don't want to see some stupid movie about a guy playing catch with his dead father, trying to change what happened. I've got my father, I've got my family—"

"No, I don't mean that. I mean, you have to decide if you can give Boone anything, any part of you."

Silence.

"You liked him, Pete." When something flickered in his face, she purposely changed tenses. "You like him and you care about him."

Pete's hands slid off his knees to dangle between them as he slumped forward.

"I liked him," he said so softly the engine almost swallowed the sound.

"Are you going to be happy having him out of your life forever?"

"How about you?"

She shook her head. "That's different. And more complicated."

"Because of me?"

Her little brother was growing up. He deserved honesty. "Partly. But there are other issues."

He nodded, looking impossibly wise for sixteen years old. "But you know what Mom says. 'Food feeds the belly, love feeds the soul and the heart.'"

"Yeah. I know."

"But you want me to butt out?"

"You can't help, Pete."

"And you can?"

"Not much," she conceded. "But I can tell you a few things. First, I'll quote Mama right back—'Do what you'll feel good about thirty years from now.'" Their eyes met, and beneath the seriousness, they shared a wry affection for Irene's sayings and their wisdom. "Second, I'll tell you, now that Angie Lee is dead, I'll have to live with regret that I didn't at least consider her request to see me ten years ago."

"I didn't know—"

"Nobody knew. Not even Irene and Ted."

She knew Pete's eyes were on her, but she kept hers on the blessedly straight road. As long as she kept the tires in the ruts, the truck could almost drive itself.

Pete drew in a breath as if to say something. She hurried on.

"Maybe, after thinking about it, I still would have said no, but I didn't bother to think. I let the old pain take control and I jumped on the opportunity to give back Angie Lee a little of her own by rejecting her." Confession might be good for the soul, but it was hell on the nerves. "What you have to decide, Pete, is if you're reacting to Boone out of fear, and if you might someday regret slamming the door on him."

When his words finally came, they were halting, confused.

"I guess . . . I don't know, Cambria. I guess the thing is I don't want anything to . . . you know . . . mess things up."

She stopped the truck and turned off the engine.

"Pete, there is nothing—nothing in this world and probably beyond—that could make us stop being a family. More than the sun rising, more than the sun setting, you can count on that."

Her brother shot a look at her from under his brows, color rising on his neck, but a smile lurking at the corners of his mouth. "Yeah, I know. . . . It's just, sometimes . . ."

She saw the sheen in Pete's eyes, and aimed at strengthening his smile. "And, I hate to break it to you, brother of mine, but no matter what Mama says, you will not be allowed to let your hair grow or skip church as long as she's around. She won't even have to say much. She has her ways. Believe me." He did smile, their eyes meeting in amused understanding. "She won't ever quit being your mama. And dad won't ever quit being your daddy."

"I do know that. I really do. But . . . Well, you know."

"Yes, I do know. I truly do, Pete. With a patchwork family like ours, sometimes you worry if the seams might come apart. But you know that antique quilt Jessa has on the wall behind the register?" He nodded. "She's had it as long as I've known her. One day in our apartment in D.C. something . . . well, something came up. I found myself staring at that quilt, and I realized that where it showed wear wasn't in the seams, but in the fabric. The fabric might split, but those seams held, Pete."

Pete stroked the initials on his baseball hat—P.A.W. for *Peter Andrew Weston*—and one side of his mouth lifted in a half grin that twisted at her heart. "Pretty stupid thing to worry about, huh?"

"No, not stupid. Entirely natural." She drew a quick breath. As long as they were being open . . . "Just as it would be natural for you to have wondered about your birth parents, Pete. To wonder what traits you inherited from them. Haven't you ever wondered where you got your long legs or your coloring or—"

"Or my big feet?" He shot a quick grin at her that triggered a simultaneous urge to grin back and to cry.

"Or your eyebrows, say."

Pete shook his head and, although those distinctive features had drawn down in concentration, his mood clearly had lifted. "No, I don't think I have wondered about it much." His frown cleared and a grin lurked. "It's like Mama always says, 'It's not what you're given, it's what—'"

"'You make of it,'" she completed in unison with him.

His smile faded almost immediately. "But what could I tell Boone? I mean, I don't want him to misunderstand or—"

"So you tell him the truth, as straight as you can. About what you want and how you feel."

"But with him gone, I don't know..."

"You might start by reading Boone's letter. I just happen to have it with me."

Giving Pete privacy to read his letter, Cambria got out of the truck and walked several yards down the road to where a bank of earth offered a seat, with the dirt at her feet, the sweep of blue sky over her head and, around her, the drying green of native grasses.

She saw none of it.

She saw the remembered words on a single piece of paper that sat in the top drawer of her bureau. Words written in a strong, upright hand in black ink on stark white paper.

I haven't told you why I love you, Cambria. I love your fierce loyalty, your blunt honesty, your straightforward approach to life and people, your tough-

mindedness—and your heart, which you try to keep hidden behind all that. Do you know how often you fail at that? Every time you smile. Every time you look at your family or your friends or your land, especially those mountains. And when I hold you in my arms, I thank God for letting me see that.

Boone Dorsey Smith had seen beneath her prickly surface, to what she was, what she could be. As he had with the old cabin. She smiled faintly to herself at the metaphor. But the more she considered it, the more true it held. He'd seen potential in the cabin, given of himself to bring that potential out, and he'd left it a better, stronger and more appealing structure.

Not a bad accomplishment for anyone.

Even when he tried to step between the people he loved and their problems, instead of standing beside them, it was because he had so much love to give.

Boone had been honest with her about secrets that were solely his. For that matter, he had been considerably more open about his childhood than she had. He'd also been more honest about his attraction to her, while she'd told herself she felt nothing.

But even lying to herself, she'd reached out for his touch.

Because she *did* trust him the way he'd talked about—at a basic, fundamental level. She raised her head, staring unseeingly at a clump of silver gray sagebrush. She trusted Boone with her secrets, with her *heart*.

Can you accept the secrets and forgive the slips?

"I think I can, Boone," she whispered to the air. "I think I can."

"Cam! Hey, Cam!"

Pete's shout brought her to her feet though she still felt slightly dazed by her own thoughts. She started toward him. He grinned, yet he somehow looked older, more mature. She searched his face, looking for similarities. She saw traces of Boone, but she also saw Ted's steadiness and Irene's generous heart. Most of all, she saw Pete, and the individual he was making of himself.

"Let's go back to the house, Cam." He looked around. "Unless you're serious about cutting firewood and not just using it as an excuse to get me to talk."

She laughed, even as a tear slipped down her cheek. She hugged him hard and kissed him on the cheek, realizing that before too long she'd have to reach up to do that.

"Hey, what's with the mushy stuff?" But he squeezed her ribs in return before releasing her.

"Firewood was a ploy, all the way. Who needs firewood in the middle of summer?"

Chapter Twelve

"Marlene? It's Boone... uh, Bodie. Bodie Smith."

"Oh. Hello." The voice over the phone line was wary.

"I'm not calling to make trouble, Marlene. I just wanted you to know... you were right."

"Right?"

"About letting the boy have his own life."

"You saw him?" She sounded almost afraid to ask, but not quite able to stop herself.

"Yes. I saw him. He's a good kid, Marlene. And he's happy. He'll turn out okay. He's got a good head on his shoulders and a good heart. And he's got a family that loves him and supports him. He doesn't lack for anything, not anything vital. And he wants nothing from us—from me. He made that clear in no uncertain terms."

"Oh, Bodie... I'm sorry."

"You're sorry?" His chuckle held little humor. "What for? I'm the one who made a mess of this—seventeen years ago and now."

"I'm sorry you were hurt."

"Well, I'm sorry, too. Sorry I wasn't the sort of person you felt you could have counted on to help and understand seventeen years ago."

"Don't worry about me, Bodie. I made it through fine. Like I told you, I have a good life."

"I know. But I'd still like to be the kind of person someone would turn to. I'm working on that."

Boone had been back in North Carolina a month—longer than he'd stayed in Wyoming. But in his mind, the past month slid away unnoticed, almost unreal, while the days at the Weston ranch stood out vivid and beckoning.

It sure hadn't been much fun coming back.

With Cambria's voice echoing in his heart, he'd vowed to clear time and energy so he could design. But he'd handled everything with Bodie Smith Enterprises for so long that it was like trying to turn the *Queen Elizabeth II* around in midocean. He couldn't just drop his responsibilities—strings, as Cully called them. He had to find someone else, the right someone else, to take charge of each one, as well as make sure the newly spread out strings didn't get hopelessly tangled.

No easy job for a man who'd never paid attention to which of his employees was good at what because it didn't matter as long as Bodie Smith did it all.

In the back of his head he'd thought his changes would stir enthusiasm among his employees. Instead they were outright skeptical. A few seemed wary of more responsibility, but most seemed braced for when the boss changed his mind and snatched it all back.

He'd had a devil of a time talking Hannah Chalmers out of quitting as head of advertising. It turned out she'd been frustrated a long time with the tight reins on her authority. Reading her memos with a new perspective, he saw that. He'd been blind to it before Cambria Weston.

At night, when he wasn't not sleeping because he was thinking about Cambria and the other Westons, he was not sleeping because he was thinking about Kenzie. Had she, like Hannah Chalmers, sent out signals for years that he held too tight a rein on her? Signals he hadn't received until the only solution his sister saw was cutting ties?

He wrote her a letter. In fact he wrote six letters, tearing up five. The sixth, sent to the last address he had for her in Maryland, came back with Addressee Unknown. No Forwarding Address across the front in smeared red ink.

He considered writing to Cambria, or calling, or catching the first flight west, or walking toward the setting sun as long as his body held out. But the same question always stopped him: what would he say to her?

Could he tell her he'd become or even hoped to become the man who could give her the love she needed?

He didn't like the answers.

All in all, he'd spent a miserable month turning his life and business upside-down. Some days wanting to return to the way things were, some days being afraid he'd do just that.

On one of the worst days, Cully Grainger visited.

When the door opened without warning, Boone turned from staring out the window toward the heavily wooded hillside beside Bodie Smith Enterprises. He dredged up a smile. "Hey, Cully. Where've you been?"

Cully took his time studying Boone before moving into the room, slamming the door behind him and taking a chair with his usual insolent ease. "Louisiana. Doing a job for somebody. You look like hell."

"Nice to see you, too."

"Boone, I'm telling you—you look bad. You didn't look that hot when you came back from Wyoming, but now..." He shook his head. Elbows on the chair arms, he steepled his fingers over his middle, and surprised Boone. "Tell me what you were thinking about when I walked in."

"I don't—"

"Spill it, Boone. What's on your mind?"

"Marlene."

If he'd been expecting surprise, or any other reaction, he didn't get it. "What about her?"

"Remember what I told you Marlene said, about why she didn't turn to me when she found out she was pregnant, why she handled having the baby and putting it up for adoption by herself?"

You would have taken over like you always did, Bodie.

"Yeah, I remember."

"I was thinking about that one night—"

"Looks more like you've been thinking about something all night, every night," Cully muttered.

Boone ignored that. "I was thinking about what she said and how I used to think that if I took charge, even if I made a mistake, I only hurt myself. And I realized it's not only me who can get hurt by my mistakes. Pretty damn arrogant, huh?"

"Not bad for a dictator."

Boone nodded. "Yeah, that's what Kenzie called me. Cambria called me general manager of the universe. And that's the other part—if I don't hurt people outright, I drive them away. Marlene. Employees who'd like to think for themselves now and then—I found Phil updating his résumé right before I left for Wyoming." One corner of his mouth lifted. "Lately he hasn't had time to send it out."

Boone sobered immediately. "Not just friends and employees, either. There's Kenzie. And now..."

"And now you're thinking you've added the Westons to the list." Cully understood. Boone was grateful for that. Even more grateful his friend didn't try to extend sympathy.

Cully tugged a sheet of paper free from an untidy stack on the desk. He cocked an eyebrow at the drawing. No more than doodling, really, but something new. "Looks like you regained at least one thing, though."

"It's a start." After a long drought, it was a blessed drop of rain. "Cully, you found Pete for me, how'd you feel about looking for Kenzie, maybe paving the way..."

"Maybe."

"What do you mean, maybe?"

"Might not need to look for her. Might already know where she is."

"You've been in touch with Kenzie and you didn't tell me? I have a right to know where she is. You should have told me—"

"So you could take over?"

That hurt. Because it was true. All his good intentions... "Cully—"

The intercom buzzed. Boone jabbed the button. "Yeah, Phil."

"Call on line two, Bodie. It's Pete Weston."

Cully's eyebrows rose. He started toward the door. "Sometimes you get a second chance to escape that mousetrap, Boone."

"Put him through, Phil."

Cully paused at the door only long enough to give him a thumbs-up sign of encouragement.

Boone let out a long breath before picking up the receiver.

"Pete?"

"Hello, Boone."

"Is everything okay? Your family, Cambria—"

"Yeah, yeah, everything's okay. Your letter said to call anytime, and Cambria said... Well, I didn't want to leave things, uh, the way they were. I, uh, I reversed the charges. Your letter said—"

"I'm glad you did. I just... didn't think you'd call."

For an instant he thought that might have been too honest. Pete sounded even more strained when he spoke again.

"I, uh, wanted to tell you I read your letter. I thought about the things you said and some stuff Cam said I needed to decide."

Boone's throat grew narrow and dry. "What did you decide?"

"I still feel the same about who's my father. I gotta be honest. Now, or thirty years from now, you're never going to be my father, Boone."

It hurt. He couldn't deny it.

"Okay, Pete. Like I said in the letter, I won't try to push into your life anymore."

"Yeah, I know. But, you know, I thought we... we did okay as friends, you know? Pretty good, really."

Boone tried to keep his voice steady through the buffeting of emotions. "Yeah, I thought so, too."

"Okay, then. So, I sort of thought, you know, if you wanted to be friends, well, that might be okay. We could try it, anyhow. But no stuff about giving me things."

Boone squeezed his eyes tightly shut again, then opened them slowly, letting go of expectations, letting go of the way he'd thought things had to be, letting go of a lot of old ideas about love and being loved.

And discovering he could live without them.

He could accept another way.

The way Pete was giving him a chance to learn, and Cambria had given him the wisdom to try.

"I..." He swallowed hard. "I'd like that."

More cautiously than he'd approached any exchange in his lifetime, Boone volunteered a tentative comment about the Colorado Rockies' pitching rotation.

Pete answered with enthusiasm heavily laced with relief.

They'd never be Kevin Costner reconnected with his father. Boone and Pete would never have that field of dreams, but Boone found himself smiling. He and Pete were starting a connection based not on the past but the present.

"I better get going," Pete said into a pause.

Boone fought the urge to keep him on the phone. "Okay. I, uh, I hope we can talk again soon."

"Well, that's... Uh." Pete's indrawn breath filled the phone line. It came out in a spurt of words. "You know you've got four days left on the month you paid for, and your cabin—the one you used—is empty Fourth of July weekend. So why don't you come on out? Your not finishing the month really messes up the bookkeeping, you know."

Boone's grip on the phone tightened.

"Did your sister say that?"

"No," Pete admitted. "Mom did."

No words coming to mind, Boone grunted acknowlledgment.

"She misses you."

Boone knew Pete didn't mean his mother. "She said that?"

"She doesn't have to. I can see it. She's my sister."

"It's complicated, Pete."

"That's what she said. She said there were a lot of issues."

"She's right."

Pete gave a huff of breath. "Well, maybe the two of you should get busy and figure out all those issues. Cam used one of Mom's sayings on me, you know, saying for me to decide what I wanted to do about you by figuring what I'd feel good about looking back on thirty years from now. Seems to me you two should do that, too."

Boone stared sightlessly out the window at the soft and green mountains of North Carolina, envisioning the stark, rough lines of Wyoming. And the direct eyes and tenacious mouth of Cambria Weston.

"Boone?"

"Yeah?"

"Whaddya think about coming for the Fourth of July?"

"I think," he said slowly, "your thirty-year plan has a lot to say for it. And I'd hate to be responsible for messing up the bookkeeping because of my shortsightedness."

Boone parked his rental car—a red one that a beaming June Reamer assured him was the "hottest" available—in the familiar spot under the cottonwood by the westernmost cabin. He stepped out, leaned crossed arms on the top of the open door and looked around. He heard a whicker from the barn he couldn't identify. The answer, he'd bet, came from Snakebit.

The new cabin stood solid and finished, complete with roof, windows, door, redwood settee, window box and flowers. By its front steps sat a compact car with North Dakota license plates and telltale white smudges on its trunk that once spelled Just Married.

An unexpected twinge caught him, and he wondered if it was the cabin, completed without him, or the car and all it implied.

His gaze carried on to the main house, as solid and comfortable as ever. Chances were the family was gathered in the kitchen for lunch right now. All the Westons. There . . . together.

And him out here.

Boone turned to the cabin he'd occupied. He could stow his gear first. It wouldn't take long, since he hadn't bothered with the fax or computer. Then maybe he'd be ready—

He slammed the car door and started across the open area to the kitchen door. He'd never be truly ready. He just had to do it.

"Boone!"

In the initial second, he saw Cambria was not there, but the other three Westons were.

Irene reached him first, because she'd been on her feet to bring a plate of sliced fruit to the table. He extended a hand to her, not sure if he'd shake her hand or pat her shoulder. She overrode that by pulling him into a clasp so tight she brought moisture to his eyes. Then she reached up, took his face between her palms, kissed his cheek and announced, "It's about time you came back." Leaning back, she studied him critically. "Don't they have barbers in North Carolina?"

"I got it cut—two weeks ago," he protested.

Ted and Pete, scraping back their chairs to come greet him, both laughed.

Ted's handshake was solid and warm. "We're glad you're here, boy."

Pete's grip was less certain, inclined to squeeze and part. Boone fought the urge to hold on as the boy backed away without meeting his eyes.

"Come sit down and have some lunch," Ted invited.

"I thought, uh, I'd put my things in the cabin, if it's the same cabin."

"Same cabin. But that can wait until you've eaten." Irene guided him to the table. "You look like you've lost any meat you'd gained here and then some. Now you sit right down."

"Might as well give in," Ted said with a smile as he returned to his chair.

"Sure it's the same cabin," Pete said with sly mischief. "Cambria saw to that."

As Boone took his old chair, he found the sight of Pete's lopsided grin easing the tightness between his eyes, but not the one around his heart.

"You told me it was empty this weekend, Pete," Boone said, accepting a plate from Irene. "I see someone's in the new cabin, but I wondered if business—"

"Business is fine," Irene said. "We've been full up quite a bit. It just so happens your cabin's empty this weekend."

"'Just so happens'?" Pete repeated. "Just so happens to be empty..." At the boy's dramatic pause, Boone looked up from putting together a roast beef sandwich from the makings on the table, and caught Irene glaring a warning at Pete that he blatantly ignored. "After Cambria kicked out the people who were staying there."

"Peter Andrew Weston," Irene began a scold that Pete continued to grin through.

Boone hardly heard it.

That sure sounded like Cambria had wanted him here. But he wanted to hear it from her. He needed to see it in her eyes.

He ate absently as the Westons caught him up on the sparse doings of Bardville. Where was Cambria?

"You know what else about that cabin I helped you with, Boone?" Pete didn't wait for an answer, hurrying his words as if anxious to get them out before he reconsidered. "Cam says I can have the profits from renting it this summer for a college fund. She's lending me some money from selling that house she inherited, too. She says I'm a lot better off borrowing from her than a government loan because she doesn't require paperwork. But she's going to make me work it off by helping with the B and B all summer. Next summer, too. Unless I can find a job that pays real well."

Boone opened his mouth, then closed it to smother the assurance that he could get Pete a high-paying job to help finance college. His reward was a flash of relief in Pete's eyes, and a subtle easing in the room.

"That's great, Pete."

Before Boone knew what she was up to, Irene took his half-empty plate from in front of him and wrapped the sandwich in foil. "Go on, get out of here, Boone."

"But..."

She clicked her tongue in feigned impatience. "I can't take watching you anymore. If you don't go ahead and get over there, you're going to wear out that neck of yours."

"What?"

"The way you jerk your head up at every little sound, and spin it around to look out the screen," she explained.

"Like a scene from *The Exorcist,*" Pete confirmed smugly.

"You aren't getting much eating done, so go ahead and look for her like you want."

Ted had the final word. "Try your cabin."

The cabin was open. Boone closed the screen door behind himself silently. The empty main room smelled less strongly of new paint and wood fires, and more of lemon polish and warm sun.

There was no sign of Cambria here, either.

Then he heard it—water running in the bathroom sink, and the faint, subtle shifting of flooring under human feet.

He made it to the doorway between the main room and the bedroom, but there he stopped.

Boone Dorsey Smith had helped keep his family together at an age most boys memorized baseball stats. He'd served in the army, learning how to kill and facing the necessity of not getting himself killed. He'd built a business, taking on a world that could shatter ambitions with arctic indifference.

He'd never been this scared.

The water shut off, and footsteps reached the open doorway.

"Oh—" Cambria jolted to a stop. "You scared me. I thought... I thought you were over at the house."

He could have looked at her for hours, just the way she stood there. In her short-sleeved, red cotton blouse, her fading blue jeans and a pair of dusty boots, she looked as good as he'd been remembering. Her shining hair was tucked behind one ear on one side and hung loose on the other to brush her cheek, and her hands were wrapped around an earthenware jug with a mop of orange and yellow flowers sprouting from its top.

She followed the direction of his gaze to the flowers. "Marigolds. They don't smell very good, but—"

"They're the ones you planted in the flower boxes."

Her eyes met his, then skittered away. "Yes. I thought they'd, uh, brighten the room."

"Thank you."

"Yes. Well... I'll just..."

She put the earthenware jug on the nightstand, then stepped back to consider their placement. With no apparent thought, she wiped her damp hands on the seat of her jeans. Boone's throat constricted and his lower body tightened.

"Cambria..."

She rushed into speech before he could say any more. "So, you saw the new cabin? What do you think? Looks pretty good, doesn't it?"

"It looks great. Pete told me what you're doing with it, using the rental money for his college fund."

"I thought, since you did so much work on it, it was fitting. I thought you'd approve."

"I do. I'm glad it'll help him."

He'd probably always want to do more. For Pete. For her. For his sister. For Ted and Irene. For all the people he cared about. But he was learning that loving more sometimes meant doing less.

Cambria nodded, accepting his answer and approving. Boone felt as if they'd cleared a hurdle. One about the size of a minor mountain. "But I thought you needed the B and B income to pay off the canyon land."

"We do. And the easiest thing would have been for me to turn over the money from Angie Lee to Ted, but he wouldn't hear of it. He insisted I put half right in a money market savings account. I couldn't budge him. But then…well, it occurred to me, since I do the B and B books and I have this extra money, Weston Ranch Guest Quarters could be sort of, uh, guaranteed of having a few real lucrative years. It's one of those secrets you talked about people having. Or maybe one of the slips. I'm not sure which."

He stared at her an extra heartbeat, then laughed out loud. The laughter calmed to a smile, then heated as they looked at each other across the width of the room.

"What's that?"

She turned to look in the direction of his nod, as if she didn't know he meant a trio of design pads and a dozen lethally sharpened pencils in the center of the spread. The laughter had helped, but it hadn't erased all her nerves.

"A welcome back gift."

They both knew it was much more than that. It was her reminder that he should do what made him happy in life. She was confident he understood that. She wondered if he also knew it was an invitation and a symbol she trusted in him enough to believe that he *could* change.

"You don't think that's maybe a little optimistic?"

"No, I don't."

"You think I can stop trying to do everything myself, can stop trying to run other people's lives, can let go of enough of those strings that I could do some designing? That maybe I can learn that keeping a balance in life's as important as it is in designing?"

She let out a long breath. He had understood. "Yeah, I do. As long as you keep working at it."

"Maybe with somebody around to keep reminding me, huh?"

"That would probably help."

He tipped his head, surveying her. "Sounds to me like maybe you believe in me a little, Cambria Weston."

It was a challenge. She met it, head high, eyes direct. "I love you, Boone. I believe in you. I trust you. I'm not saying it'll be easy. Or smooth. I guess we're both too hardheaded for that. But I am saying..."

"What? What're you saying, Cambria?"

"I'm saying I'm glad you're here." Her chest felt so tight she wondered that she could speak at all. "I might have had to come after you if you'd waited much longer. Even though I would have been scared. I'm scared now. I'll probably keep on being scared. And you were probably right that some of it comes from people walking out on me. But even when I'm scared, I know down deep that you won't. So I don't know why you're still standing there in the doorway holding your bag like you might walk out any second."

The bag dropped to the floor beside him with a *chunk* that might have made her jump if she hadn't been concentrating so completely on Boone. He took a step forward.

Cambria started across the room to him. They met in the middle.

Just after Boone swept the paper and pencils from the bed and just before he lowered Cambria to it, they heard distant voices floating in through the open window.

"Well, he's not exactly a newcomer." The familiarity of Pete's voice made his words more easily identifiable. "His name's Boone Dorsey Smith. You'll probably meet him later. He's, uh, I guess you could say he's a friend of the family."

Cambria kissed the taut skin over Boone's jawbone.

"But—" A glint of mischief lit Pete's final words. "I wouldn't mind having him as a brother-in-law."

"How long are you going to stay?"

It was nearing suppertime. They'd have to get out of bed sometime. If only to assure her family that all was well. Cambria smiled as she rested her elbow on the pillow and propped her head on her palm so she could watch Boone. All was better than *well*.

"I thought maybe a month."

"A month? How can you do that with work and—"

He rolled his head on the pillow and grinned at her in reminder of her questions and doubts when he'd arrived the first time. "We're not going to go through this again, are we?"

"I'm not complaining," she clarified. "I'm just surprised you can take that much time away from Bodie Smith Enterprises."

"I've made changes there. A lot of changes. Shifting things around to give myself designing time." He quirked an eyebrow at her. "Letting go some of those strings. In fact—" he shifted to his side, bringing their eyes nearly to a level "—I had this possibility in mind of dividing my year."

"Dividing your year?"

"Yeah, you know, something along the lines of mid September through May in North Carolina, then June to September someplace like, oh . . . say, Wyoming."

"Really?"

"Really."

"It's an interesting concept. Were you thinking of doing this year-splitting alone?"

"Not if I can help it," he said fervently, then resumed his pseudo casualness. "I've been playing with a design for a house that would be great up the canyon a ways—it would have great views without intruding up top or in the meadow."

"Very interesting. That's rather a long-term project, isn't it?"

"I've been thinking pretty long-term lately. Matter of fact, did you notice how my year-splitting matches school opening and closing?"

"Ah." She trailed her fingertips along the line of his collarbone, then across the top of his shoulder to his neck. "But there are short-term considerations, too. For example, did you know this cabin's got to be vacated by Tuesday morning?"

"I know a motel the other side of Bardville—"

"Don't you dare go to the competition. We'll just have to find you other accommodations."

"Like where?"

"Oh, there's a cabin that's never rented out. One of the oldest ones we've got. I suspect you can share that one."

"I'll take it." He sat up enough to snatch a kiss. He dropped his head and pressed his lips to the inside of her bent elbow. "But, Cambria?"

"Hmm?"

"Does your daddy have a shotgun?"

"What?"

"Ted. Does he have a shotgun? Rifle? Pistol? Revolver?"

She blinked out of the distraction caused by the gentle assault of his lips and tongue. "You want to go shooting?"

"No, I *don't* want to get shot."

"What are you talking about?"

"I'm talking about if I'm sharing your cabin we better get married. Fast."

She laughed and slid a would-be soothing hand over his chest. It might have soothed his worries, but it didn't soothe his desire.

"You don't think they already have a pretty good idea why we haven't come out all afternoon?"

"There's a difference between having a pretty good idea and having it shouted at you."

"You're old-fashioned," she said in discovery. She had a feeling she'd keep discovering things about this generous, complicated man for quite a while. It sure wouldn't be boring.

"About some things." He sat up suddenly to look at her closely. "Why? You mean getting married? I'm damned old-fashioned about that. I want to marry you. I want the whole damned world to know we're together."

"It won't bother you . . . I mean, your relationship with Pete. . . ." With strained wryness she added, "I'd hate to think of how a genealogist would chart that. So, if it's a—"

He stopped her words with a hard kiss. "I'll be proud—and happier than I deserve—to have my position in this family be as your husband, Ted and Irene's son-in-law, and Pete's brother-in-law. Okay?" The seriousness in his voice eased. "So that's settled. Now, to get back to shotguns . . . I want a church wedding. And I *don't* want your family hating me in the meantime because I'm seducing you."

She flicked her tongue over his flat brown nipple, which immediately tightened in pleasure. "I thought the seduction was mutual." Desire lit his eyes, but she could see he still wasn't totally convinced. "Boone, I'm a grown woman. Ted and Irene know that. I make my own decisions."

"In that case, we still better get married. Fast." He kissed her. "I don't want to risk your taking back this decision. And I want to get started on long-term as soon as possible."

"Not to mention mutual seduction."

He agreed with actions that spoke louder than words.

* * * * *